# Acclaim for
# Kristin Billerbeck

### *A Billion Reasons Why*

"Katie and Luc dance off the pages of this book, making you fall in love with them and New Orleans. A nostalgic trip full of surprises and romance."

— Carolyne Aarsen, author of
*The Baby Promise*

"A sparkling and lively romance . . . featuring the spunkiest heroine of the year!"

— Denise Hunter, bestselling
author of *Convenient
Groom*

"*A Billion Reasons Why* is a fun, sophisticated romance with Kristin Billerbeck's unique voice and quirky characters. I loved it!"

— Colleen Coble, author of
*Lonestar Homecoming* and
the Mercy Falls series

### *She's All That*

"Snappy dialogue and lovable characters make this novel a winner."

— *Publishers Weekly*

# The Scent of Rain

# Also by Kristin Billerbeck

*A Billion Reasons Why*

*Split Ends*

## THE ASHLEY STOCKINGDALE NOVELS

*What a Girl Wants*

*She's Out of Control*

*With This Ring, I'm Confused*

## THE SPA GIRLS SERIES

*She's All That*

*A Girl's Best Friend*

*Calm, Cool, and Adjusted*

# The Scent of Rain

## Kristin Billerbeck

THOMAS NELSON
*Since 1798*

NASHVILLE   DALLAS   MEXICO CITY   RIO DE JANEIRO

Published in Nashville, Tennessee, by Thomas Nelson. Thomas Nelson is a registered trademark of Thomas Nelson, Inc.

Thomas Nelson, Inc., books may be purchased in bulk for educational, business, fund-raising, or sales promotional use. For information, please e-mail SpecialMarkets@ThomasNelson.com.

The author is represented by the literary agency of Alive Communications, Inc., 7680 Goddard Street, Suite 200, Colorado Springs, CO 80920. www .alivecommunications.com.

**Library of Congress Cataloging-in-Publication Data**

Billerbeck, Kristin.
  The scent of rain / Kristin Billerbeck.
    p. cm.
  ISBN 978-1-4016-8565-2 (trade paper)
  I. Title.
  PS3602.I44S34 2012
  813'.54—dc23                                              2012014942

*Printed in the United States of America*

12 13 14 15 16 QG 6 5 4 3 2 1

*To my brother Gary Compani*

# Chapter 1

Daphne Sweeten's knees buckled beneath her, but Sophie, her maid of honor, kept her from reaching the marble floor. She straightened and stared into her best friend's eyes, which were softened in pity.

"He's not coming?" Daphne mouthed the words. As she searched the vast gothic church in front of her, the crowd stared back. The rows reserved for the groom's family were empty. "They knew," she murmured.

Sophie nodded and pulled the bouquet from Daphne's clenched hands. "Let's go." Sophie caught hold of her elbow, but Daphne couldn't take her eyes off the long aisle that she wouldn't be walking down. "Daphne, come on."

She should be fleeing in humiliation. All those faces, familiar and foreign, had her in their scope. But something kept her there. Her feet remained firmly planted as she registered the peppery scent of freesias and the slightly musty smell of the rental runway carpet. She turned to Sophie, ringed by the rest of her bridesmaids.

"Where's my father?"

At the distant opposite end of the white carpet, the Reverend Riley stood alone at the altar. He cleared his throat as though preparing to make some kind of announcement, and Daphne held her breath. If she allowed so much as a tiny sob to escape, she would echo like a Swiss yodeler in the cavernous cathedral. But what was the point of saving face now? She may as well take it all in or she might miss something, and then how would she ever fix it?

"Daphne, let's go," Sophie whispered as she tugged at her arm.

Resistance was futile. Daphne followed Sophie out of the great double doors, turning one last time to face the altar under its three grand stained-glass windows, littered with white rose petals and dotted with violets. The altar was like the end of a rainbow, a destination she'd never reach, and the petals were like the remnants of her heart. Mark wouldn't be back.

"That was my wedding day."

"You're scaring me. Let's get in the limo."

"Did you see his side of the church? No one was there. He knew he wasn't coming! Why did he bother to rehearse last night?"

"I don't know, Daphne."

She allowed herself to be led outside the church, which stood atop Nob Hill in San Francisco. It was an idyllic June day, no fog. Probably a bad omen. A light breeze and pure California sunshine marked the day, mocking her in its perfection. The steps between her and the limo appeared endless, and she wondered if her legs would carry her the distance.

"Why did you just stand there forever?"

Daphne looked down at her gown and shrugged. "I'm wearing Monique Lhuillier. Face it, if you're going down in a blaze of glory, this is how you want to be dressed."

Sophie laughed. "That's the first sign I've seen of the real you all day!"

"I had a feeling he wouldn't show," Daphne said. "He must have given me some sign that I didn't want to face. I figured all brides probably had that little inkling of fear, but now I wonder if I noticed something subconsciously."

Mia, her friend from high school, lifted the back of her skirt. "I'm sure you did. It's always been frightening, the details you notice. Sometimes it's like being friends with the Mayan calendar."

"Did you notice anything?" Daphne asked.

Mia shook her head.

"Keri?" She looked at her coworker, who also shook her head.

Daphne and her four attendants huddled in a circle on the steps of the church. "We look so good," she said, making light of the situation. "What a waste."

"You don't have to be brave for us," Marguerite said. "Go ahead and cry if you want to."

Daphne's blood ran cold as awareness settled in her veins. "I missed it. I missed something."

"Did you?" Sophie raised an eyebrow. "What did I wear the first day of kindergarten?"

"A purple dress with heinous flowers on the skirt," Daphne replied automatically.

"There. Rest assured: your obsessive nature is still well intact.

Sometimes it's just easier not to see certain things." Sophie skipped down the long set of stairs toward the limousine, and Daphne followed.

"What are you trying to say, Sophie?"

Sophie's flawless skin looked nearly plastic in the bright sunlight of the afternoon. Her strawberry-blond hair was wrapped in an elegant updo, and the simple strand of pearls around her neck was the perfect complement to the dark sapphire gown they'd selected. One thing was certain: Daphne hadn't missed a detail in coordinating the look of her wedding.

"I'm saying . . ." Sophie twisted around so quickly, Daphne nearly crashed into her. "Maybe there *weren't* any signs. Maybe things were too perfect."

"Too perfect?" Daphne blinked mechanically. "Is that possible?"

"What was wrong with Mark? I mean, name his imperfections. Just a short list."

Daphne turned to make certain the others weren't in hearing range. "Lots of things."

"Name one."

"He couldn't get a job in Paris, for one. I had to give up mine to get married."

Sophie continued down a few more steps, and Daphne called after her, "Just because you spend all day dealing with psychological problems does not mean Mark has one."

"Then where is he?"

She hated it when Sophie got like that, so certain in her assessment of another person. "I'm sure he has a perfectly good

4

excuse. Maybe he never wanted to get married at all. Maybe I pushed him into it."

"So it's your fault again. Like the excuse he had for not being employable in Paris. He left you out like yesterday's trash, and you're standing here making excuses for him."

"You never did like him," Daphne accused. Did Sophie really think she needed any reminders of her fiancé's faults at this moment? She was standing alone in a trumpet gown, tailored beautifully, with detailed Chantilly lace on the bodice. Every detail was perfect save one. The absence of a groom. "Maybe that's why he ran! Maybe together we scared Mark off."

As they spoke, random tourists applauded from the sidewalk below, where the limo waited. Rather than point out the obvious, Daphne just waved. They probably thought she and Sophie had just gotten married anyway.

"Call Arnaud and ask for your job back," Sophie said.

"Not an option. Arnaud said if I left the perfumery, he wouldn't save a spot for me. He was so mad at me." She looked across the park at the Fairmont Hotel. "Look, there's another bride. Her groom showed up."

"Daphne!" Sophie's expression lightened and she looked back up toward the church. "Oh, there's your dad."

Daphne turned to see her father standing on the church steps, blinking wildly, cupping a hand over his eyes and searching for her. A dark shame washed over her, and she ran back up the steps to be swallowed up in his embrace. "I'm sorry, Daddy."

He patted the back of her head. "It's not important now. I want you to take the car and go home and get your things.

You'll just start your job in Dayton early. Your mother and I will clean up this mess. Leave it to us."

Her head spun. "But I want to go back to Paris. Sophie thinks I should ask Arnaud—"

Her father released her. "You'll go to your new job in Dayton. That will prove to your boss in Paris that you can follow through on something. In the meantime, I will sue that kid for everything he owns."

"Daddy, don't." She backed away, still wanting to defend Mark and find a reasonable explanation for his absence. "He doesn't own anything anyway."

Her father lifted something from his tuxedo pocket, and it glistened in the sunlight. A key chain. She waited for an explanation.

"The keys to your new house."

"My new house?"

"In Dayton. It was to be your wedding present. Mark went to Dayton two weeks ago to finalize the details. He gave me the keys so I could present them to you at the reception." He raked his stubby fingers through his gray hair—a monument to his long work hours. He looked as if he'd aged a year in the past day.

Daphne watched the keys jangle but made no effort to reach for them. She didn't want a house in Dayton, Ohio. She didn't want anything in Dayton, Ohio. She wanted Paris. Perfumery. Mark. *In that order?* She wasn't sure.

"I want to go back to Paris," she repeated. "I want to be a professional 'nose' again. I only took the formulation job to be with Mark." She looked at her feet. She just admitted she'd been pathetic enough to take a job she didn't want for a man. A man who cared so little about her he didn't even give her a reason for leaving. Talk about casting pearls before swine.

Still, she wanted to cling to the idea that he was the man she loved. Mark was the one thing that would finally have been hers alone. She'd counted on him to take the sting out of her lonely childhood. With hindsight, that felt like the dumbest belief system she'd ever embraced. But when she thought of Mark's eyes and the way they looked at her, she knew she'd do it all over again.

"You're not going back to Paris," her father said. "Take them!" He shook the keys. "You have a job in Dayton, and you need a place to live. Now stop living in your dream world and get out of here. The guests will be out soon." He jutted his chin toward the limo.

A fresh wave of shame washed over her. It was a natural response. She'd never measure up. Maybe Mark's behavior only confirmed what her father had thought all along—that something just wasn't quite right about Daphne.

"No offense, Mr. Sweeten, but Daphne will live where she wants to live." Sophie snatched the keys from his outstretched hand, placed her other hand in the small of Daphne's back, and guided her firmly down the steps toward the limousine.

"Sophie, isn't part of being a therapist letting people take responsibility for their own lives?"

"Just get in the car, Daphne."

"I'm only doing what's best," her father called after them.

Daphne did as she was told and climbed into the car with her fluted gown shoved from behind by Sophie, who then ran around the other side and climbed in beside her. From behind the darkened windows of the limo, Daphne felt detached from the scene playing out above her. The people filing out of the church with shock and awe on their faces. The other bridesmaids milling about on the steps. On some level she was enjoying the spectacle. Like a guest at her own funeral.

"Other people just get married. Nothing happens. Their daddies walk them down the aisle and send them off in majestic triumph." She smelled the soiled leather of the aged limousine and knew the latest scent of failure.

The driver didn't ask her where they wanted to go; he just headed toward the bay. Sophie rapped on the window that separated them from him, and it slowly came down. "Where exactly are we going, Mr. Driver?"

"Tony," the man said, his brown eyes twinkling in the rear-view mirror. "My name is Tony. I'm going to the Embarcadero. I thought you'd enjoy the fresh air."

Daphne looked at Sophie. "He knows I've been dumped."

"Of course he does. You're in the limo with your maid of honor and no groom. There's no shame in this, Daphne."

The driver kept talking. "First I thought about the Palace of Fine Arts, but there will be too many tourists there on a Saturday. I think what our bride needs is peace."

"I'm not a bride," Daphne said. "I just play one on random Saturdays in June." She looked at Sophie. "If I ever choose to be humiliated again, remind me to pick a weekday. Fewer crowds."

"You should powder your nose. It's red."

Daphne shrugged. "I'm a bride without a groom; do you think anyone is going to look at my nose?"

"Looking good is the best revenge, and that gown is sheer perfection. You have a reputation to uphold for the designer."

"I don't want revenge," Daphne said. "I just want to know what happened. Maybe Mark is lying in a coma somewhere and can't get to me."

"Oh, Mark is brain-dead all right, but I can assure you, he's perfectly alive somewhere. Otherwise, his family would have been at the church."

Daphne pouted. She crossed her arms and touched the soft silk of the embroidered flowers on her bodice. "If I want to live in a fairy tale today, I think I should be allowed."

"I agree," Sophie said.

At the edge of the Embarcadero, a quiet portion of San Francisco's bay front, Tony pulled into a parking lot and turned toward them. "You both look beautiful. Go out and enjoy the day." He turned around, draping his arm over the front seat. "You're not the first bride I've seen left at the altar, and you won't be the last. But you are the prettiest, so go out and revel in your future without this guy. He'll never do better."

The stranger's words made her smile, but suddenly she shook her head and grabbed Sophie's leg. "We have to go to the reception. The cologne I made for wedding favors for the guys. I need the bottles back to send to Arnaud so he'll remember that I'm worthy of the position he offered me once."

She didn't dare say the real reason. She was afraid Mark

would get his hands on the bottles and claim he'd created the scent. If they were both going to be in Dayton working at the same company, that would be awkward enough. But if he tried to take credit for her work, her grace would officially run out for Mark Goodsmith.

"Your parents will grab them," Sophie said. "Let's go get some air."

Daphne tried to feel Sophie's sense of calm, but Mark was a chemist and had most of her formula. "What if—" But she didn't want Sophie to know it was even a fear.

"What if, what?"

"Nothing."

Tony opened their door, and Daphne felt the rush of wind off the bay hit her with its murky, foul scent. She searched for motivation to get out of the car. When she failed to move, Sophie opened her own door and tugged at her arm. "Let's go. Air, remember?"

"I'd rather have chocolate. Lots and lots of chocolate, and I wouldn't even care if it left little dark spots all over my dress."

"Yes, you would. We're selling that baby on PreOwned WeddingDresses.com, and it's going to buy me a trip to Dayton." Sophie hesitated. "If you go there, I mean. Come on, we're getting air." She breathed in deeply. "Ah, that is so refreshing!"

Sophie was the epitome of sweetness and light, with a side of control issues. Something like this could never happen to her, because the singing birds that flew around her head like a happy halo would never allow it. Her warm and compassionate disposition drew people to her like fresh honey, but cross one of her friends and you would rue the day. That was the side dish of control that apparently came with her degree in psychology.

Sophie was engaged. *Her* fiancé loved her unconditionally. At least it seemed that way from the outside, and even though Mark asked Daphne to marry him before Gary asked Sophie, it felt as though Gary and Sophie had been first. Daphne could just smell things. Her lost relationship was just one more way the friends were traveling in disparate directions.

"What if you catch whatever bad-luck disease I have? Do you ever worry about that, hanging out with me?"

"What?" Sophie yelled over the wind off the bay.

"Nothing." What did it matter? Everyone would avoid contamination soon enough when she was quarantined to Dayton, Ohio.

They stood under the grand silver structure of the Bay Bridge. Daphne worried that a turbulent wind might catch her gown and cause her to take flight over the concrete barrier, tossing her into the choppy surf. The sight of the immense silver structure and the historic yellow streetcar on its rails, along with the embrace of the gusting wind, lifted her spirits. She was good at being alone in the world. Maybe she was meant to be alone.

"It's beautiful here." Sophie came up beside her and leaned over the concrete wall to see the surf slapping into the barrier below. "You forget, when you live in one of the most beautiful cities in the world. You take it for granted."

"I don't," Daphne said. "I was thankful for every day in

France and Switzerland. I'm thankful for every day here. But what if I can't feel that way in Dayton? Is that why God is sending me there?"

"He's not sending you there. You don't have to go."

"I have nowhere else to go."

"Stay here. Open up your own perfumery."

"I love how you believe I can do anything I set my mind to."

"Because you can."

"I can't stay here. I've brought shame on my parents. My mother will never let me hear the end of it, and my father will remind me daily what it cost him. Dayton will be fine until I can get back to Europe."

"But formulating—chemistry and analyzing data—there's no art in that." Sophie's lip rose. "You hate formulating."

"I don't hate it. It's just not my calling. I was meant to make the world smell better." She held down her hair from a rogue gust of wind.

"No, Daph. You hate it."

"It's temporary. I'll be fine." The sea lions barked in the distance. "Hear that? I wonder what new sights and sounds—and smells, of course—await me in Dayton."

"Maybe you could wait a few days to make a decision. You don't have to leave town because your parents' society friends will gossip. Come stay with me on the Peninsula."

"Nope. There will be fewer distractions in Dayton. I'll be able to think. Plan."

"And if Mark shows up to work?"

Maybe a tiny part of her wanted to go to Dayton for that

very reason. Just a sliver of her. "I gave up the Holy Grail of per-fumer jobs for love."

"We all do crazy things for love. Who was it who said it is better to have loved and lost than never to have loved at all?"

"Someone who ended up alone."

"That's precisely why I don't want you in Dayton. You'll be alone."

"I'm good at being alone. Maybe too good. I thought giving up my dream was sacrificial and beautiful. Now it seems ignorant and based on one too many chick flicks. I gave up my dream job for a tool."

"Well, you didn't know then that he was a tool."

"How is it I didn't sniff Mark out? How is it *you* didn't figure him out? With all that Stanford schooling under your belt, you'd think you'd have some insight."

"I'm going to put him under the category of sociopath—he's so adept at charm skills that he flew under our radar. And sociopaths don't have empathy, so anything you feel for him now is wasted on the likes of him."

"This is a fresh diagnosis."

"It makes me feel better, all right?"

"I thought I was the luckiest girl alive because Mark wanted to marry me."

"So did he. Think you were the luckiest woman in the world for getting to marry him, I mean."

Daphne stared across the choppy water and pondered what life would look like without Mark Goodsmith by her side. Tomorrow she would allow herself to feel the full depth of the day's events and book her one-way ticket to the Midwest. Without a doubt she'd be the talk of her parents' social circle for years to come; crushing failure was always a favorite topic among the city's elite. But she could rejoice over one thing: she'd be in Dayton, Ohio, far out of ear's reach. It wasn't exactly Paris, but it wasn't San Francisco either. That alone was cause for rejoicing.

"I still need to get the cologne bottles back from the reception," she said abruptly. "Volatility! is my best work, and I want Arnaud to smell it."

"It's not your best work; it's just your first work. You have so much more to create, Daph. But maybe you need to smell it again to know you're capable of more great things."

Sophie reached into her pocket. "And you thought the pocket in the gown was tacky. I can powder your nose and produce Volatility!" She pulled out the cobalt blue bottle. "Not so tacky now that it's practical, is it? I snatched a few for souvenirs when we were dropping them off at the hotel last night. Maybe you should give one to Tony the limo driver."

Sophie grasped the bottle so that Daphne couldn't see the writing in gold: *Mark & Daphne Goodsmith, June 4, 2011.* "Smell it!" she ordered and lifted the stopper from the bottle.

"I don't want to smell it. I just want it shipped off to Arnaud so that he remembers what I'm capable of."

Sophie kept waving the bottle underneath Daphne's nose while she wrestled to move away.

"Stop!" Daphne said. "You're going to spill it on me, and then we can't sell the gown. I know what it smells like. I designed

14

it. Besides, I can't smell anything out here with all the competing odors on the wharf."

"You've forgotten how good you are. Mark didn't inspire you. *Love* inspired you, and if you can love that guy, you have to believe there's another one out there with a shred of decency. One who's worthy of you."

"Wait a minute!" Daphne grasped the bottle from Sophie's hand and lifted it to her nose. She inhaled deeply. "I can't smell it!" She narrowed her eyes at her friend. "Did you put water in here?" If this was some kind of joke, Daphne didn't find it funny. She searched the air for the pungent fish odor she'd just been smelling.

Sophie looked indignant. "Why on earth would I do that?"

Daphne inhaled deeply and smelled nothing. Not the Indonesian patchouli, the bergamot, not even the rosemary or the hint of citrus. "I can't smell it. I can't smell anything."

Sophie grabbed the bottle and took a deep whiff. "It's still incredible. Is that what you need to hear?"

Daphne shook her head and felt her throat tighten. She was trained to identify over five thousand scents, and suddenly her whole world, the aromatic world, had gone silent. "I must be getting a cold. Or maybe the tears are messing with my olfactory system."

"You haven't cried yet. It's just stress, Daph. You'll be fine when you're in your jeans and have a plan."

Daphne nodded. Emotion finally bubbled from within the pit of her stomach. "But what if it isn't just stress?" She'd used everything she had to create Volatility! Like a desperate Victorian poet, maybe she was dried up at twenty-seven.

"It is," Sophie said, as though she could will it into being so. "Relax, and everything will be fine by the time you get to Dayton. But you have to promise me: if you feel too alone, you'll come back. You can stay with me, and your parents won't even need to know you're here."

But what if Sophie was wrong? What if creating Mark's scent had destroyed her most valuable asset: her sense of smell? Without it, she was utterly worthless. Even in Dayton, Ohio.

# Chapter 2

On Wednesday morning Jesse Lightner eased into the chair in his home office and checked the numbers again. His predecessor had forecast a 10 percent increase in sales. It hadn't mattered that the stats were optimistic at best; now Jesse was responsible for meeting those numbers for the stockholders. Ben played on the floor with his wooden trains, making choo-choo noises. Jesse smiled down at his son, and the feat of making impossible numbers work paled in importance.

His cell phone rang, and he saw his boss's name on the display.

"Ben, Daddy has to take this call. Can you be quiet for a minute?"

Ben nodded and continued his noises at a quieter pitch.

"Jesse here."

"It's Dave," his boss answered. "You figure out a way to get that nose in the budget? How are those forecasts coming along? We've got shareholders to answer to."

Jesse waited for the barrage of questions to subside.

"Well?" Dave asked.

"I've been over the numbers a dozen times. I have to say that I can't see an expensive nose helping our bottom line. Lemon floor wax will smell like lemons, and it doesn't take an expert to tell us what lemons smell like. My four-year-old could tell us that."

"Did you read the statistics I sent you on how P&G raised its sales with professional noses?"

"I read it. P&G has the money to hire professional noses." *And to make a mistake,* he added silently. "We have to do what they do on a fraction of the budget." He covered the speaker. "Ben." He tried to keep his voice calm as he looked down at his son. "Ben, take that out of your nose! Right now."

Ben peered up with his wide, innocent eyes, two prominently displayed dots sticking out of his nostrils. "Raisins, Daddy!"

"Raisins are for eating, Ben. They don't belong in our noses."

"Jesse, you there?" Dave's imposing voice boomed over the line.

"I'm here. My sister went to get her hair done. It's just Ben and me this morning."

Dave cruised over the fact that Jesse had a life outside Gibraltar. "Excuses, Jesse. What separates the good from the great? Excuses. I'm giving you the chance of a lifetime with this nose. She can put us on an international playing field."

If playing on an international field was just a matter of hiring one employee, he imagined he'd have done it long ago. "I have nothing against your professional nose, Dave. I just want

18

her to come out of beauty's budget. Why put her in household products?"

"Daddy, it's stuck." Ben tilted his head back to show a raisin clear in the back of his nostril.

"I have to go, Dave. We'll talk about the professional nose when I'm in the office. I'll be there in about an hour."

"Just wait until you meet her. You'll see."

"Look, Daddy! I'm a profeshnal nose." Ben had stuck more raisins up his nose, which he wiggled proudly.

"Ben, you can get those stuck. Come here."

Ben scampered in the other direction.

"Dave, I really have to go."

"Didn't you want that new piece of equipment for the lab?"

Jesse nearly stopped in his tracks. Catching up with Ben in the hallway, he swooped the boy up with one arm and answered his boss. "Are you saying if I hire the nose, I can have my formulation equipment?" His stomach actually fluttered. Automating Gibraltar's processes would enable them to compete on any level, not to mention be a hundred times as productive and enter new product categories. "You know what this formulator costs?"

"You sent me the procurement papers. I'm trying to show you how to work smart, not hard. You give this nose a chance until the shareholders' meeting. If you can keep her on staff and utilize her to increase market share, you can have your equipment. But I'm saying I don't think you'll need it. She does things the old-fashioned way, and I think that will appeal to buyers with the uptick in quality."

"Daddy, hurts."

"Dave, I'm sorry. See you in an hour." He pressed his phone off and focused on Ben. "Why did you put those up your nose? You can get things stuck there, and then you won't be able to breathe."

Ben started to cry. "It hurts, Daddy."

Jesse took his son into the bathroom and set him on the toilet. "We've got tweezers here somewhere." He opened the medicine cabinet and searched until he found a pair. At the sight of the silver tool, Ben burst into tears.

"No, Daddy."

"Ben, that's why we don't stick things up our noses. It's not pleasant to get them out."

He held Ben down while the boy wiggled to get free, and carefully inserted the tweezers to pull the last raisin out. Making his quarter was overrated. He felt all the satisfaction he needed for the day in plucking that raisin out of Ben's nose.

"What are you doing?" Abby appeared in the doorway. She reached for Ben and cuddled him in her arms. "What's Daddy doing?"

"Aunt Abby, Daddy hurt me," Ben cried.

"Why, you little— Abby, he stuffed raisins up his nose."

"Yeah, he's going through a phase. He does that a lot."

"Well, make him stop!"

"He probably will now that you've traumatized him." She snuggled Ben and rocked him. "It's all right."

"Quit babying him. He can't stick things up his nose."

"Go to work, Jesse. Ben and I will work on not sticking things up the nose. Won't we, sweetie?"

Jesse rolled his eyes. "I have to get to the office. Everything rides on this new product launch if we plan to make Dave's numbers. And now I have to account for this nose's salary in my expenses."

"I can't wait to meet her," Abby said. "I wonder if her nose is huge." She caressed Ben's hair. "I know you're not happy about her, Jesse, but she may be just what your funky environment at Gibraltar needs. She's from Paris, for crying out loud. I've never met anyone from Paris."

"She's not *from* Paris. She's from San Francisco."

"I've never met anyone from there either."

Jesse changed the subject. "How long has this phase been going on, anyway? Where he's sticking stuff up his nose?"

"Just a short time. He's trying to get your attention, Jesse."

"Ben, Daddy will take you to the zoo this weekend," Jesse said firmly. "Stop sticking stuff up your nose." He failed to see how the two things had anything to do with one another—the zoo and the sticking of things up one's nose—but Abby seemed to approve. His sister was wonderful with Ben, and Jesse was grateful. What would he do if he had to work for Dave and raise his son alone?

His phone rang again.

"We seem to have been cut off," Dave said. "You can fit this nose into your budget, Jesse, or I wouldn't have trusted you with her. Push the sales team, or find a way to lower production costs. No one ever made it easy on me, but I never got ahead by complaining."

Jesse walked back to his office, his jaw clenched. "I hesitate to mention that I could lower production costs by not having a nose on staff. Or is that stating the obvious?"

"Procter & Gamble didn't get ahead by thinking in the short term, and neither will we."

*No, but some middle manager probably paid with his job for overzealous sales predictions by senior management.*

He'd seen it happen many times. Before his life went awry, Jesse had been the youngest vice president of product development for the largest employer in Cincinnati. He had a reputation to live up to, and Dave made sure he understood that daily, asking him every time he made a mistake how he'd ever made it work for Procter & Gamble.

Jesse knew how things worked. If Dave didn't make his numbers, he'd just pull a success from another department and even things out. If Jesse didn't make his quotas, he'd be pounding the pavement looking for work in a terrible economy, and his résumé was a mess. Middle management meant all of the responsibility and none of the power.

"So when does this miracle nose of ours start?"

"She'll be here today. That's why I called."

"Today! What?" Jesse stared at his calendar. "I thought she wasn't supposed to start for two weeks." He sat down at his desk and groaned, staring at the numbers, the numbers that relied on an unproven product selling at a clipped pace. He quietly calculated how he'd have to rearrange them based on this new information.

"Her wedding got canceled. She's coming early. And be sure you account for her signing bonus in the budget. I left her contract information with Anne."

"Great," Jesse said. *An overpriced pair of nostrils, complete with excess baggage of a failed wedding. This ought to be fun.*

"Daddy!" Ben reappeared in the doorway. If it was possible, his son seemed to have garnered energy in the seconds they'd been apart. "Daddy, I went pee-pee!"

He covered the speaker again. "That's great, Ben!"

"Want to see?"

"Yes, I'll be right there." He tried to follow what Dave was saying.

"Givaudan trains just five a year, and most of them stay on and work in the perfume industry. A twenty-billion-dollar industry, I might add, and Givaudan's doing about 20 percent of the market share. If our nose can help us capture .001 percent of that, she'll be worth the money. We only got her because her fiancé took a job with us in sales. But it turns out he padded his résumé, so he's gone. Just the nose is left. We should be dancing in the halls."

"Daddy!" Ben was doing his own dance of impatience.

"Dave, I'll be in the office in an hour. We'll talk then."

"Just so long as you understand, this nose is gold to our shareholders. You absolutely have to hold her until Christmas. Six months. Got it?"

"I've got it," Jesse said. "I'll be in soon."

"This job isn't getting to be too much for you, is it?"

His boss knew to attack right in his Achilles' heel.

"You know it isn't. I just think a perfumed-trained nose belongs in the perfume industry. How long is she going to be interested in the chemistry of floor wax formulation? Would a lotus-raspberry-scented cleaner really sell more product than lemon?"

"If you're what you used to be at P&G, you'll figure it out. Find me when you get here. I want to see those spreadsheets."

"No problem." He wished the nose had lied on her résumé. The sales guy was someone else's problem.

Jesse looked down at the toilet and roughed his son's hair. "Way to go!" He flushed the toilet, and Ben started to cry.

Abby appeared in the doorway with her arms crossed over her chest. "Ben doesn't like the noise of the toilet."

"Sorry, buddy, but you have to get used to it. An unflushed toilet makes women mad. The earlier you learn that, the better."

"Jesse, did you talk to your boss about these hours? It's ridiculous how much you're in the office. And when you are home, your phone rings constantly."

"It's just temporary, Abby. After I make my numbers this quarter, Dave will let up."

"You've said that for the last three quarters, and you're still like a ghost in this house. You know I'm happy to help out, but Ben needs his father."

"I know it. I never should have left P&G—but what would I have done with Ben all day if I'd stayed in Cincinnati?"

"Things happen the way they do for a reason," Abby said. "But this Dave has some kind of hold over you that I don't understand. You had a bigger job at P&G, and you were never gone this much."

The words hit him hard. He looked down at Ben's wide eyes. "I promise I'll do better," he said. He didn't have a clue how he'd make that happen, but he'd have to.

"Ben's going to be in school next year," Abby reminded him.

Jesse rubbed his forehead. "Let me go into the office and take care of this. I've got to find this nose's salary somewhere."

"Stop calling her a nose or you're going to think of her that way instead of as the person she is."

"Without a face on her, it's easy to see her as just another impediment to making my numbers work this quarter." And if he didn't make those numbers work, he'd end up just as his predecessors had: out of a job.

"God will work it out," Abby said. Faith rolled off her tongue so easily . . . when it didn't involve her. She had a way of ignoring facts that were inconvenient to her sunny way of looking at life.

"You're right, as usual. I've got to focus on that equipment Dave is promising. It would speed up formulation and make time to market shorter. One successful quarter with the nose—I mean Daphne—and I'm home free. But Dave is wrong; I won't change my mind about the equipment upgrade because someone has the ability to discern five thousand scents. How many scents does one need in floor cleaner?"

"That's the spirit."

"If sales can get us that shelf space in dish-washing pods, my troubles are over."

"See?" Abby brightened. "There are lots of ways around this if you stop and think."

Jesse walked toward his sister and kissed her forehead, then he bent down and lifted up Ben. "You're going to be good today for Aunt Abby?"

Ben nodded.

"Nothing more up the nose?"

Ben shook his head wildly.

His phone rang again. "Jesse here," he answered while he winked good-bye at Ben and made his way toward the car.

"Jesse, it's Anne." Anne was the office manager and Dave's right-hand woman, and she was married to Jesse's pastor. Jesse thought if patience was a virtue, Anne must have received a double dose to handle Dave as easily as she did. The staff jokingly called her "the Dave Whisperer."

"Hi, Anne. I'm on my way in as we speak."

"I'm calling because Dave wanted me to make reservations for you and Daphne for lunch."

"The nose?"

"Yes, the nose. Dave wants you to take her on a tour of the place, then out to a nice lunch and perhaps see RiverScape. You know, show her all Dayton has to offer."

"That should take a good hour," he quipped. "Anne, I'm against the wall on this budget. Can't Kensie or someone take her? You maybe?"

"Dave specifically said you. I'm only calling to see where you'd like me to make reservations."

"Reservations? That means somewhere fancy. I don't have time for that. Call the Spaghetti Warehouse and tell them we'll be in around noon."

"Jesse, can't you at least pick a place with clean tablecloths? Think of it as practice for a date. It will serve two purposes."

"It's not serving any purpose." Jesse opened his car door and tossed his laptop case onto the passenger seat. "Because I don't have time to take the nose to lunch."

"Daphne," Anne corrected him. "You know I wouldn't say this if it wasn't true: you need to take Daphne Sweeten to lunch, and you need to show her why Gibraltar and Dayton are perfect for her. Dave says that P&G will be chomping at the bit to get her. And Givaudan is opening offices in New Jersey soon."

Anne mothered the staff. She baked a cake whenever someone had a birthday. She bought baby gifts and passed around the cards to be signed; she made certain the coffee was always fresh. Anne's own children were grown and gone, but her motherly instincts got plenty of use at the office.

"The Spaghetti Warehouse is fine, Anne. This girl—" He corrected himself. "Daphne. If her wedding didn't come off for some reason, she won't feel like going to a quiet restaurant that seems like a date any more than I would."

"Maybe you're right."

He started up his car.

"I'll let the Spaghetti Warehouse know you're coming. But, Jesse, since we're talking about it . . . Daphne might not be ready to date, but it's certainly time you started thinking about it."

"I don't have time to do my job now, Anne. Sometimes Ben and I barely make it to church, so you'd better talk that suggestion over with your husband."

"I'll pretend you didn't say that."

"Shoot. I forgot a file. I have to run back to the house. Stall Dave if he gets restless, will you?"

"I always do. We'll see you soon."

He appreciated Anne more than he could say. With her gentle spirit, she redirected his boss as if he were no more difficult than a toddler in her Sunday school class. And Dave certainly threw tantrums right up there with a few toddlers Jesse knew.

When Jesse tried to reenter the house, he walked right into the door. Abby was downright paranoid when it came to security. He inserted his key into the lock and opened the door to find Abby and Ben on the living room floor with an enormous wooden track set up.

"Did you do all that since I left? I was only gone for a second."

"Ben's a builder. Aren't you, Ben?" Abby stood up. "By the way, I forgot to ask—are you coming home for lunch?"

"Not today. It seems Dave has offered me up to show the no—I mean, Daphne around. You know how good I am at small talk."

"Bring her home for lunch!" Abby said. "I'm dying to see what she's like, and I can keep the conversation going. I'd love to talk about something more than *Thomas and Friends.*" Abby looked down at Ben and back to Jesse. "No, take her out. You don't even know how to talk to people anymore. Remember how you used to make everyone feel important? I miss *that* Jesse. Now even when you're sitting here, it's like you're somewhere else in your head."

He gave a half smile. He missed that Jesse too, but that Jesse was long gone, buried under the weight of huge responsibilities and a lack of time. He grabbed the folder he needed and listened to the sweet sounds Ben made for the trains.

"I might be late tonight. I don't know how it's going to work with this new girl."

"Are you afraid to take her out because she's all cultured and stuff? I mean, she's been in Paris. We haven't even been to Paris, Texas."

"I'm not afraid of anything, other than not getting the equipment my scientists need to stay competitive."

"Ask Daphne if she's willing to sell her wedding dress."

"Why? Do you have something to tell me?" He stared at Abby's apple cheeks and marveled at how much Ben looked like his sister. No wonder everyone believed the boy belonged to her when they went out anywhere. Pride filled his heart as he looked at the two of them. They were the reason it was worth working for Dave. "Doesn't a failed wedding dress have bad mojo or whatever it is you say?"

"Not if it's from Paris. Besides, we don't know why the wedding was called off, right? Maybe she dumped him because he was a total dog and her gown had magical powers that told her so and she had to shed both him and the dress to be free of his dark evil."

"You need to get out more. And quit watching all those *Housewives*! I regret ever telling you about Daphne coming. There is no drama, other than that I need to keep her around until the next shareholders' meeting in order to get my equipment, so let's hope I have some interpersonal skills left." He switched gears. "What's this about you needing a wedding dress, anyway? Spike hasn't proposed, has he?"

The last thing their house needed was another mouth to feed, and Spike wasn't exactly the working sort.

"Not for me. I was thinking for you. Maybe if you had an elegant wedding gown hanging in your closet, you'd remember that there is an opposite sex and get out there and date again."

He chuckled. "When would I have time to do that? Besides, you and Anne seem to have my future all planned for me, so why should I go looking? Won't you both tell me when you've found Ms. Right?"

"Yes, we will. This one just fell into our laps, though, so I'm hoping she's a believer."

Jesse sighed. "She's from California, so don't get your hopes up. Besides, if she's a nose, I doubt she's going to like the smell of soured milk and discarded french fries that fills my car. I am to a nose what Pepé Le Pew is to that kitty he fell for."

"Love makes all things smell beautiful."

He groaned. His sister's romantic view of the world made a jobless guy like Spike look like marriage material. "I have to get to the office. Ben, be a good boy."

"If she's been in Paris and you have to make Dayton seem equivalent, you'd better put on your game face. Show her the romance of Dayton. And remember that she's probably just had her heart broken."

"I can't afford to feel sorry for her. Can't afford much of anything with her in my budget."

"You can always afford to be kind, big brother, or you might turn into Dave. I already like this girl. Can't tell you why, but I have a good feeling about her."

Jesse shut the door behind him. Why everyone thought he needed a woman in his life was beyond him. Abby nursed a romantic dream that having a ready-made family was the stuff of fairy tales. Sleepless nights, endless laundry, and a man with a hole in his heart didn't exactly add up to Camelot. If this Daphne had the laser-sharp senses everyone said she did, she'd understand instinctively that he was not an option, and they could move forward to get him the machinery his scientists needed. If she wanted to stay on after that, they'd be able to formulate Basil Lemon Verbena hand soap that much faster.

# Chapter 3

After San Francisco, Dayton seemed . . . flat. From her taxi, Daphne scanned the landscape. The buildings, the dry brush, everything was one level and mostly an inherent beige color. She hoped the lack of color wasn't indicative of the new life before her. She sniffed hastily, to the point where the cabdriver turned around to see what she was doing.

"I'm just smelling. I'm a nose," she said, but it had sounded a lot better in her head than aloud.

"I have nose too. My cab doesn't smell," he said, obviously offended.

"No, your cab doesn't smell. Nothing smells. I can't smell anything."

He blinked several times in the rearview mirror before he pulled up to the curb. "We are here."

She stared up at the high-rise that housed Gibraltar Industries, and her first thought was of Mark. Would he be there? What would she say to him? He hadn't called her since leaving her high and dry at the church four days earlier. Hadn't left so much as a note, though he'd gone to the trouble to "unfriend" her on Facebook. The fact that he'd handed her father the keys to "their" house didn't seem like a good omen.

The cabdriver got out of the car, and she wondered if she'd made a mistake. She had come to Dayton because she had nowhere else to go, and a new environment sounded better than the pitying glances of friends and family. Healing would not come easily, but perhaps that's why she'd been brought to this fair, flat city. At least that's what Sophie claimed, and since Daphne had no better explanation for why her life had taken this turn, she went with her best friend's logic.

The taxi driver stood on the curb holding her two small polka-dot suitcases. She opened the door, handed him a wad of cash, and tried again to smell.

"Crazy!" The driver rolled his eyes and scurried back into the car away from her. Men seemed to be doing a lot of that lately.

*This is it. Your new life.* Daphne wasn't ready to see her new house. She'd gone straight to the office from the airport, lugging two suitcases, an archery bow, and other less visible but more significant baggage with her. Meeting Dayton without her sense of smell to guide her was like being the walking blind.

She stared up at the building, which loomed over the city in its importance and made her feel even smaller. She pushed through the door, pulling her suitcases in one at a time. The interior boasted shiny granite walls in eighties colors of peach and green. Her heart sank. Somehow the building had looked more modern when she'd come with Mark for their interviews. Her stomach fluttered at the thought of him, and she silently hoped that he'd be here already and rush to tell her what a huge mistake he'd made. She closed her eyes and imagined all the smells she was missing: the rubber of industrial carpet, the formaldehyde on the modern birch chairs, the benzene from the rubber plants.

People bustled around her, and she stood watching as if invisible. *This is home now.* She read the directory on the wall and reminded herself that Gibraltar was on the sixth and seventh floors. She stepped onto the elevator.

At the third floor the door opened for a man in a gray pin-striped suit with *lawyer* written all over him. "You going on vacation?" he asked. "If so, you're headed in the wrong direction. The exit is down. Wish I could go with you."

She shook her head. "Just arriving. Came straight from the airport. I'm starting a new job today." Her enthusiastic over-sharing didn't seem to spark any sort of interest in her fellow rider, and she retreated into silence. Like an overzealous bloodhound, she kept sniffing in each new space, hopeful. She got out on the sixth floor.

Gibraltar's offices were nothing special, like the offices of Givaudan, but then, Ohio wasn't France. Then again, without a sense of smell, she wasn't the woman they'd hired either. She looked about for any sign of humanity, but saw no one.

"God help me," she whispered.

"Well, you must be Daphne!"

She startled at the sound of her name and turned to see a middle-aged woman with a dirty-blond bob and warm blue eyes. The woman wore a frumpy polyester suit and sensible shoes, but she carried herself with a natural elegance that would have helped her pull off a visit to Chanel in any outfit.

"I feel as if I know you already. I'm Anne Robles." The woman enveloped her in a hug. "I talked with you on the phone, do you remember? My husband was off preaching out of town the day they conducted interviews, and I'd gone with him. It's so lovely to finally meet you in person." Anne pulled away and stared at her. "Aren't you the prettiest thing?"

"Oh yes, Anne, such a pleasure." Somehow over the phone she had imagined that Anne smelled like simple pleasures: Dove soap and honeyed hand crème. After meeting her, she'd be willing to bet on it.

"I knew you'd be pretty. I just didn't imagine you'd be *this* pretty," Anne said. "My, you are a stunner. Wait until the lab gets a load of you. That should pull them out of their own little world." Anne laughed to herself. "Or maybe not. The lure of obsessive projects to you scientists will never cease to amaze me. Would you like some coffee?"

"No, thanks, I don't drink coffee very often. Strong tastes interfere with my palate."

"Ah, of course."

Daphne tugged at her jacket sleeve. "I must be a sight after the plane ride. Is there a place I could freshen up?"

The truth was, Anne's warmth made Daphne want to cry. Her own mother hadn't offered her a hug after the failed wedding; this total stranger had given her more emotional support for simply showing up. It messed with her emotions somehow. Made her want to run and not look back.

"If this is you a sight, then I don't want to see what you look like in top form. Have some mercy on the rest of us. You pretty girls always make it look so easy."

Daphne gave a nervous laugh and felt heat in her face. She could tell by the way Anne went on that she must know about the wedding. "You're too kind." She longed to get the niceties behind her. "I'm so embarrassed that I've brought my suitcases with me, but I was anxious to see the lab again."

"What's that in the bag over your shoulder?" Anne asked. "Something I could take to the lab for you?"

Daphne shifted the canvas bag. "It's my bow. An archery bow. When I can't think clearly, I go to the archery range. It helps me think."

"Ah, isn't that clever?"

Daphne had thought she'd find more support for her archery habit in Ohio than she had in California. Perhaps not.

"Well, we've heard so much about you from Dave. He's gone on so about your credentials that we almost believe you've got magical powers."

Daphne swallowed hard and felt her mortality. "I'm not sure I can live up to that kind of talk." Or any talk, come to that. She looked around the office again, at the bank of cubicles that housed her coworkers. "Will any other new employees be starting today? Or soon?" she asked cryptically.

Anne stared at her as if she had three noses. "I don't think so. We're a small company. You're the first laboratory hire in a long while. I'll take your bags and put them in the storage room if you don't need anything in them."

She bustled through the office, past the glass bank of walls toward the cubicles, then suddenly stopped and dropped the luggage at her feet near the front desk while she focused intently on Daphne. "I'm so excited for you to meet everyone. We need some new blood in this office."

Daphne stayed quiet, feeling the weight of expectations. If everyone believed she possessed the power to turn Gibraltar around with a single Superman-like leap, they were in for disappointment.

"Is Mark going to be here?" she blurted, unable to contain her curiosity any longer.

"Mark?"

"Mark Goodsmith. He was hired the same day I was— for the sales department—and I hadn't really heard if . . . you know . . . if he'd be starting the same day as me." She didn't mention that she was nearly two weeks early, sans honeymoon.

Anne's mouth moved into a round O position. "You mean— I'll let your boss discuss that with you. Legally, I can't comment on employees."

The atmosphere suddenly had grown chilly.

"I just want to know if he'll be here. You don't have to tell me anything more than that."

Anne stopped in the wide hallway before they entered the cubicle section behind the glass walls. She lowered her voice. "Your former fiancé—that's Mark?"

Daphne nodded.

Anne pulled her into the nearby ladies' room and waited for the door to close behind them. "They rescinded his offer. He lied on his résumé, so he won't be here." Anne took Daphne's hand in hers. "I'm sorry."

"No, no," Daphne said lightly. "That's fine. I just wanted to know, that's all. I wanted to know what I should expect."

"Of course you did."

One of the bathroom stalls opened, and a tall, lanky brunette with flowing dark hair and an outfit straight out of *Vogue* emerged. An unfriendly smile overtook the gorgeous face, and the woman exchanged a look with Anne that Daphne didn't like. She washed her hands and exited without saying a word.

"That's Kensie. She's in marketing, and you'll meet her soon enough. The restroom didn't seem like the place for a proper introduction. But if I were you, I wouldn't mention Mark to her."

At the sound of Mark's name, Daphne plunged lower emotionally. "He's not coming . . ." Her voice trailed off as reality sank in. Mark was gone. The man she thought she'd spend the rest of her life with . . . She might never see him again.

Anne put her arm around Daphne. "I promise you, the best is yet to come."

Out in the hallway once again, they walked to the front desk. Anne rolled the luggage toward a door behind the desk, opened it, and the luggage disappeared from view. "Let me get you to Jesse. He'll be anxious to meet you. And if you want a shoulder to cry on, you come to me. All right?"

Daphne nodded. "Who is Jesse?"

"Your boss."

"I thought Dave—"

"You were Dave's idea, but you're Jesse's formulator. He

was at a conference when you were here before. Wait until you meet him."

*Yes*, she thought. *Just wait until he meets this magical nose who can't smell a thing.*

She sucked in a deep breath as she followed Anne. If she had known Mark wouldn't be in Dayton, would she have come? Maybe this had only been her pathetic attempt to get him back. She wanted answers; knowing Dayton held none, she was ready to retreat. She wasn't as ready for healing as she'd thought.

Anne turned briskly, and Daphne practically ran into the older woman.

"Sure you wouldn't like something to drink?" she asked. "Some water maybe?"

"No!" Daphne lowered her voice. "I'm sorry. No, thank you. I'm a little nervous."

"About Jesse?" Anne grabbed her wrist. "You really are nervous, aren't you?" She motioned toward a chair in the office's lobby. "Why don't you have a seat and let me know when you're ready. He's got plenty to do."

"That will only give me more time to worry. Let's get it over with." She prayed her sense of smell would miraculously be back before she met the man.

"As I mentioned, my husband is a pastor," Anne said out of the blue. "I know you're not likely thinking of dating yet, but we have an excellent singles' group. I'm sure you'd enjoy it."

Daphne gasped slightly. "Sounds lovely," she lied.

Anne led her to an office door with its shutters to the hallway closed and its inhabitant a mystery. Daphne read the nameplate on the wall. *Jesse Lightner.* He sounded innocuous enough, but with the way Daphne's life had been going, she knew better than to make rash judgments.

Anne tapped on the door. "We have an open door policy here at Gibraltar. Even a closed door isn't off limits if you knock first."

"Wonderful," Daphne said, trying to catch a glimpse of Jesse when Anne opened the door. She only heard his deep voice.

"She's not here already?" he said, before he noticed her presence. "Ah, you are here." A tall man approached them with long, assured steps. He made a quick assessment of her, but she couldn't tell what conclusion he came to.

His dark hair was cut close to his head, almost in military style, and his sharply cut features emitted an air of intensity that felt almost criminal. She shuddered unwittingly as he approached, but her eyes were glued to his form. His tailored suit did nothing to diminish the rough-hewn masculinity beneath. Her eyes fell to a tattooed wedding ring on his left ring finger.

Anne waved her in. "Daphne, meet your brand manager. This is Jesse Lightner. Jesse, this is Daphne Sweeten, the famous nose of Gibraltar."

For a fleeting moment she smelled the essence of baby powder, and she filled with excitement that her nightmare had ended. "You're a father!" she said too enthusiastically, as if no one on earth had ever parented before him.

"I am," he said. "How did you know?" He narrowed his eyes and looked at her warily, as if he'd encountered the paranormal.

Daphne longed to grab her bow and find the nearest archery range.

"I—uh—I thought I smelled baby powder," she explained. A frame on Jesse's desk faced away from her, and without thinking, she turned it toward her and saw the future she'd lost. An infant was curled up in Jesse's arms and a gorgeous blond woman stood next to them, looking at the two as if they were pure magic. The sight of the happy family made her stomach churn. If Daphne were blond, would she be more attractive? Better able to keep a man? She struggled to regain composure. "Your family is beautiful."

*Love does not envy,* she told herself.

She searched for words that would take that judgmental skepticism off Jesse's face.

"Your wife looks like she'd wear Gucci's Envy. Have you ever smelled it? Peonies, jasmine, pomegranate, and teak. It sounds like it would be really heavy, but it isn't. The combination totally works."

He stared at her darkly, and she scrambled to explain herself. Something about his intensity stripped her of composure.

"She seems to have the elements of the most feminine qualities, but she also seems so warm, so the wood would ground her. If you're looking for a present, I'd recommend it."

He reached for the photograph and planted it facedown on the credenza behind him. She was rattling on, she realized. And she hadn't gained back her sense of smell; it had only been a fleeting gift, taunting her with the essence of baby powder.

She stared at her boss again. Most people had no idea how to select a scent for themselves. Jesse's flavor would be a Hermes cologne with notes of berries, balsam wood, and dried mosses: manly and rugged, a protector with berry overtones hinting at accessibility under the gruff exterior. His type was true, she decided, not the sort to wander. The thought made her envy the blonde in the photo even more.

He was glaring at her now the way a wild animal stares at its prey. "We're not big on perfume at my house."

She cleared her throat. "It's one of my gifts, sensing signature scents for people. By their personalities. Am I right?" She looked toward her feet. "About your wife, I mean?"

"I'm not married," he said.

She wanted to point out the tattooed wedding band, but *Even fools are thought wise if they keep silent*, she reminded herself, and bit her tongue.

Somewhere during this disastrous conversation Anne had slipped out of the office.

"Please sit down." Jesse motioned toward the chair, and she sat immediately like a well-trained dog. He closed his eyes for a minute as if her presence had already worn him out.

*God, please. I can't take any more. Help me out here.*

When Jesse opened his eyes, she noted their color—a blue-green like she'd never seen. The blue parts were like a deep periwinkle, the green a soft, mossy earth color. She felt mesmerized by their uniqueness until he blinked and woke her from her momentary peace.

"I hope I didn't—"

"I'm not married," he said again, as if she might have missed it the first time. "What exactly can you do for Gibraltar?"

Jesse stared across his desk at his recently acquired liability of Daphne Sweeten. How was he supposed to keep such a worldly creation cooped up in the dank halls of Gibraltar? At the sight of her, he'd instantly had the image of trying to keep a hummingbird still. He'd expected her to be beautiful—after all, she'd come from the fashion industry in Paris—but he hadn't expected her allure to have any effect on him. He thought himself above that weakness since Hannah's death. But his reaction betrayed him. There was nothing inappropriate about her attire or demeanor; she wore a knit suit that hugged all the right curves and yet was the essence of modesty. But he struggled to find words to speak to her. Instead he barked everything he said in cold staccato.

He tried to redeem himself. "I hate to be unprepared, but I had very short notice you were coming today. I confess I'm not sure what to do with you." He stared down at her portfolio that lay open before him on the desk. "You're a perfumer, and as such I realize you're highly sought after in the field. But you're also overqualified for our needs here." He rapped his fingers on his desk. "I make floor wax and dishwashing liquid."

She gazed at him with wide blue eyes. With her dark hair and full red lips, she looked like a model on a magazine cover in the grocery store. But the picture came to life, and she came back at him with the same force he'd used himself.

"Perfume is no more glamorous than floor wax," she said. "Maybe Switzerland and Paris are more glamorous settings, but the job is essentially the same. A little less art and a little more science, perhaps, but I assure you I'm up to the task. I have the chemistry background and am quite capable of formulation at any level. I've worked with the latest in formulation software and machinery."

"The latest in software and machinery we don't have," he said bitterly. *We do have . . . you.*

She shifted in her seat but otherwise seemed unfazed by his forthrightness. "You're getting me for a good price, since I'm fresh out of my internship. I'm sure you're aware of what Givaudan graduates make."

"I'm aware of it, but from my standpoint it hardly seems worth it. I'm just not sure we need a Givaudan graduate on staff."

"Have you ever had one?"

"No," he admitted.

"That's because you don't understand scent. All brand managers think they understand scent, but they don't grasp the power that scent creates in a person's life. Maybe when you've had a chance to see me work, you'll think differently. Why don't we wait and see?"

He tried to escape the pull of her blue eyes, but he couldn't. "Tell me how you see the two connecting: dishwashing liquid and the professional nose."

"I've changed my mind about you," she said. "I think you'd have a musk foundation with cardamom. Maybe some teen angst in the form of sandalwood."

"I think I've been insulted," Jesse said. "But I'm not educated enough to know for sure."

She laughed in a melodious tone. "See, I can help you with that."

She wasn't afraid of him. Maybe that's all it was that intrigued him about her, but that would be his downfall.

The fact that Daphne could afford to lose this job was exactly why Dave shouldn't have hired her. She'd probably already booked her flight back to Paris. She'd leave him in the lurch, with some half-designed floor wax no one else could formulate.

"Back to your question of how I'll fit in here . . ."

She flicked her hair over her shoulder. He noticed its glimmer and forced himself to focus on her words, but then he found himself thinking again about how red her lips were.

"It's the same job. Less romance, as you pointed out. But as the Bible says, there's a time for everything under the sun. A time for sensual pleasures and a time for washing the dishes. This is my time to wash the dishes and make that job a more pleasurable experience."

Her allusion to Scripture caught him off guard. Neither Paris nor California was exactly known for its faith. He saw his own prejudice coming out in his thoughts, and he wanted to give her the benefit of the doubt. Which scared him. She was the kind of woman who wasn't easily shaken, but he couldn't afford to take his eye off the prize. He needed to make his department profitable this fiscal quarter.

"I see on your résumé that you worked on a perfume for a

new movie coming out." He tapped his pencil on the desk rather than meet her eyes.

She nodded. "I'm not into Hollywood, and the scent isn't my favorite. It will tank eventually, but by then it will have sold too many for anyone to care. Sometimes it's all about the marketing, not the quality of the product."

He raised his eyebrows. "You created this product to fail?"

"We didn't create something to fail. My team created something, and the top brass on the movie selected the final product. I assume you've gone against your own ideals to please the customer. Ultimately, we gave them what they wanted, and sadly, that dog will follow me around on my résumé until I have something to replace it."

"And do you?"

"I have the scent I created for the men's gifts at my wedding. I plan to market it myself."

"Is it good?"

"It's perfect. I named it Volatility! to reflect—well, never mind. I think I'll be renaming it. Something manly."

Jesse shrugged. "Afraid I can't help you there. I'm not much of a cologne wearer."

"Back to why I can help you," she said curtly. "Most scientists create with an end product in mind, and that is a completely reasonable way to go about product introduction. I am different, as are most perfumers, in that we create based on emotion. You, the brand manager, give me the *feeling* you want your customer to have when interacting with your product, and I create a scent around the emotion. Maybe you don't even know what that feeling is? In that case, I can offer up samples, and you can tell me what they make you feel."

She may as well have told him she got her ideas from the Ghost of Christmas Past; it would have made as much sense. He scratched at the back of his neck. "What kind of 'memory' does one want when washing the dishes? You've got your lemon-lime, your fresh apple, citrus—it's like fruit salad in your sink. Most people just want their dishes done. They're not looking for an aromatherapy experience."

Did she just scowl at him?

"Fake scents only strengthen your resolve to get the dishes done. I've smelled your products, and quite frankly, I find them nasty. In fact, I might become a hoarder if I had to smell that every day—just let the dishes pile up in the sink, or start using paper plates."

Daphne Sweeten was a spitfire. And he needed that in his life like Dayton needed another great flood from its four intersecting rivers.

"You're not shy with your opinions, are you? Do you happen to know the market share we've got with our dishwashing liquid?"

"I know you can use more, or your boss wouldn't have hired me." She leaned back in her chair and crossed her arms.

The peacock blue of her suit highlighted her eyes, and he imagined she knew that. She understood how her fluid movements captured attention. She had to. Anyone that in tune with the smallest details in life knew the effect her appearance had on others.

"I'll be frank with you." He laced his fingers together on the desk. "I don't want to count on you for a product, only to have you fly off to Paris midcycle and leave me high and dry."

Daphne's eyes softened, and for the first time Jesse realized she might not be as tough as the front she presented. She looked thoughtful, and he waited for her to speak.

"You don't have to worry about me leaving. Presently, I have nowhere to go." Those blue eyes looked directly into his own. "I'm as stuck with you for now as you apparently are with me, and I promise you that when I get the opportunity to leave . . . *if* I get the opportunity to leave, I'll give you as much advance notice as I can possibly manage. Deal?"

She reached her arm across the desk, and he took note of her feminine hand and the soft pink nails, probably still manicured from her wedding.

He grasped her hand, and it felt small and vulnerable in his own. He quickly dropped it and cleared his throat. "I appreciate that. Would you like to visit the lab before I take you to lunch?"

She reached into her bag and pulled out a small, oddly shaped, cobalt blue bottle. She set it gently on his desk. "This is Volatility!"

"I don't really wear cologne," he said. Then he caught sight of the gold lettering on the bottle and realized it had been her wedding favor, and empathy welled within him. He uncorked the stopper. The scent filled his nostrils. Truly, he'd never smelled a cologne like it. It wasn't heavy or overbearing, but it was distinctly masculine. "I think I get it."

"I'd like to have a bottle designed and trademark the name. I really believe in this scent. It took a lot out of me. The ingredients aren't overly costly, so it's something that can be mass-produced pretty easily. And I have reason to believe it will be—with or without me."

What did she mean by that? He couldn't figure her out. Of course, he'd never been able to figure women out, which was why he'd been such a failure as a husband.

"Maybe you should talk to Ken. He heads up beauty and grooming. He could help you."

"Won't you help me?"

Were her eyes starting to swim with tears? He lifted the bottle. "I told you, I don't know the first thing about cologne."

"I don't know the first thing about Ken, but this scent, you're exactly who it's designed for. Manly men, men who wouldn't be caught dead spending more than five minutes in front of the mirror," she said. She glanced about his office. "You may not know cologne, but you know how to market products. How to package them."

He laughed. "Laundry detergent. I know how to package laundry detergent and get it to market on time."

He looked at her eyes again and was afraid she'd break into sobs at his desk. That tough exterior really was nothing more than an act. And Lord help him if he wasn't a sucker for a crying woman.

"You're trustworthy. I can see it in your eyes. This may sound ludicrous to you, but this fragrance is about taking back my power. I need this. And if we can help each other, why not?"

He knew he'd regret his words, but they came tumbling out anyway. "I'll do what I can."

She smiled all the way to her eyes, and Jesse knew his troubles with Daphne Sweeten were a lot bigger than his budget.

# Chapter 4

Daphne had laid all her cards on the table and realized shortly thereafter that she had far fewer reasons to trust Jesse Lightner than she did Mark . . . and look how that had turned out. Mark used to tell her she tended to give the game away in negotiation, offering up too much information up front. How ironic that his best advice would echo in her ear a moment too late.

She'd always found his take on negotiation, and people in general, to be slightly paranoid. He'd certainly kept his cards close to his chest when it came to his wedding escape.

"Maybe I should do this myself," she said as she lifted the cobalt bottle from the desk.

"You made this scent for your wedding?"

She nodded.

"The one that didn't happen, I'm assuming."

"Yes." She supposed that was the only thing that could be worse: having two weddings that didn't happen. She wished she could run from view and hide the red heat she felt on her face.

"Well," Jesse said, stacking papers on his desk, "I'm sorry that happened, but it appears you and I are meant to work together for this season."

He looked sincere, and she appreciated that. Though at this point, alone in a city she didn't know, she'd probably cling to any port in her current storm.

Jesse wasn't hard on the eyes. His soft smile implied empathy, but not pity. As her superior he was off limits, but it didn't hurt to look.

"I just need you to stay until Christmas," he said.

When she looked at him, he shrugged.

"You were straight with me. I figure being straight with you is the least I can do. It will build some trust between us. This is how trust is formed."

"By being bad negotiators?"

He laughed. "Why not? It doesn't appear either one of us has a choice presently, so we may as well prove our combined worth."

She never should have shown him the cologne, nor let him know she had nowhere to go. She could apply for other jobs. She had options. Why did she make herself sound so completely pathetic?

"I'll do what I can for your cologne. Bob's our packaging expert. I'll tell him this is private; you can trust him. In return, you'll stay through Christmas. Is it a deal?"

Jesse reached out his hand, but her eyes were locked on the tattoo wedding band.

"It's a deal." Christmas was only six months away. It would take her that long to find a decent placement.

The phone in his office rang, and he looked toward the display. "Excuse me, I need to get this." He lifted the phone. "Jesse Lightner." He paused and twisted around in his chair so he faced the window. "Sure, send her in. I'll have her take Daphne to the lab." He turned back around and put the phone down. "Good news. Marketing has arrived and is going to tour the lab with you while I get some paperwork done. We'll meet for lunch and talk about your first assignment. Maybe we can find an emotional aspect to dishwashing after all."

He tried to hand her the cologne bottle.

"Don't you need it for packaging?"

"Right."

He curled his hand around the bottle, and she tried to decipher if he'd ever pick it up again. Six months wasn't a lot of time; she'd make good on her word even if Jesse wouldn't. She only hoped that he was a man of honor who would do as he said. She needed that at the moment, if she was ever to believe in love again. She needed to believe a man could keep his promise, no matter how trifling it seemed.

There was a light tap on the door, and then it opened to reveal the beauty queen of epic proportions whom Daphne had seen in the bathroom earlier. She had to be nearly six feet tall in her heels, but even if she'd been five two, Daphne would have felt looked down upon. The woman looked very French and very elegant in her white, high-waisted nautical pants with a stylish blue rope for a belt. Her look was both impeccable and timeless. She tossed her long, dark tresses as if she knew the cosmic disturbance she'd cause with the action.

Discouragement gripped Daphne. Not because she wasn't the belle of the ball—she hadn't been the belle of her own wedding—but because she wasn't even the most elegant woman in a small office in Dayton, Ohio. Maybe Arnaud never had wanted her back and had been relieved at the opportunity to let her go.

"Kensie Whitman," the woman said from atop her Barbie waist and under her Kardashian-worthy mane. "You must be Delilah."

"Daphne," she corrected. "Daphne Sweeten."

"Isn't that sweet? I knew it was something biblical." Kensie smiled.

Daphne thought it useless to correct Kensie on Greek mythology versus the Bible. Something told her it would fall on deaf ears.

Kensie seemed young for her marketing position. Maybe twenty-four at the oldest, Daphne surmised, but the confidence she showed in what must be five-inch stilettos said that Kensie wouldn't be held back by anything, much less age.

Daphne couldn't stop staring. She wished she possessed that kind of spark that gathered attention like flowers gathered bees. A woman like Kensie would never be left at the altar, and that made Daphne feel sorry for herself all over again.

"What's that?" Kensie asked, noticing the bottle on Jesse's desk.

Jesse opened a drawer and put the bottle inside. "It's nothing. A sample from a company wanting to do business with us. You know how they are."

Daphne looked to Jesse, and then to Kensie, confused. If

Kensie was marketing, wouldn't she be involved in a discussion about packaging?

"What time should I bring Delilah back?"

"Daphne," she and Jesse said together.

Daphne didn't think for a minute that Kensie didn't know her name. The woman didn't get to be marketing products by forgetting people's names.

"Have her back by noon," Jesse said, barely acknowledging Kensie's presence. "Do you like Italian food, Daphne?"

"You're not going to take her to the Spaghetti Warehouse! Jesse! That's where he took me when I started. Now he knows better than to take me to that dump."

"I like Italian food," Daphne murmured.

"Jesse, look at her suit. She does not want to sit in a vinyl booth in that suit." She turned toward Daphne. "St. John, right?"

"Yes," Daphne said, not adding that it was from her trousseau and she'd never owned anything like it before and probably never would again. It was the one and only thing she owned with a label that she hadn't picked up at a Paris flea market. Working in chemistry, one rarely invested in clothing for work. And now that she'd learned that formulation at Gibraltar was done by hand, she never would again.

Jesse looked bruised.

"I'm fine, really," Daphne said. "I like comfortable restaurants. We don't even have to do lunch today if you're busy. You can just let me read over the product information on what you want me to start working on. I'm very much a self-starter."

There she was again, making excuses to be ignored. She'd

allowed it with Mark, she supposed. Best not to get in that dynamic again.

"Make him take you to a nice lunch. Trust me, it's the only perk you'll get around here. Moths fly out of Dave's wallet—but first you'll have to fill out a requisition form to get him to open it at all."

"Kensie, take Daphne to the lab, will you?" Jesse said.

"Your wish is my command." She saluted Jesse in unspoken homage to her nautical outfit. "The lab's upstairs. I'm sure Jesse plans to get you out to the manufacturing plant at some point."

Daphne grabbed her handbag and briefcase, and struggled to keep up with Kensie's long strides. "How do you walk so fast in those shoes?"

"I've been wearing them so long, I'd probably have more trouble in flats. Shoes aren't important to you, huh?"

Kensie looked down at Daphne's shoes, and they suddenly felt very cheap and last year. In truth, they were just practical, and they weren't cheap. Comfort didn't come cheap.

"I have to be able to walk around the lab all day and protect my feet from any toxic chemicals. Friday night, sure, I'm all for heels."

Even as she said it, she sounded ridiculous. As if Kensie would believe Daphne had any nightlife to speak of. On a Friday night, Daphne was either at the archery range or testing scents in her home office—maybe if she was really feeling wild, she'd knit. She wondered if it showed, how incredibly boring she was. Yet another reason Mark probably escaped.

"Well, don't spend your money for good suits in our lab.

Even if the guys are neat, they're easily sidetracked." Kensie smiled. "I should know. I've had a few chemicals splashed on me giving tours to prospective customers. Wear your lab coat and keep some distance."

Daphne finally caught up with Kensie at the elevator. "I have a chemistry background. I know my way around a lab." The comment sounded full of herself, and she tried to recover. "When I was in Paris, I only used to dress up when we met with a client. I suppose that's your area of expertise, so I won't need suits here."

"Did you ever meet anyone famous?" Kensie asked as though she might hear a chewy morsel of gossip.

"I did, but we're under strict confidentiality rules at Givaudan. I can't give away proprietary information."

"Please. You're kidding, right? Tell me who!"

She leaned in, giving Daphne an up-close view of her absolutely flawless skin. So flawless, in fact, that Daphne forgot what she'd been asked.

"Didn't they fire you? I mean, that's why you're here, right? I doubt it matters if you tell me who you met there in your secret building."

"I wasn't fired," Daphne clarified. "They offered me a position, actually, but I left of my own free will."

"I've never left a company that didn't beg to get me back."

Daphne wanted to ask how many jobs she'd had in her infinitely short career, but she bit her tongue. "That's great. I hope it stays that way forever."

"Why wouldn't it? That guy you toured with the first time

Kristin Billerbeck

didn't get the job, by the way. Turns out he lied on his résumé.
I didn't think you science sorts were sly enough to do that, but
I have to admit, I was intrigued when I found out. A bad boy
scientist is, you know, kind of intriguing."

"That's too bad," Daphne said.

Kensie pressed a slender manicured finger toward the elevator's button. "I know, right? Because he was hot and he was
totally flirting with me, and this office could use an influx of
good-looking men. Well, what office couldn't, right? The bores
we have around here are not worth a second glance. Jesse would
be hot if he wasn't so hung up on his dead wife."

Daphne gasped at the callous comment. "Jesse lost his wife?"

"Some say 'lost.' Some say she did it on purpose. I suppose
with as quiet as he is, we'll never know."

"That's terrible!" Daphne felt suddenly very protective
toward her new boss and didn't want to hear any more. "He
must have been crushed. Any rumors are just that, I'm sure."

"Are you for real? Or did Laura Ingalls Wilder just get off
the train from California?"

"I just think . . . I think it's none of my business."

"Rumors are usually based on something, in my experience." Kensie turned and looked into the mirror on the elevator
as the doors opened. "Fine. We'll talk about something safe.
What's your favorite perfume?"

Daphne followed the elegantly timed clicks of Kensie's heels
across the wide hallway and into the bright white lab. "I guess
it's—"

"Mine is Toxic Love," Kensie said. "Have you smelled it?"

"Yes," she said without commentary. In truth, she might have picked the scent for Kensie without asking.

"It's, like, got pheromones or something in it. All I know is when I wear that stuff to a club? I'm, like, irresistible to men."

"I'm sure that has something to do with the way you look, Kensie."

"Why? You don't like Toxic Love?"

"No, it was a compliment. I meant because you're so pretty. That's why men find you irresistible. But I bet if you smell great, it only adds to the allure."

"Sure," Kensie said. "So this is the lab."

The pristine white room was lined with windows overlooking the city of Dayton. "Wow, it's amazing. The lab and the view." She loved how the lab was expansive and allowed the scientists to work together, but separately.

Kensie looked at her. "You're easily impressed, I'd say. Are you planning to live downtown?"

"Um, I'm not exactly sure. It seems my fian—father purchased a house here, but I haven't seen it yet. I plan to stay in a hotel first and get situated."

"Your dad . . . your dad bought you a house?"

"As an investment. He does real estate development for a living." She longed to change the subject. "So tell me about the lab."

"It's a lab." Kensie shrugged her delicate shoulders. "I don't see how it's any different from any other lab. It's got scientists who are all brains and no street smarts, certainly no chivalry or dating sense. That's what I'm here at Gibraltar for—to bring common sense into your world so you can focus and I can get your products to the market."

Daphne couldn't find her voice, as two of the scientists were within listening distance. Luckily, the roar of the hoods probably drowned out Kensie's running commentary.

"Here's a lab coat. Put it on." Kensie tossed her a coat and slipped out of her heels and into hard-toed shoes. "Nylons aren't acceptable as leg attire when you're working. You'll need to bring pants. Oh, and no jeans."

"I think I've got the lab rules down." Chemistry was chemistry, and the rules didn't vary that much from lab to lab.

One scientist stood over a centrifuge in his safety glasses and gloves, but without her nose, Daphne couldn't tell what he was mixing. There was a pang in her stomach from all she missed. The roar of the fume hoods filled the lab. There were only two scientists in the room, and neither looked up or took notice of their arrival. She didn't want to draw their attention anyway, since without her sense of smell she had no way of knowing the volatility of the chemicals they were using. And she didn't need any questions.

It dawned on her that her job might be more dangerous without her nose. It wasn't just the matter of measuring proper values in a pipette. Now she'd be working with more cleaning agents. But she hoped with the loss of one sense, her others would only get stronger until scent came back to her. As she took in her surroundings, Kensie patted her on the shoulder and yelled over the noise.

"This is the formulation lab. Fragrance is down at the other end, but both Willard"—Kensie motioned toward a man who wasn't old enough for the name Willard; he was maybe fifty and stood with a volumetric pipette measuring solution— "and John"—she pointed to the younger man at the centrifuge machine—"count on fragrance to work well with their formulations. If they don't, trust me, you'll hear about it in the staff meeting. They can't confront, so they have to tattle like second graders. Around these parts, the scent doesn't come first. Marketing is first, product second. Scent is discussed in marketing. Beauty works out of its own lab and has four scientists on staff. They don't usually mix. I suppose you'll be in the fragrance lab by yourself."

Kensie had been shouting to be heard, and as Willard flicked off his fume hood, the room got eerily quiet.

"Is that so?" Daphne crossed her arms. She'd never heard of a company that placed marketing over product, but it might be the reason Gibraltar was still so small. If the company followed Kensie's sashaying hips, it was bound to lose focus. Her father had always told her to be careful with upper management who hired model-like assistants; he claimed their love of beauty clouded their ability to run a company and do the hard tasks. She wondered what dear old Dad would say about a marketing manager with those same qualifications. "Did you go to school for product marketing?"

Kensie whipped around and stared at her. "Do you mean, like, college?"

"Well, yeah. I suppose so."

"While others were letting Daddy's trust fund pay for their

tuition and buy houses, I was off in the school of hard knocks learning to be the best marketing manager there is. You don't need a degree to be good at something." Kensie swung her hair with force. "I'm adamant about that, you'll find out. I don't care what the degrees on your wall say; I only care that you can do the job."

"Of course," Daphne said. "I had a stellar sense of smell before I became a nose. School just honed my skills. It helped me to understand how the business of fragrance works. It was like getting my MBA in smelling." She smiled.

Kensie didn't seem impressed. "Some of us have to find ways other than graduate school to hone our skill set." She held her arm out and walked toward the older man as if she were solving the puzzle on *Wheel of Fortune*. "So this is Willard. Say hello, Willard."

Willard noticed their presence at that point and gave a short nod. Maybe Daphne had expected too much of Gibraltar after Anne's warm welcome. It wouldn't be the first time her high expectations let her down. Willard seemed like a stuffy man in his short white dress shirt and Buddy Holly glasses. A typical science nerd. At least fragrance chemists held conversations in the lab. Or the ones she knew did anyway. They spoke so quickly in French that she caught about every sixth word, but the activity around her made her feel a part of something. In Paris, the space was so confined; it felt like she was among friends even if she was sitting alone in a corner café. At the very least, the waiters would flirt with her.

"Is he always so quiet?" she whispered to Kensie.

"He nodded. That's a full conversation to Willard. Over there is John."

John walked away from his machine and came toward them. Everything about him seemed intense: with his shock of dark curls and mascara-length eyelashes that aimed the intense green of his eyes like a laser pointer, he looked more like a character actor than a scientist. Daphne would have cast him in the role of a CSI suspect because he simply looked too good to be true. Like Mark, he had that coiffed appearance that suggested he spent a fair amount of time in front of the mirror. His very look made her uncomfortable, and she shifted her hips. He was probably in his early thirties, though his receding hairline made him look slightly older, but she was immediately on edge. His smooth exterior seemed more salesman than scientist.

He reached out a tanned, buff arm toward her as if he was flexing to make the movement. "You must be the infamous Daphne."

She giggled, then immediately regretted her reaction as Kensie stared her down. It wasn't as if she'd planned it. John made her nervous. The way a seventh-grade girl feels on her first slow dance. Not because he was handsome, but because he was so much like Mark in his self-assuredness. On some deeper, insane level, she subconsciously felt as though he had answers for her. As if a perfect stranger could tell her why Mark had left her at the altar . . .

"I'm Daphne." She shook his hand, still thinking, *Do you know why Mark left me?*

When had she become so dependent and pathetic? She was

in Dayton to heal. On her own. She'd been perfectly healthy in Paris, with a bevy of friends. She hadn't needed Mark then, and she didn't need him now. Though knowing that logically and believing it emotionally were two different things.

John looked at her with his piercing eyes as if he could see inside of her. She waited for him to speak.

"Willard doesn't like change. Don't be offended."

"No, it's fine."

"Come on over and smell what I'm working on. It will be good to get a trained professional's opinion."

"You're a trained professional," she answered. "I simply have a few more years of developing scent based on the emotion it creates." The pit of her stomach felt hard at this first query to use her skill set. A skill set she was without.

"Humor me," John said as he walked back to the metal fluted hood at his station.

"How do you design your scents now?"

"Most of them are standard. We generally don't create new scents for products. Do we, Willard?"

"No one cares what their floor wax smells like," Willard grunted.

Daphne wanted to retreat to Jesse's office. She may not have a *friend*, exactly, in her new boss, but they'd struck a deal.

"Let Daphne be the judge of that. Come here." John led her by her wrist to his station and stuck a pipette in a beaker. He held it up to her nose.

"Don't you think your expectations might be high?" Kensie said. "She's a nose, not a miracle worker." She stuck her own nose in between them. "It doesn't take a nose to tell you that smells awful. Like dirty feet. Do you even have an olfactory system?"

Daphne wanted to come to John's rescue, to tell him the formulation smelled wonderful, but she couldn't say either way without lying. She'd like to think he knew enough that it didn't smell like dirty socks, but then again, she couldn't decide what motivation lurked behind Kensie's fashionable front.

"Maybe she is a miracle worker," John said. "Beauty didn't get her, and that's a miracle in itself."

"Beauty already has four scientists," Willard said. "We only have two. Do the math."

"You're that small?" She hadn't meant to say it out loud, but she'd hope to create a new family of friends in Dayton, and statistically things weren't looking good.

"We are small, but we're growing," John said. "As long as we don't eat it this quarter. We're growing with our organic lines. People are all over that stuff now. Maybe you'll have something to offer in that area, coming from perfume. We're anxious to learn." He turned toward the older gentleman. "Aren't we, Willard?"

Willard grunted.

"That's thrilled for Willard," John explained.

"If you cared about the girl, you'd tell her the truth—that this division is one bad quarter away from being brought down," Willard said.

Daphne flinched. "That wasn't the impression I got from Jesse. He's planning for new equipment." She was the means to his end, she supposed, as he was for her—she wanted to get back to Paris and fragrance.

"He's also planning for the Easter Bunny to visit this year, but it's not going to happen."

Daphne's stomach tightened. "It's that bad?"

"Don't listen to Willard," John said. "He's a sky-is-falling type. Jesse will get the equipment, and with your creativity, I imagine that equipment will be put to good use."

"I just don't want to see another good man go down. If your expertise can't save Jesse with new products, you should quit now, young lady. He's got mouths to feed at home. Not just a new pair of shoes for you women to stumble about in."

"Willard, that is a sexist comment," Kensie said. "Daphne's not responsible for Jesse making his numbers. That's his problem."

"Kensie," John said, "you may not care if Jesse loses his job, knowing yours is safe, but we've been here long enough to know that nothing good comes from starting over with new leadership. Not in this place. It's time the board of directors looked at the real problem."

"Aw, leave her be, John," Willard said. "Kensie knows which side her bread is buttered on. She's not going to see the truth even if you draw her a picture."

"That's fine, but she can keep her wagging tongue out of my lab. If I need marketing to know something, I'll be sure and get out the memo."

"It's not just your lab. I was asked to come up here, if you must know. I don't like being here any more than you like having me." Kensie slipped out of her lab coat, tossed it at John, and stormed out of the lab, grabbing her shoes on the way.

Daphne didn't know if she should follow or not, but her feet stayed planted because the lab was where she felt most at home. The tension with Kensie present was positively explosive by lab standards, and she wanted to get a feel for the room without the other woman's presence. She also wanted to flee to Europe and beg Arnaud to take her back. How could she possibly be responsible for Jesse's success or failure when she couldn't smell a thing?

"That's an angry young woman," Willard said, but the comment seemed out of his character. "What right does she have to be bitter in her short years?"

John turned toward him. "Willard, I never thought you noticed Kensie."

"How could I not notice, the way she slithers in here with Dave and her foul marketing reports that stink of nothing good. Young people think they know everything, and they're too proud to learn what they don't know. That girl doesn't know a lot, but boy, can she stir up trouble. And I'll go a step further: I think this division's downturn is the result of her flawed reports."

Daphne had never seen office politics so violently displayed. And while she hadn't known anyone long enough to make an assessment, it seemed to her that no one had much faith in Jesse Lightner. And she'd just made a promise to the man. For someone who noticed every detail around her, she didn't have the slightest ability to discern people. She trusted everyone until they burned her . . . a few hundred times. It was time for her to leave that kind of innocence behind. Until she learned more, she wasn't going to take sides.

The door was yanked open, and Kensie stuck her head back into the lab. "You coming or not?"

"Yeah, I'll be right there."

Willard put down a pipette and ambled toward her. When he reached her, he stopped and pulled off his safety glasses. Misty gray, middle-aged eyes narrowed to focus on her, and she swallowed hard under his scrutiny.

"Go back to Paris, young lady. Or wherever it is you came from."

John shifted his weight. "Willard, don't say that. She'll think we don't want her here."

John gazed right at her with his intense eyes, and she wondered how a man with that much charisma had settled into a life of science. "We do want you here," he said. "Dave was very excited about a real nose on staff."

"It's for her own good," Willard said and turned his attention back to Daphne. "Go back to Paris."

With his gloved hand, John grabbed her and pulled her toward his station. "Come here, I want you to smell something."

Her heart pounded and she tugged her hand, but he didn't relinquish his grasp. "Kensie's waiting for me." She pointed toward the window to the hallway.

"I want to show you something first. Right now Gibraltar is living off royalties from our home dry-cleaning agents, but I think I may have something here." He let go of her hand and lifted a beaker to her nose. "Here, smell."

She sniffed but had no idea what her reaction should be. Should she be sickened or enthralled? "I, uh—wow."

"Wow, good?" he asked.

"What's it for?"

His enthusiasm diminished. "Can't you tell?"

Her stomach swirled. "I—I'm getting used to all the new sights and sounds of Ohio. I think my sniffer's off. Nerves, you know?"

He set the beaker down. "I understand. I want you to come back and let me know, though, because the formulation is proved, tried and true, but I don't feel we ever had the scent right. New and improved packaging could remind consumers what it is they love about the product."

Daphne had no idea what John was talking about, but she admired his enthusiasm and his implicit trust in her. She felt like Humpty Dumpty, and all the king's horses and all the king's men couldn't put her back together again. Part of her was left in Paris, another portion in Switzerland, and her heart? That she'd truly left in San Francisco, and with a man who'd never wanted it in the first place. The way John embraced her opinions as if they mattered so deeply created a sense of unworthiness in her. She felt like such a fraud. The great nose who couldn't smell a thing.

*Closure and healing.*

*Closure and healing.*

That would be her mantra until her sense of smell returned. Until Paris called. She'd find a new ministry at a new church and that would take her mind off her problems. No one ever got better by focusing on life's traumas. And she really had nowhere to run. Her parents didn't want her home. Sophie was getting married. And Paris was only a distant memory until she could prove to Arnaud that she was worthy of his loyalty and she wouldn't leave again. If only she'd placed that loyalty with her mentor rather than the young and charismatic Mark Goodsmith, she wouldn't be in this mess out in the wilderness of Ohio.

"If you don't like it, you can tell me," John said.

"It's not that, John. It really is as I said. Nerves. Maybe I'm getting the rumblings of a cold from traveling. I'm going to see a doctor tonight. I promise, the minute I can distinguish one note from another at my usual skill level, I'll give you an honest opinion."

If Daphne had hoped to find refuge in the quality of her work, she realized that probably wasn't going to happen. From what she could glean, Gibraltar was on the brink of bankruptcy, and it was hard to cover up the stench of failure with a signature scent.

# Chapter 5

Jesse exhaled as Daphne left for the lab, and he cradled his head in his hands. Her presence was a diversion that his department didn't have time for. He had to find a place, a project, and a salary for her—all for the dog-and-pony show that was the shareholders' meeting. It wasn't enough to make and sell good products; he had to show constant growth and movement within his department. Under Dave's direction, most of that movement seemed to be backward. But maybe that was only sour grapes talking. Leaving his vice president position at Procter & Gamble hadn't been easy; answering to Dave only made things worse.

He tapped a letter on his desk, with its professional stationery and Mark Goodman's name emblazoned across the top. He wouldn't have remembered that Mark was Daphne's former fiancé until the letter arrived, and clarity with it. There was a knock at his door, and he shuffled the letter under another paper and looked up. "Anne, how's everything going?"

"Since I saw you ten minutes ago? Fine, why?" Her eyes narrowed suspiciously.

"No reason. Always want to make sure my pastor is taking care of his wife, that's all. I'm concerned like that."

"You are," she said, but her arms remained crossed in front of her, as if she wasn't quite buying it. "I wanted to let you know I made a reservation at the Spaghetti Warehouse. You sure know how to impress a girl."

"I do my best."

"Why wouldn't you take her to the lab yourself? You've taken every other new employee. Is it because you didn't want to hire a nose? Or because she's so pretty?"

He sighed, exasperated. "Look at my desk. You can't even see the wood. It's because I'm busy and didn't expect a new employee today. Nothing more to it than that."

Anne looked past him out the window. "Is she very much like Hannah?"

"She's nothing like Hannah," he said through a clenched jaw. "Nothing at all."

"She's obviously artistic. Wasn't Hannah an artist?"

He loved Anne, but sometimes she overstepped her boundaries. Saying that Hannah and Daphne were alike simply because they both harbored artistry in their blood was like saying Winston Churchill and Hitler were alike because they were both leaders.

"Anne, I'd rather not talk about it. Daphne is no wilting flower who needs your support, I can promise you that much. If you'll excuse me . . ." He looked back down at his desk.

Anne gave him that consoling look he'd come to hate. "Fine, she's nothing like Hannah—only be nice to the girl. I wanted to keep this from becoming a sermon, but Dave is just looking for an excuse. He's been threatened by you since you came; don't give him the reason he needs to let you go. Just show Daphne the same respect you'd show any other formulator." Anne walked out of his office, and he stared at the place where she'd stood.

Jesse had never heard her talk like that. To anyone. It served as a reminder that Daphne was probably brought in for the specific reason of becoming the cause for Jesse's firing. He'd get no credit for any of the financial troubles he'd solved, but he'd take all of the blame for what Dave deemed as his failures.

The new nose had waltzed into his office in her peacock-blue tweed suit as if she owned the place. The fact that she'd smelled baby powder upon sight of him made him feel about as masculine as a drag queen. And the way she plucked his family photo off his desk and offered her opinion. Daphne had no need of him, or anyone else for that matter. Life wouldn't overwhelm a woman like Daphne.

In that brief instant when she'd helped herself to his family photo, he'd connected to her—because he wanted a part of that confidence again. She'd reminded him of how proud he'd been of his accomplishments and his family. The way her soulful eyes lit up as she discussed powerful memories—as if she could swim deeply in their joy by pulling them up at will. He coveted that ability. Memories brought no joy for him, and that made him feel guilty. He had a lot to be grateful for.

The space Anne had vacated was now complemented by Daphne in his doorway. He drank in her appearance with fresh eyes. She possessed an exotic, alluring beauty with her long, silky dark hair and deep blue eyes . . . In spite of all she'd recently endured, her eyes sparkled with an inner light that reminded him joy did not come from circumstances.

He glanced down at the letter from her ex, a skunk of a man; now he folded it and shoved it into his top desk drawer. After reading the letter, she was a complete mystery to him all over again.

He and Daphne looked at each other in a silent standoff, neither of them certain what to say to the other, like a bad first date.

"Is this an inconvenient time? Do you want me to come back later, after lunch?" Dave, a foreboding man who never lost his high school quarterback swagger, had stuck his head in the doorway and tapped twice on the door frame, as was his custom.

Jesse's boss oozed what he would call a false confidence; at least it wasn't based on any accomplishments that Jesse could observe. Dave's father-in-law had started the company, and Dave's marriage apparently deemed him qualified to run it. His successes always came at the expense of others, but that wasn't how the man saw it. In Dave's world, he had done everyone else a favor by hiring them, and in return he expected unquestioning loyalty. Jesse did his best because, after all, God had commanded that he respect the authority put into place, but it was a struggle.

"So, I see you've met your nose. What say you on the matter?" Dave asked in his pompous way.

"I'm anxious to hear Daphne's amazing ideas. But we were just about to leave for lunch. You wouldn't care to join us, would you?"

"Me?" Dave said. "No, I've got back-to-back meetings all afternoon." He towered over Daphne in a way that made Jesse want to get between them. "Daphne, welcome to Gibraltar. I assume you're getting all the help you need to get started and work effectively here."

Daphne looked toward Jesse. "Absolutely."

The woman's raw emotional state after a failed wedding made her a perfect target for Dave's entrapment mode of unfettered loyalty. Jesse himself had been a prime target because of his loss and desperate need of a different job at the time. His experience with the competition only made the snare that much more effective. He'd have to make sure Daphne didn't end up like him, stuck at Gibraltar.

"I noticed there were some ticks in your employee files at your former company." Dave looked at the window as he spun his web. "Not enough to deter me, obviously, but enough where I thought you should be aware that we don't put up with that kind of thing here at Gibraltar."

"How did you get a look at my employee file?"

Daphne appeared confused. Her employee file probably said something as innocuous as her French wasn't very strong. Dave wouldn't release the details. As was his custom, he'd let her wonder what terrible sins her former employer scribbled into her file.

"Nothing is secret in this day and age," Dave said. "That's

why it's always best to be forthright. I can't help you further your career if you're not honest with me."

Dave was so transparent, Jesse could almost hear a sinister laugh emanate after his statement.

That was Jesse's true job: to entrap Daphne so she felt there was no option for a job elsewhere. Wasn't that Dave's modus operandi? *Make your employees desperate and grateful, and they won't leave you until you're ready to cut ties.*

Daphne swallowed, and Jesse stood up. "We're off to lunch, Dave. Anything else?"

Jesse didn't understand men like Dave. The man didn't accept input. He hired the best and the brightest, listened to nothing they had to say, and then when his plans failed, he'd fire the employees who did what they were told. The dynamic was maddening, and it kept the office in a state of paranoid turmoil. They were all so worried a coworker would turn them in, conversations were riddled with subtext and stealth.

Dave looked at Daphne. "You're going to see that Dayton isn't missing anything that Paris or San Francisco has. This is going to be home before you sneeze over a scent strip."

Jesse couldn't stand to watch her confidence dissipate further. He had to get her out of there. "We'll miss our reservation," he said. "You're sure you can't join us?" He knew Dave's schedule didn't have room for small talk.

"Now wait a minute." Dave motioned his palm down to tell Jesse to sit. "Maybe we should discuss those marketing reports before you two go to lunch. I'd like to hear how you plan to utilize this nose here. By the way, did you hear we've got your nose insured?" Dave rocked back on his heels, looking pleased with himself.

Daphne stared at Jesse, and he wished he could read her mind. She gave a half smile. "Will you excuse me for just a minute?" She exited the room quicker than she'd done the time before.

"I don't think she's ready to work yet." Jesse shrugged.

"You give everyone too much leeway. You give an inch, they take a mile. That's why your employees don't have the respect for you that's needed. Don't baby her, and she'll be fine. She has to sniff stuff, for crying out loud. How hard could her life be?"

Jesse ignored the part about his employees not respecting him. The dig had no merit; he knew it wasn't true. "Daphne says she creates on emotion. If her emotional state is not great, that's going to come out in the product. As it would with any artist."

Dave rolled his eyes. "I didn't expect this from you. It's your job to get the business side out of her. Kensie can make recommendations for her to work on products that will make money. It's more than pretty-smelling water here. She needs to understand that."

"Kensie's ideas all have to do with how to make housecleaning sexy. She's not exactly our market. I don't think she's ever actually cleaned something in her life."

*More importantly, none of her ideas have worked.*

"I'll never understand why you're so hard on Kensie. Are you jealous of her success because she's so young?" Dave yanked the top of a chair and pulled it under him. "Being a good leader does not mean being in competition with those under you, those you can grow."

It took every ounce of strength Jesse possessed to keep quiet.

"I'm looking at the results. Not one of Kensie's studies has produced a profitable product yet." Jesse slid a report across his desk toward Dave. "That doesn't make you nervous—putting your faith into another one of these marketing reports?"

"What do you have against that poor girl? Is it because she didn't go to college? I'll remind you, I worked my way up as well."

*Married your way up is more like it.*

"She's ineffective. That's all. Her studies haven't proven to be of any use in the market."

"Daphne's not pregnant, is she?"

"What?" Jesse said. "Why would you even ask that question?"

"She was going to get married and she didn't, so I thought maybe it was a shotgun wedding gone wrong. And she's excusing herself in the middle of an important meeting. You don't think that's a little strange?"

"Who thinks like that?"

"Maybe if you did, we'd have a profitable quarter. Nothing wrong with seeing the world the way it really is."

Jesse knew better than to speak. No good could come from anything he might say.

Dave cleared his throat and leaned back in the chair. "I handpicked you for this project, Jesse. You make this investment pay off, and they're going to pay attention at the board meeting." Dave kept his voice low and turned to swing at the door behind him until it slammed shut. "You understand that even having a nose on staff can increase the stock values. All we have to do is convince the stockholders we've got the ability to do something special. You too busy for it? Want me to pass it off to beauty? I know they'd be thrilled to get her."

"No, no. I appreciate your trust in me, and I will make the most out of it." All he needed was the tired accusation that he wasn't a team player.

"And she's obviously available," Dave whispered. "You just have to wait until she lets go of this other guy in her head. Timing couldn't be better."

"I didn't notice." Jesse wanted Dave out of his office. He wanted to know if Daphne was off crying in the bathroom. "This lunch is strictly business."

"You worry too much. But you're not a married man, Jesse, and that's why you've got this promotion in your sights. You've got no wife to hold you back."

Jesse winced at the thought that a wife held one back. Statistics didn't support that notion, actually, but Dave saw the world differently, and there was no sense in arguing facts. Life was one big business opportunity to Dave, and for all the man's faults, in the guy's head he was doing Jesse a favor. So Jesse tried to be grateful.

"This is just the start. I expect you two to visit the fashion shows, the bridal shows to get ideas for new scents. That's how Procter & Gamble does it."

"Procter & Gamble has money."

"Got to spend money to make money." Dave tapped the desk twice.

Banks weren't lending, and Gibraltar's P&L sheet would hardly entice them anyway. Even Dave would eventually have to come to the conclusion he had tried to warn him about. Until then, he would continue to charm the skin off a snake and sport an aura of success.

Dave wasn't finished. "This woman, Daphne, has the ability to transform household products for us and give us a real shot at a greater market share. Have you thought of a way to get her to stay yet?"

Jesse had indeed thought of a way; in fact, he'd wrangled a promise out of her to stay until Christmas. But he didn't think he had the heart to force her to keep it. How could he put her in the same position he found himself in—at the mercy of Dave?

"Excuse me, Dave, but we're going to be late for our lunch reservation. I'll grab Daphne on the way out." The concept of a lunch reservation at the Spaghetti Warehouse was laughable, but if he had to listen to any more of Dave's "pep talk," he wouldn't be able to focus.

"Right," Dave said.

Jesse's phone trilled, and he glanced at the caller ID display. "That's my sister—I have to take this." He waited for Dave to exit and picked up the phone. "Abby, everything okay?"

"Yeah, no problems. I just need you to take over early tomorrow night, okay? If it's a problem, I can take Ben next door for an hour."

"No, I can be home at a decent hour. What's up?"

"Spike made dinner plans and told me to dress up."

She gave a little giggle, and Lord forgive him, Jesse's first thought was of himself. What if Abby went on with her own life—which she should do—where would that leave Ben and him? Maybe the only reason Dave's ways annoyed him so much was that he possessed the same flaws.

"Jesse, did you hear me?" Abby asked.

"Yeah. Sorry, what time did you want me home?"

"Is five okay?"

"No problem. I have to run. Kiss Ben for me. And, Abby?"

"Yeah?"

"Never mind. Just kiss Ben for me."

"I will. He's watching *Thomas the Tank Engine*, or I'd let him talk to you. Face it, you're no competition for James the Red Engine."

"No, I'm not. See you soon." He hung up the phone, grabbed his sport coat, and ran to meet Daphne. Standing outside the ladies' restroom, he felt ridiculous.

Kensie emerged, and he tried his best to appear casual.

"Jesse. Waiting for someone?" She stood with her arms wrapped tightly about her and her lips pursed.

Jesse didn't answer. That girl made Scarlett O'Hara seem low maintenance.

"I took her to the lab, as you know. John and Willard are both working on projects for me, and I want them done. Daphne stayed in there jabbering, and I have nothing to present to Dave. Can you let your new employee know to keep her chitchat to a minimum so the rest of us can get some work done?"

He rolled his eyes. "Kensie, could you at least let her have a full day of work before you disparage her reputation?"

Kensie shrugged. "Suit yourself, but when you find yourself ensnared, don't come running to me for help."

"Duly noted."

"They work together so well in there, and you wouldn't want to mess with that dynamic. Not to mention, the fragrance lab is rarely used, so she can have that space all to herself. Plus, she's got all that emotional baggage from being dumped."

Jesse stifled a laugh. "How do you know she was dumped? What if she dumped the fiancé?"

Kensie shook her head. "No, she didn't. I looked her up on Facebook. She's public. You should talk to her about that. She needs to change her privacy settings if she's going to be living alone. Her status update said, *Sorry for the inconvenience, Mark changed his mind.* She totally got dumped. Right at the altar! That is harsh."

As if she had any empathy for her latest competition. Kensie was used to being the center of attention, a spark of light in a colorless lab.

"Why don't you take her to lunch tomorrow and see if you're right?" Jesse suggested. The last thing he needed was Kensie's green-eyed monster rearing its head in the midst of the company's crisis.

"Seriously, there's malice in that. Guys don't just leave you at the altar. It's like on *48 Hours* when someone is stabbed forty times versus being shot. There's emotional rage. It's an act of passionate rage, leaving her at the altar."

"I'll take your word for it."

"Unless she wouldn't let him go, and he couldn't break up

with her rationally. Then he didn't know how to get away from her, so he bailed. You see that all the time on *Cheaters*."

"On what?"

"*Cheaters*. It's a television show where they catch cheaters in action."

"I think you watch too much TV."

"She probably didn't get her way. I know how these princesses work; I went to high school with a ton of them. Mommy and Daddy buy them everything they need, and—"

"This is fascinating, but I have work to do." If life's lessons had taught him anything, it was that he wasn't a great judge of stability. His mother was depressed most of his childhood, so he couldn't discount Kensie's judgments rashly. But he did consider the source. He was probably looking for a rationale for why he'd noticed Daphne's beauty in the first place.

"Women know other women. You men, you think people say everything they're thinking, but women know they're like an iceberg. There's a huge amount of communication that goes on underneath the surface." Kensie's mind changed gears. "Are you leaving now? Because I have some marketing to discuss with John, and if he won't be preoccupied with Daphne, now's a good time."

Daphne came out of the restroom, and suddenly he felt like a stalker, waiting there for her. But his heart squeezed at the sight of her, and her electric smile dispelled his fears. Her doll-like waist, those eyes that created an invisible connection inside of him—they endangered him. If he allowed it to happen, Daphne would shatter his carefully constructed world. He needed to help her out of the trap of Gibraltar, and yet some unseen force drew him toward her. He thought again of the letter and wondered how much to reveal to her. He had to think of Ben and himself, but that's exactly what he'd said before Hannah died. What if his priorities were screwed up again?

"Is it time to go?" Daphne's wide blue eyes met his, and he focused on his loafers rather than give her any power over him.

He fought the urge to step toward her. "Yes. Then I'll take you back to your place, and you can rest up for tomorrow."

"I haven't been there yet." She pulled out a scrap of paper from her handbag. "This is the address. It's not too far out of your way, is it?"

He perused the address. "Nothing is too far here in Dayton, but this is actually quite close to my place." He rubbed at the back of his neck again.

She had a *house*. She was committed to Dayton. He took the news like an unwelcome houseguest. He didn't want to feel any obligation to Daphne. He had enough obligations in his life.

"My father bought it for me. Well, for us. My fiancé and me. It was supposed to be a wedding gift. Now I guess it's an independence gift." She looked at the address in his hands. "I'm going to make a hotel reservation on my phone. That's best until I know . . ."

"Know—?" He tried to understand what she was wrestling with, but she was tapping something on her phone.

Kensie was still standing there, listening to their conversation and smiling. She gave Jesse a look and then spoke to Daphne. "Is it true you got jilted at the altar?"

Jesse clasped his eyes shut.

"It is," Daphne stated plainly. "Then I sneaked into my own reception and took the top layer of the cake and the cologne bottles I'd made as gifts for the male guests. Oh, and my maid of honor and I ate the whole layer of cake in one sitting."

Jesse chuckled. "Good for you. No sense in letting good cake go to waste."

"Why didn't he show up? Did you guys have a fight or something?"

"Marriage was going to get in the way of his dating life, so we decided to call it off. Anything else you want to know?"

Daphne winked at Jesse, and he smiled despite himself.

"No," Kensie answered meekly. "That will about do it." She crossed her arms over her chest again. "Oh, but, Daphne, I'd like to meet with you tomorrow once you're settled and let you know which products I'd like you to work on."

Daphne smiled sweetly. "Sure, Kensie. I'm looking forward to it."

# Chapter 6

J esse realized his mistake at once. He may as well have
taken her to McDonald's. The red-and-white checkered
tablecloths stained with former patrons' meals, the Chianti
bottles dripping with wax and dust, the sticky menus, all fused
together in a perfect storm of degradation. It made it look like
he'd railroaded her into agreeing to stay and he wasn't going
to put in any kind of effort whatsoever. As if he took no pride
in his position. If Dave observed them in this run-down pizza
shack, he'd think Jesse's main objective was to rid Gibraltar of
Daphne's presence as soon as possible.

He searched for conversation to fill the awkward silence.
"We should go somewhere else."

"This is fine," she said as they were led to their table.

The waitress, who smacked her gum and wore too much
makeup, including drawn-on eyebrows in the shape of an exagger-
ated rainbow, set down two scratched jelly jars full of iced water.
"You ready to order?" she asked as she pulled a standard number
two pencil from behind her ear.

"We'll need a little time, thanks," he said.

Daphne's eyes scanned the room, but he couldn't begin to know what she was thinking. She had that way about her, as if there was an entire world spinning in her head and she released none of it to the public.

"I should have asked for the name of a nicer restaurant, but I go out so rarely. My sister and I used to come here because it was loud, and if the baby cried, no one cared. It's time to update my repertoire."

Daphne crossed her hands in front of her on the table. "I don't know what you mean. I prefer this over something fancy. Especially today."

"Most of the restaurants I frequent give free toys away with the meals."

She grinned and lifted her menu. "I hope I can hear you, is all. I'm anxious to know what my first project will be. Dave seems pretty anxious for us to get started."

"Dave's always that way—get used to it. Let's order first. You have to be starving. They don't feed you on planes anymore."

"No, but my mother packed me a meal." She perused the menu, then looked back up at him. "She's Greek."

"Huh?"

"Greek mothers like to feed you. They have a tendency to think their children are nothing but skin and bones. Even when they're spilling out of their clothes."

He wasn't going to touch that with a ten-foot pole. Everything looked exactly right with her skin and bones.

Daphne dropped her menu on the table and with laser

accuracy aimed her blue eyes directly at him. "Kensie told me your wife died. I'm so sorry. I felt like I should tell you so you didn't think I was gossiping."

"I'm sure she did. I bet it was a real struggle for her to keep her mouth shut for three minutes."

"When you said you weren't married earlier, you didn't explain, but I couldn't help but notice you have a wedding ring tattooed on your finger. It seemed a relatively benign thing to know about your boss. If he's married. How many kids he has." She shrugged her shoulders.

He opened his mouth to reply when the waitress reappeared. "You ready?"

"No," he said, rather gruffly, and she vanished again.

"I thought maybe you were avoiding the topic of marriage with me because you knew I just got dumped."

Jesse thought about what Kensie had said about communication being a large percentage underwater. No wonder he didn't understand women.

"No, that wasn't it at all." He lifted his ring finger. "My wife was allergic to metal, so rather than rings, we both had this design made." He dropped his hand again. "My life's not for the faint of heart. I just figured you had enough to deal with, and we'd keep this strictly professional."

"Except for me needing help to get back to Paris and you needing me to stay through Christmas. Professional besides that, you mean?"

"I guess I do. You're very direct, aren't you? Not a lot misses your attention."

"It comes from having your senses deepened in perfumery. I don't miss much. The exception being that I was about to be left at the altar." She laughed.

"You're laughing?"

"I figure if I missed that, I missed something even bigger, and this is God's way of sparing me. Not that it feels that way at the moment."

She didn't know how true that statement was, Jesse thought. But he had read Mark's letter, and he did know.

"Can I get you something to drink here?" The gum-smacking waitress stood over them again, with her pad uplifted.

"Uh . . ." Daphne seemed discomfited by the interruption.

"I'll have a Coke," Jesse said, to hurry the waitress on her way. "Daphne?"

"Coffee," she answered.

"Any appetizers?" the waitress asked.

"No." Jesse shook his head and focused on Daphne again. Every time they started to find their footing, the blasted waitress interrupted.

"Ready to order?" she asked.

"Not just yet," he snapped. "I'm sorry," he said to Daphne. "You were saying?"

She paused and lifted the wax-covered bottle. "Interesting decor. Some of the old-school restaurants in North Beach have these." She blew on it, and dust flew into a cloud and forced a cough. "I'm so sorry," she said, laughing. "I don't know what made me do that!"

"Probably the fact that you're used to dining in better

establishments. You have a great laugh, by the way." He fiddled with his salad fork and noticed its water spots. "You may not believe this, but I used to be good at wining and dining clients when I was at P&G."

"I'm sure you were," she said, laughing again. "And I'm only laughing because I would totally do this. I'd remember some place fantastically in my mind, recalling the scents that lured me back, and then reality would strike when someone else asked what I'd been thinking. So I like it. It makes you very human." She shook her head. "But don't bring a date here."

"Duly noted." He set the fork back down. "Did Kensie also tell you that there was suspicion that Hannah took her own life?"

"Well . . ." Daphne looked at the red-checked tablecloth rather than meet his eyes.

"She didn't commit suicide. She had an allergic reaction to the wrong medication. She was so young, and she knew about her allergies, so there was an inquiry into her death and time for rumors to get started. It turns out the pharmacist had filled the prescription wrong and gave her an antibiotic that caused anaphylaxis."

"You don't owe me an explanation. I haven't taken anything Kensie said seriously."

"I appreciate that, but I don't want you to look at me like Kensie does—like I'm a monster in a true-crime novel. If Kensie bothered to Google the event, the inquiry's findings are public."

Daphne laughed. "You don't seem like a star in a Lifetime movie, but I'll keep that in mind."

The waitress slammed the coffee cup to the table, spilling some of its contents. Daphne ripped open a salt packet and poured it into her cup. Jesse opened his mouth to say something, but after she sipped it and had no reaction, he supposed it was some French delicacy.

"I mean, the thing is," Daphne said, "usually people say, 'I'm divorced,' or 'It's complicated.' Or even 'I've never been married.' But you said, 'I'm not married,' so it made me wonder if you were trying to spare my feelings. And I just wanted to say you don't need to worry about that. I know I was dumped. It's not going to interfere with my work, just as I'm sure all of your history doesn't interfere with yours. It's a strange world we live in when our business is so public, isn't it? That's why I'm public on my Facebook. I figure if someone wants to know it, they'll figure it out anyway. May as well hear it from me."

Her forthright way left him dumbfounded. Hannah was always so reticent to share herself with him, even after four years of marriage. If she had told him more about her problems after Ben's birth, could he have changed the outcome?

"Willard told me I should go back to Paris."

"He did?" Why didn't that surprise him? "You'll find out there's no shortage of opinions at Gibraltar."

"It was nothing against you. He seems to really admire you. He just isn't sure that your department is going to make it, and he thinks I might be out of a job soon."

"I think you'll be fine. It's me who may be out of a job. But if you were my sister and not the employee sent to save my department? Yes, I'd probably tell you to go back to Paris too."

"I can't go back. At least not yet."

"Rigatoni all right with you? It's the house special."

She shook her head. "Just soup for me. The rigatoni might be too strong for my palate."

The waitress brought him another Coke and refilled Daphne's coffee.

"Two minestrone soups to start." He handed her the vinyl-covered menus. "Thank you." He looked back at Daphne. "Isn't coffee strong on your palate?"

She pressed her cup to the table, her pink fingernails still wrapped around the white utilitarian cup. "Usually, but . . ." She reached for her water and gulped half the glass down.

He pulled his reports from his briefcase. "How did you get into this business?" he asked.

"I've always been fascinated by the smell of things, how scent is so connected to memory. I guess you could say it was the way I escaped as I child. Into my imagination."

"Escaped from—?"

"Boredom. My family was small, and my parents were busy. I love the power that scent has, the ability to transform the energy of a place—like an earthy smell, or something as simple as a scented candle. It made me happy and made me feel loved when no one was around. Like an imaginary friend I could call up anytime."

"You light up when you talk about it. What's the scent say about the energy in here?"

"Listen to me talking about myself. What's *your* favorite smell in the whole world?" she asked. "I should know something about my boss if I'm going to design for him, right?"

He thought for a moment. "I'm not sure it's marketable. My son. It's a mixture of baby shampoo and him. Can't really explain it, but that smell calms me like nitrous oxide. Reminds me that the struggle to do it all is worth it."

"Most people can't explain it. That's why you hire marketing geniuses like Kensie. And why I create on emotion and not from a marketing plan. An emotion will stick with you in your memory and make your connection to a scent stronger. It creates loyal customers—that's why perfumers are always looking for the next Chanel No. 5. A scent that is fairly inexpensive to make, but one that customers are willing to pay for over the next one hundred years."

Their soup came, and the waitress set the bowls before the two of them. Daphne bowed her head and said what must have been a silent prayer, then she did the oddest thing. She took the sugar container and sprinkled a heaping helping of sugar into her soup.

"Uh . . ." He reached his hand up but thought she must know what she was doing. Maybe with that special palate there were things a girl had to do. No doubt she had some quirks, with such strong senses.

She nodded as she tasted the soup. "Good."

"You like it with sugar?"

She looked at the sugar container and then back at him. "Sure." She stirred her soup zealously. "Doesn't everyone? Takes the bitterness out."

"I didn't notice it was bitter. I guess my palate isn't as refined as yours."

She smiled. "Let's talk about my first project, shall we?"

He felt so comfortable talking to Daphne. Maybe because this stranger shared her vulnerable thoughts over the sticky glass table. Maybe because she poured sugar in her soup and didn't care what others believed about her. He felt himself relax around her. It felt so good to not be so tightly wound.

But just the thought of opening up emotionally and making a fool out of himself made him shovel his soup into his mouth to avoid speaking.

Everyone carried baggage, she supposed, but the way she saw Jesse's, with his tortured eyes and his lack of faith in a job he obviously had done well, enlightened her to her own set of faults. No one probably saw her situation as dire as she did. Resilience was required. Life was meant to be lived triumphantly, not passed in the dark corners of one's worst moments. She saw where she'd gone wrong with Mark, believing what she wanted to believe about him, creating her own hero in her mind and pushing away the shadowy questions she had—all in the name of love. Love, or denial?

"We have an idea for a sports detergent," Jesse said. "It can be marketed toward mothers, but also to single young men. The idea behind it is that it wipes away the memories of sweaty athletics, but reminds people you're an athlete. A contender."

"The emotion?" She tapped her bottom lip. "Competing?"

"Winning. The emotion is how it feels to win," Jesse said.

"Think of the World Cup after a qualifying soccer game, an iron man after a track meet."

They stared at each other, then both broke into laughter.

"So not us?"

"Basically, yes." Jesse chuckled. "You said to create an emotion."

"An emotion I've felt." She ripped off a piece of French bread. "But I guess no one is going to buy a detergent called Loser, huh?"

"So we have to reach back a little further. Like the quarterback who peaked in high school. What's your last win?" Jesse handed her the cup of butter pats.

"Getting one of the spots at perfume school when my father told me it was a waste of time to apply."

"Why did he tell you that?"

"My dad's all business. The odds weren't good, but I had faith. What about you?"

"When I became one of the youngest VPs at P&G."

They gazed at each other again, and an unseen connection formed between them.

"It's not all in the past. Our wins." She didn't know if she meant it, but it felt like the right thing to say as a believer.

Jesse shook his head. "I know. God has always come through for me."

She nodded, surprised by his taking it to a place of faith. "Not always the way we imagine it. I'm wondering what my time here will teach me."

He cupped his hand over hers. "Me too."

She cleared her throat, and he pulled his hand away. "So back to Loser . . . which I think should be the code name for our detergent."

"I love it. That will take the pressure off while we create a winner."

"What scent were you going to start with?"

"Something woodsy, I think. But that's what we're paying you for, correct? What makes *you* think of winning? A spicy wood? Cedar? Balsam?" He slid the report toward her. "This is your budget, and all the notes will need to be included as well as the formulation. Here are your formulation costs." He pointed to a number.

"This is it?"

"This is the difference between a spicy-fruit water and home products."

"We don't want to make it too woodsy, or it will be too masculine. I think we need top notes of citrus to add energy to the sport. The feeling of winning is one of exhilaration. Citrus tingles the senses."

She rummaged in the briefcase at her feet and pulled out a wooden kit, which she opened to reveal several vials that he could only assume were her key ingredients.

"What do you think of starting with this?" She pulled the stopper from one of her vials and with the dropper dripped a few drops of oak moss.

"You always carry that with you?"

"You never know when inspiration will strike. I just carry the basics."

"Oak moss is a basic? That's what sugary soup will do, I guess. Inspire."

She ignored the comment. "Now this is predictable, expected. Wait until I add something to lighten it." She looked into the depth of Jesse's eyes. The dark swirl of blue and green made her think of a triumphant navy ship, its men lined up on deck in perfect uniform. "Patchouli for health." She swirled the mixture, and Jesse sniffed the concoction.

"Strong."

"Too strong without the energizing citrus." She looked through her vials and found apple and pineapple. "What about this for starters?"

He nodded and looked pleased. She took great pleasure in the thought that her mind and memory could work without her sense of smell. At least in the early stages.

"It's incredible."

"Maybe it needs an oceanic note for that feeling of freedom."

Jesse smiled. "I honestly feel like we can win again."

She put the stopper back on the pineapple vial. "We *can* win again, Jesse."

"What's the cost of this, though?"

"We don't have to go organic. Everything can be created in the lab. Synthetic can be done cheaply for scent, and we can use the organic detergent granules."

"This gets me so inspired," Jesse said. "I feel like we could expand the lines. Even consider some of Kensie's crazy ideas."

"Such as?"

"Sexy fabric softener."

She nodded. "I get it. A fresh market. Single women. Maybe even single men. Think about it—everyone loves how fabric softener makes your clothes feel. And there's nothing better than climbing into clean sheets, fresh from the dryer. It's like a warm cloud surrounding you. A cuddly baby blanket effect. But if you're single, and you're going out for a night on the town, do you want to smell like silky sheets or a baby's blanket? Silky sheets have an appeal." At the way he looked at her, she instantly backed down. "Not that I'd know. I've just been in Paris, you know. Everything is about being alluring and—"

"You don't have to explain. I didn't think you were ready to hit the singles' bars. It's just that I can't remember the last time I went out for more than a church potluck, so I'm not this market." He smirked. "My sister does the laundry. I doubt she's concerned about my being sexy. The mere thought would probably make her laugh."

As fresh as her breakup sting was, Daphne had little problem imagining Jesse as sexy. In fact, she suspected that fact was hard to miss by most women, whether he smelled like baby powder or musky leather. For the first time since losing her sense of smell, she felt excited about creating.

"Granted, asking men to buy fabric softener is probably far-fetched, but single women? What if you added some spice notes, like amber or cloves? Add a top note of musk or woods? Package it in red, and Scents & the City is born."

Jesse cocked an eyebrow, and she wondered how it was that she felt she could trust someone whose story she knew so little of—who left so many unanswered questions. But she did. She even *liked* him, and that's what worried her the most, she supposed. He made the feeling of wanting to shoot arrows for hours on end go away. He reminded her that her ability to create went beyond her sense of smell.

"I have to admit that when you didn't say anything about my car on the ride over here, I was worried."

"Your car?"

"The spoiled milk smell. I found a sippy cup full of milk curdled into a solid this morning. I was worried you might vomit upon getting in."

Her eyes went wide. "Nope. You don't give me enough credit."

"Then when that skunk smell on the road didn't dissipate—"

As quickly as confidence had filled her, it puddled around her ankles, and she corked the vial of the scent she'd created at the table. The scent she had no ability to test herself. "Maybe we should get back to the office."

She didn't meet Jesse's gaze. God forbid that he discover what a fraud she was. Maybe Mark had known instinctively that her career would fizzle as quickly as it ignited. For some reason, she wished she could show Jesse otherwise . . . that she could retain some sense of what it meant to win.

# Chapter 7

Daphne finished her tasteless soup and her first day at work and took a taxi to a hotel nearest to an all-night clinic. The hotel was close to Wright-Patterson Air Force Base, and she seemed to be the only overnight guest without fatigues.

She dropped off her bags and her bow but took a few scents with her to test her olfactory systems with the doctor on call. Freshly expelled essential oils from ylang-ylang and sandalwood, which she'd steam-distilled herself before she left California. She also grabbed the bottle of Volatility! just in case. She'd called ahead and let the clinic know she was coming and had spoken with the doctor himself. He'd taken her Visa number and said he'd meet her at the clinic. She didn't think that was a very good sign, but how many options did she have, on her own in a brand-new city? She rushed out of the hotel before she talked herself out of getting immediate help.

The clinic was a squat brick building with few windows.

The doctors hadn't spent much on landscaping, but that was probably due to their laser focus on medicine.

"You're sure someone is here?" the taxi driver asked her.

"I'm sure," she said, but she took his card for a ride home. She tugged on the glass doors and was met by a young man in a lab coat.

"Daphne?"

She nodded. "Are you old enough to be a doctor?" As a child interested in science, she'd loved Doogie Howser, but she didn't want to be his patient. She stammered, "Thank you so much for staying late. I just started a new job today."

"I assure you, I am fully licensed. Dr. Seghal Seema," he said, reaching out his hand. "What new job did you start?"

"I—I work for Gibraltar Industries."

"Ah. They're a nice stronghold in this town. I guess laundry detergent doesn't suffer too much in the down economy."

"No."

"Let's go into my office. Katy," he said to a mousy woman behind the receptionist's desk, "you can lock the doors now."

Katy stared at them with an eerie calm, and Daphne shuddered as she followed the doctor into his office.

"Have a seat."

She sat in a bright orange dental chair, and the doctor pulled a stethoscope from his pocket. "You say it's your sense of smell?"

"Yes, and it's crucial I get it back." She didn't mention her position, nor did she plan to. Who knew how small of a town Dayton might be?

"How long has your sense of smell been gone?"

"Nearly five days now."

"Are your taste buds affected as well?"

"Yes."

"Did it leave you suddenly, or did you lose it gradually over time?"

"Suddenly."

He took his two hands and felt her neck. "Your glands don't seem swollen. That's a good sign. You haven't had rhinoplasty—a nose job—recently, have you?"

"If I had, it would look more like Angelina Jolie's."

Not so much as a smile.

"Were you hit by anything? Any blunt-force trauma?"

"No."

He took out a scope and looked into each ear. "You don't appear to have excess fluid. Any colds recently?"

"None."

"Allergies?"

"No."

"I'm going to check your nose for polyps now."

She winced automatically. "My nose is very important to me. Can you try as much as possible not to touch the edges of it?"

"Of course," he said as he stuffed in the speculum with what could only be described as blunt-force trauma. Her eyes watered.

He set the scope down, placed his hands on his knees, and rolled backward. "It must be allergies. I don't see anything."

"Is it—is it possible that an emotional trauma could cause this?"

"Anything is possible, but I highly doubt it."

"Is there anything that can fix it? I really need to smell." She forced the desperation from her voice. He didn't seem the type to respond to hysterics.

"This type of thing is usually caused by an underlying infection."

"So what can I take?"

"Well, I can give you some antibiotics. Of course, we don't like to prescribe them unnecessarily. Maybe some steroids would help with any inflammation that may be causing the problem. You can take zinc. Of course, that can cause a problem if you take too much. You haven't been upping your intake of zinc, have you?"

"Not unless zinc is in wedding cake."

The doctor blinked. "No, that wouldn't cause an overload of zinc," he said with all seriousness. "But if it doesn't go away, I think we'll want to do a CT scan. We'll want to make sure there're no lesions or tumors that could be causing this."

"What about stress? Can stress cause it?"

"You said you just started work today. How much stress could you be under?"

"Well . . ." She paused. "I moved across the country." She preferred not to tell him that she'd been left at the altar. Something told her he wouldn't get the emotional connection.

"This is short-term. I'm certain of it."

"What about Botox?" she said desperately. "Could that make my sense of smell work again? I saw your poster in the entryway."

He shook his head. "No. If anything, it's more likely to cause the problem. Maybe if you took your mind off of getting your sense of smell, it would come back. Do you have any hobbies?"

"Yes, I have hobbies," she said, annoyed. "I like to make perfumes."

"Well, that won't be easy if your nose isn't working."

"You think?"

He started scribbling on his prescription pad. "This is for steroid spray. Come back and see me in a week if you don't have your sense of smell by then. We'll run further tests." He stopped writing. "Are there any toxins you may have inhaled? I'm not a fan of at-home chemistry."

"I'm a chemist!" she protested. "Not a kid with a chemistry set."

"Were you working with any solvents? Something that might be considered toxic?"

"Only if you count my ex-fiancé." She took the prescription.

"Pay Katy at the front." He stood and then gazed at her hard. "Do you want me to fix that lip while you're here?"

She covered her mouth with her fingertips. "My lip?"

"It's larger on one side." He shrugged. "If it doesn't bother you, it's no big deal." He handed her a mirror.

"Well, it bugs me now." She'd never noticed that her upper lip was fuller on one side than it was on the other, but now it was all she saw when she looked at her face. She wondered if that had something to do with Mark leaving. Maybe he didn't want his kids born with disfigured lips. "You can fix it?"

"A little filler and you'll be as good as new."

It was scary how quickly Dr. Seema had a syringe in his

hand. Almost as if he had itchy fingers to get started on her. She fretted for about a second, but then thought of her warped lip. Maybe fixing it would make her other problems disappear. Maybe she'd been subconsciously freaking out about her lip, and her anxiety transferred to her sense of smell to get her attention.

"Will it hurt?"

"This is numbing gel. I'm barely going to use any, so you'll be back to normal soon." He rubbed her lip with the gel.

At the prick of the needle, she exclaimed something guttural and Gollum-like. "Are you kidding me? What's that numbing gel? Toothpaste?"

"Stop moving your lips or this will turn out badly."

As far as she was concerned, it was already turning out badly.

"Now I have to add a little to the other side to even it out. Don't move."

"No," she protested. "You are not sticking that syringe anywhere near my lip again. I'm not in a position to make great decisions, and I think this proves it."

"You can't go with your lip half done."

Daphne grabbed her sweater and her handbag and made her way to the door. Dr. Seema followed her with the syringe in his hand.

Katy sat in her mousy state the same way they'd left her. The girl wasn't reading. She wasn't working on a computer. She was simply sitting behind the desk waiting for life to happen to her. Maybe she was onto something.

"I need to pay for my visit."

Katy looked up, and Daphne noticed the girl's eyebrows

were in the middle of her forehead, inching toward her hairline. Though she wore no makeup whatsoever, she'd clearly come into contact with some of Dr. Frankenstein's magic syringes. "Is he finished with you?" Katy asked as she stared at Daphne's lip.

"I'm done. What's my total?"

Katy exchanged a glance with the doctor and came up with an amount. An amount that said Daphne would not be staying in a hotel long. Whether she wanted to face her love nest or she didn't, that was all she'd be able to afford after tonight.

Rather than call the cab, she decided to walk back to the hotel. She pulled out her cell phone and dialed Sophie.

"Daphne? Where are you? I didn't want to call you because I didn't know how long you'd be at work. Did you get your smell back?"

She shook her head.

"Daphne?"

"No," she blubbered. "Now my wip is bollen."

"Your what?"

"My wip is bollen. Filler. Filler in my bip."

"Filler in your bip?"

"My bip! My bip! Under my bose!"

"Your lip?"

"Uh-huh."

"Why is your lip swollen?"

Daphne grew frustrated at the translation troubles. "Mark? Did anybun hear from Mark?"

"No, sweetie. Did you?"

"No."

"How was work? Do they know you can't smell anything?"

"No."

"I prayed for you this morning. Prayed you'd have it back before you got there. Can you taste anything? It didn't seem to stop you from downing that wedding cake."

"I had something to prove."

"That sounded better. Maybe your lip is going down."

"I want to come home."

"I know you do, but Arnaud hasn't even had time to receive Volatility! It will be better if you continue to work on the packaging there. Arnaud will know he's not your only option. When I sent the package, I told him you were pursuing other avenues."

"What would I do bitout you?"

"You'd survive. Listen, Gary bought me a plane ticket to come see you. He says it's pointless to sit here worrying about everything when I can just go to Ohio and see for myself that everything is lovely."

"You'd do that bor me?"

"I'd do anything for you. Just like you'd do anything for me. That's what friends are for, Daphne."

"What if I don't have a job when you get here?"

"Then we'll play the whole time. God's in control, right?"

"Right now, it beels like PongeBob is in control."

"That's just because you're in the midst of a trial. We all have trials."

"But usually when one thing is going badly, something else is going well. I'm missing what's going right."

"You have me. I'm here."

"You're there. I'm here."

"I'll be there soon enough, and Gary has friends looking into where Mark might be. Did Gibraltar hear from him?"

"He fudged his résumé, so they never hired him."

"Why doesn't that surprise me? Okay, just sit tight and do your best until your sense of smell comes back. It has to return soon."

Just hearing Sophie say that, Daphne felt her sense would return. Sophie embraced happy thoughts like a cartoon princess, and somehow they manifested before her eyes. If anyone could prayerfully will the good life into being, it was Sophie.

"I hope so."

A truck roared past her on the road and honked a few times.

"Where are you?"

"I'm walking back to my hotel."

"In a city you don't know?"

"I'm on the outskirts of the city. More like a country road."

"That's even worse!"

Daphne looked around her at the barren road and the grass growing alongside it and came to the same conclusion Sophie had. "I'm almost there. I have to call my parents anyway. That should do till I'm back at the hotel."

"Call a taxi! And why aren't you at the house anyway?"

"I'm not ready to see it."

"That's just weird. You're acting weird."

"I know. You're not going to diagnose me with anything, are you?"

"I should. Your parents aren't home, by the way. Your dad's in Europe on business and your mother left on a cruise."

"How—"

"Just get off the phone with me and call a taxi. I don't want to hear you were found in a ditch somewhere."

"I can see the hotel from here." She wanted to keep Sophie on the line. "No one's heard from Mark? Not even his parents?"

"If you spend one more second worrying about him, I'm going to scream. He's fine. He's probably basking in the sun somewhere on someone else's dime. Does that make you feel more for him?"

"I just don't understand, Sophie. What did I ever do to him to deserve this? He knew how my parents are about money, yet he let them spend all that money on the wedding he wasn't going to show up for. He let my dad put a down payment on a house for us."

"You're trying to make sense out of something that makes no sense. Would you call a taxi? I can't stop worrying about you in the middle of nowhere."

"I'm fine."

"Maybe you should come home. You can stay with me until you figure out what's next."

"I promised my new boss I'd stay until Christmas."

"Daph! It's okay to take care of yourself first. Why do you always do that? You're in Dayton for one day, and you're already putting someone else's needs before your own!"

"He's a single father."

"That's not your problem."

"He just needs me until Christmas for the shareholders' meeting, then I can go. In return, he's going to help me package Volatility! Maybe by then Arnaud will be ready to take me back."

"I called around for some churches in the area. I sent them to your Gmail address. You need to get a posse there if you plan to stay six months. I'm planning to see you soon, though."

"I'm at the hotel."

"Thank goodness. How's your lip?"

She touched her mouth, and it still felt huge. And painful. "Swollen. Even if I had my sense of smell, I couldn't sniff around this lip. What was I thinking?"

"At least you can talk now. Just forget this, Daphne. When Mark couldn't get a job in Paris, you made all these concessions, and now you have nothing to show for it. I'm worried you're going to do the same thing for this single father. He's not your problem. This company isn't your problem. Come home and regroup. You can get a job anywhere in the world."

"I *could have* gotten a job anywhere in the world. Past tense. I don't know why yet, but I feel like I'm supposed to be here. It's only been a day, and I see my piece of the puzzle fitting. At least for now."

The problem was, could she trust that inner calling after all she'd been through? It wasn't just that Mark left her at the altar; it was that he'd *left* her, completely and utterly. No phone call. No good-bye. No closure of any kind. Just left her to imagine the worst about herself. Everyone could tell her that his actions said more about him than they did about her, but being abandoned was not unfamiliar to her. There was some message in his action that she felt compelled to understand if she wanted to correct it.

After she hung up, she entered her hotel room and dropped her handbag on the bed. She stared into the mirror over the dresser and clasped her eyes shut, only to open them and see shiny, reddish-pink lips the size of a child's inflatable toy on her face. She couldn't help but giggle.

"Why do you have to be the sacrificial lamb?" she asked her reflection. "Jesus did that already. He doesn't need your help!"

How would she go to work the next day? She looked as if she were wearing fake wax lips from Halloween. Well, if she'd hoped to take the attention off her nose, she'd certainly succeeded. Oddly, her mind went to Jesse and what he'd think. He already thought her slightly off-balance for adding sugar to her soup.

She opened her suitcase and pulled out her Bible. She had all the scent passages marked, including the ultimate image of humility that inspired her. *"Then Mary took about a pint of pure nard, an expensive perfume; she poured it on Jesus' feet and wiped his feet with her hair. And the house was filled with the fragrance of the perfume."*

How could God take away her most precious gift? It made her wonder if she'd done something wrong, something she wasn't aware of that harmed another. But God wanted good for her, for all of His children, so she kept looking for the lesson in her affliction. God had His reasons. Reasons she might never understand, but still she ruminated on possibilities.

The perfume market, with its glut in the marketplace, was oversaturated. She didn't want to miss the message this time.

She'd ride God's wave that had brought her to Dayton. For the next six months anyway. She'd rely on her chemistry background to get her through. Her nose might not work, but her science skills did. Chances were, Gibraltar Industries would never know she couldn't tell the difference between an iris and a rose.

# Chapter 8

J esse watched as Daphne entered the office, once again weighted down by her suitcases and what appeared to be a weapon of some kind. Her ruby lips looked as if they'd been stung by a thousand bees in the night, and he knew he couldn't let her enter household's department meeting without asking a few questions.

"Have a seat. You really didn't go to your new house yet?"

She shook her head. "That involves all sorts of things. Groceries. Turning the heat on, making sure there's furniture. I'm just not ready for that yet. I want to focus on the task at hand. Our laundry detergent. I have a good feeling about this, Jesse."

"I'm glad, don't get me wrong. I have a new enthusiasm for what it is you do, but I think you may want to take some time to get yourself settled before moving straight into Gibraltar's production schedule. It moves very quickly and becomes grueling once the process is started. If you're not prepared for it, I'm worried you won't make it through the cycle."

"I'm ready for it," she said, straightening in her seat. "Totally ready for it."

Jesse recognized her avoidance immediately. It was a tactic he used well. "Daphne, after my son was born, my wife worked herself to the bone to be the perfect mother. She was so weary and didn't even know it. I'm concerned you're not quite up to this yet."

"I'm fine," she said flippantly.

"Let me finish."

She sank farther into her chair. Her posture reminded him of Ben when he found out his time-out wasn't quite over.

"I was so excited about Ben and how my life had changed, I failed to notice that Hannah wasn't sleeping—even when the baby was. I was so lost in my own bliss, being the youngest vice president and a brand-new father, I missed what was really important. I can't help but wonder, had I helped more, been more aware, could I have changed the outcome? What if I'd been there when she took her pill? What if I'd been the one to give it to her? I would have seen her allergy signs." He paused as it took all his strength to say the final part. "Ben would have a mother."

Daphne pressed her lips together. "I don't believe my circumstances are anywhere near so traumatic. Jesse, I got dumped. By a tool. Really, I was saved from a miserable life, and one day I'll get to where I know that's the truth. But until then, I don't want to wallow in it. Did you want people to let you wallow in your sorrow, or did you want to get on with life?"

Now who had overstepped his boundaries? How could he make her understand that one didn't move forward without dealing with the pain of the past? Maybe it wasn't his responsibility, but as he gazed at her he saw so much of himself, it felt unbearable. He couldn't stand to watch her be swallowed up by one mistake and give up the future she really wanted. He knew how Dave worked, and he wanted to make sure she didn't lose her dream to keep their agreement.

"What did you do to your lip?"

She pressed them together with force, and he wondered if she really thought she could hide the fact that her mouth would enter the conference room before she did.

"We're going to be late to our meeting," she said. "Can't we discuss this later?"

He drew in a ragged breath and did what he had set out to do—make sure she wasn't taken by surprise. He withdrew the letter from Mark and placed it on the desk between them. "Do you recognize this?"

Her fingers twitched as though she wanted to reach for it, then her strength of will won over and her hand muscles relaxed. "Our personal lives shouldn't matter. We've got a job to do, Jesse, and we'll do it and then we'll go on our merry ways. You'll be the hero of Gibraltar, and I'll go back to Paris."

"I don't think that's possible with Mark at Givaudan."

He watched the fight seep out of her. And then, acceptance.

"Mark's at Givaudan?"

"I think it's best if you sit this meeting out. It will give your lip a chance to deflate, and we'll have more time to discuss the formula." He pushed the letter from Mark toward her. "And, Daphne . . . you can't live in a hotel the entire time you're here."

"Who are you to tell me where I can live?" she snapped. "There's plenty of time for the house. I want to get to the lab and get my station set up and finalize the scent for Loser."

"By the way, you can't have that here." He nodded toward the bow. "It's against company policy to have a weapon in the office."

"It's not a weapon, it's a bow. For archery."

"People hunt with them. It's a weapon."

"We had an archery team in France."

"*We* have a softball team. You can't keep your bat in the office either. After a few weeks of working here, you may have a better understanding of why." He chuckled.

She nodded. "Jesse, what is it you want from me? Why do you care so much how I'm dealing with my failed wedding?"

He felt their connection weakening in her accusatory tone. She wasn't ready to connect the dots of how they both came to Gibraltar in weakened states. But he was determined that she not get stuck there forever. Six months was all she had to give him, but already the idea of her leaving squeezed at his heart. Which made him more determined. A beauty like Daphne didn't belong at Gibraltar. She had so much more to offer, as he'd had once.

"Your lip is the size of Texas, I haven't given you the base notes we want you to create from, and that letter may have an effect on you. It may not, but it often gets rough in there. So why don't you plan to sit this one out?"

She looked at him with a determined set to her jaw. "I'll just tell Dave I'm not ready with my creative process yet. It's only been one day. I'm sure he'll understand."

"You haven't met the real Dave yet."

She reached for the letter, stuffed it into her pocket, and left for the conference room without looking back. She definitely wasn't lacking in confidence.

Jesse dropped his head in his hands. Daphne hadn't even read the letter, and he took that as a bad sign. When he was grieving, he kept bad news at bay because all he could deal with was the grief at hand. He'd hoped seeing what a dirtball her ex was would help her move forward, but apparently she wasn't ready.

If she crashed and burned without finishing their sporty laundry detergent, Jesse's hopes of keeping his numbers high were hopeless, and he'd exposed himself for nothing.

Well, maybe he was wrong. Maybe avoidance would work for her. In any case, he had a meeting to run.

As he walked into the room, he realized he was too late. Dave was already in the conference room and had hijacked Jesse's meeting. Daphne was wide-eyed and her breathing shallow as Dave paced behind her, waving a series of scent strips. Daphne turned around and eyed them as if they were medieval torture devices.

Jesse suddenly remembered two very important things: Anne had told him that Daphne didn't drink coffee for her palate, but not only had she ordered coffee at lunch, she'd sprinkled salt in it.

Was it possible that she was having trouble with her sense of smell?

"I can't wait to show you all what this little machine of a nose can do," Dave was saying. "There are formulators, and there are noses, and I'm about to show you, my team, the difference. I realize that some of you"—he glared at Jesse—"think that bringing Daphne on was a mistake, but when you see the difference in creating fragrance versus covering the scent of a cleaning product with another scent, I think you'll understand."

Jesse watched Daphne carefully. Her deep blue eyes darted about the room in fear. Maybe she had a cold and wasn't up to par, but it seemed deeper than that. By the stone-cold expression she wore, he knew he had to buy her some time. Why he felt the need to protect a woman he hadn't even wanted on his staff, he didn't understand. Maybe he'd suggest she take some time to get settled in Dayton before really starting to work, and that would take care of whatever was wrong with her nose.

Dave fanned and shook the scent strips for effect. "I have in my hand a few scent strips. You're all familiar with these." He raised his eyebrows toward Jesse, and Jesse instinctively knew this was for his benefit. It wasn't enough that Dave had hired Daphne without asking him. His boss simply had to humiliate Jesse in front of the staff to undermine his authority.

Jesse cleared his throat but caught himself before he said anything out loud. What good would it do?

"Did you have something to add, Jesse?" Dave asked.

Jesse tried to recover a poker face. Dave *didn't* want Jesse or his department to succeed. They were bleeding money, and Jesse would either be a hero or another zero, like the three department heads before him. No one had successfully managed Jesse's group to a profitable quarter since Dave himself had done it, many years before. Jesse may not have understood the motive, but he suddenly felt as though he was nothing more than a pawn in whatever game Dave was playing.

Dave stood at the head of the room, his impressive stature demanding full attention. Jesse was forced to take a backseat in his own meeting.

"I hold in my hands ten scent strips with various scents, courtesy of our lab." He looked toward Willard and thanked him with a nod.

Willard tapped a pencil, anxious to get back to his lab.

Across the table, Kensie grinned as if taking pleasure from Daphne being on trial.

Jesse stood. "Dave, I'd like for this department to start working as a team, and I fail to see how this display will help the team know they are all of equal value."

Jesse couldn't begin to explain his protective stance toward the nose he hadn't wanted to begin with, but he felt as though God had appointed him her protector. Left without a friend in a town where she knew virtually no one, the fiancé who abandoned her taking her job in Paris, no one with her to help her get settled into a home she hadn't even selected. It seemed like a pile of wrongs he somehow wanted to right.

"Precisely my point. If we don't know what each member of the team is capable of, we have no idea how to make full use of their skill set. Isn't that right, Daphne?"

Daphne offered a half smile, but with her blown-up lips, it looked like she'd blown Dave a kiss.

Willard sighed. "I know what a nose does, Dave. Is this necessary? I've got product curing, and it's not going to wait forever.

I'd just as soon get to the meat and potatoes of the staff meeting and find out my marching orders for the week."

"Dave," Jesse said with a forced chuckle, "I appreciate your zeal, but Daphne's got nothing to prove to me. We've got a full agenda this morning." He watched as the blood drained from Daphne's face. "We all know what a nose does. I fail to see how a demonstration is going to help us this morning. She's well on her way to creating our new scent, and I don't want her nose getting corrupted. You don't mind, do you?"

Dave quickly regrouped, pressing the fanned scent strips together. "Of course not. Whatever it takes to keep her asset in tune, I'm for that. We'll cut it short, and I'll give her shallow scents that won't corrupt her finer tuning. Daphne, will you come up here, please?"

Jesse clenched his teeth at how easily Dave dismissed him.

Daphne's fingers were trembling, but she opened her notebook. "I'd rather sit. It helps me concentrate."

"Very well. Don't want to mess with the process," Dave said, still waving the strips maniacally.

"Dave, Daphne doesn't only recognize scents, she creates based on an emotion. Ask her to describe a feeling and put it into a scent, so Willard and John can see how she works differently. They know how to decipher a scent."

Dave dropped the scent strips on the table. "All right, Daphne, describe love." He looked toward Kensie and winked.

"Romantic love?" Daphne asked. "Motherly love? First love? They're all different. One is like fire, one like a warm towel from the dryer. First love is sweet and soft, like carnations."

"Okay, love is too many emotions. I get it." Dave tapped his chin. "Happiness. Make me a scent full of happiness."

"Happiness has a special kind of energy. It has zing, so I'd definitely have citrus involved, something universal for the top note, so that when you open the container your first experience is exhil—"

"We know all this from marketing studies," Kensie interrupted. "No offense, Daphne. I'm certain your gift makes a difference somewhere, but I just don't see it happening here. I don't see that she has anything to offer that John Banks doesn't already do." Kensie looked across the table at the scientist. "John, do you think there's something we're missing here at Gibraltar?"

"Well, obviously there is," John said. "Or we'd be profitable. I think we should get back to business so Willard and I can get back to the lab."

"Kensie, you were the one who told me we needed to have better scents to get noticed in the marketplace," Dave said. "Isn't that what your focus groups said?" Their boss glowered at Kensie. He wasn't used to her not backing him up readily, and his feeling of betrayal showed.

"Well, y-yes," she stammered. "But I didn't mean we needed to have a nose on staff."

Daphne squinted at Kensie, a questioning look on her face, and for the first time Jesse found himself wondering what kind of power the young marketing manager had over a man like Dave, whose very presence invited respect. Kensie rarely offered it to Dave.

"You didn't, huh?" Dave walked over to Daphne and swept a scent strip under her nose. "What's that, Daphne?"

The strong scent of sour apples permeated the air. Honestly, anyone who'd ever had a Jolly Rancher would have guessed it, but Daphne remained silent. Whatever was plaguing her nose was serious. Jesse set his finger on her notepad beside the word *apple*.

She glanced up at him, and he gave a curt nod.

"Apple."

"I know it's an apple. What kind of apple?"

Jesse cleared his throat and pretended there was something in his eye and puckered his lips.

"Green," she said. "Sour . . . Granny Smith."

Dave appeared unimpressed.

Jesse was worried that the strips and their scents would get progressively harder. He had no clue what he'd do if Dave came up with bamboo or iris or something equally complicated. Daphne fidgeted in her seat as Dave waved the next scent in front of her. This one was a wood of some sort, but Jesse couldn't have placed the type if his life depended upon it. He slapped the table, startling the chemists on the other side.

"It's a wood," Daphne said, understanding his odd game of charades. "There are a lot of competing scents right now. I'm having trouble placing it. It's better for a nose to keep the scent strips far away from each other so the scents don't mingle."

"Dave, any of the chemists in here can do this," Kensie said.

"I think what Kensie is trying to say is we've got chemists on the clock," Jesse said, trying to regain control. "Time is money, and we've got a lot to cover today. Why don't we start with you, Willard? How's your current formulation?"

Willard, who was like a cross between the Quaker Oats man and Regis Philbin, stood up. He liked to make things official. "Marketing tells me that a sink cleaner is needed that's gritty enough to get grease off of stainless steel but wipes away clean. Apparently women"—he paused—"excuse me, brand users, are complaining that the grit leaves a film. They like the springy lemon scent, but the residue has to go. I'm working on that formula."

"Excellent," Jesse said, hoping to regain control of his own department meeting. "Any success yet?"

"So far it's not as effective without the gritty texture. I'm hoping to add more vinegar solution to thin it without lessening its impact." Willard checked his watch. "Anne, can you get me the minutes for the rest of the meeting? Because Dave wants Daphne to perform circus tricks, and Kensie wants us to worship the marketing god, and I have real work to do." Willard exited as if the walls of Jericho had come down around him.

The chatter rose in the room, and several conversations were going on at once. Normally, Jesse would rein it back in, but at the moment he just wanted Daphne to escape Dave's party tricks.

"All right," Dave said. "I guess no one's in the mood for this week's staff meeting. Let's all get back to work."

Jesse watched his staff close their notebooks and portfolios as the meeting exploded in a wave of disrespect. He tried to maintain a modicum of control. "Leave your current reports for me. If I have any questions, I'll contact you this afternoon."

Jesse had inherited Team Catastrophe. Before that morning, he thought he'd made progress in bringing them together, overriding their individual loyalties to Jesse's various predecessors, but it was an uphill battle. Between Dave's constant meddling and overriding his authority and Kensie's stirring up dissension, gaining control always felt slightly out of reach.

The room had cleared except for Daphne, who sat there looking bewildered, and Dave, who paced like a rabid animal.

"Jesse, Daphne was supposed to help you bring this team together," Dave said. "They look worse than ever. Willard is doing just as he always does: whatever he pleases. You're going to end up exactly where your three predecessors did unless you find a way to make that group work together as a team. When I hired you, you said that you had management skills, but I'm not seeing them."

"You excused the meeting," Jesse said in shock.

"Because nothing was getting done!" Dave exclaimed. "I didn't expect this from a vice president at Procter & Gamble."

Jesse's jaw twitched. He was used to Dave's demeaning manner, but being reamed out in front of a new employee brought in a whole new need to stand up for himself. "I never had one failed quarter at Procter & Gamble," he said quietly. "Not one."

"I didn't get to corporate by making excuses. Anybody can make it at a company where they have money to throw at every problem. Figure it out, Jesse."

Dave got to corporate by marrying the owner's daughter, but what good would it do Jesse to say that? He felt two feet tall, getting chastised in front of Daphne. His skin seemed too small for his body, and he took a swig from his coffee, which was cold. He turned back to face his boss and met Dave's hard glare. "I have a plan, and you'll see results or I'll quit the job myself and spare you the trouble of firing me."

Dave left without another word, tapping the door frame twice as hard as usual on his way out.

A cold shadow of air brushed Jesse. Daphne stood and faced him. She swiped the scent strip from the table and sniffed it. Her eyes filled with liquid, and she tried to blink the would-be tears away.

"I'm sorry you had to see that," he said, feeling like a sorry excuse for a man.

She breathed deeply in and out. "You did that for me." Her soft voice barely registered. "Why?"

"I did it for both of us. We're going to win, Daphne. It's our turn."

Daphne's bright eyes sparkled with hope, and he wondered what she must have been like before Mark. She possessed enough resilience that she'd learn from her experience. In contrast, he still wanted to rescue every person in need because he couldn't save his wife.

"I was so selfish this morning. You were trying to tell me about Hannah."

He shrugged. "It doesn't matter. The past doesn't matter. Winning is what matters now."

"The past matters to you, and so it matters to me."

He nearly teared up at her words. It felt so good to have empathy.

He pulled the cologne bottle she'd given him out of his pocket. "Can I keep this?"

"I wouldn't wear it if you don't want to be married. It's pretty potent," she said with the essence of a smile.

"I'll take that into consideration."

"Ben's a lucky boy."

The depth of Daphne's blue eyes stunned him. Each time he looked deep within them, it was like seeing them for the first time. He couldn't allow her innocence to capture him; it wasn't fair to her. But he loved the idea of their newfound alliance. For once in his long career at Gibraltar, he felt as if he could actually win.

# Chapter 9

Daphne piled her bags and her bow into the back of Jesse's small, electric-blue hatchback. He'd insisted on taking her to her new house, and she was grateful for the company. She'd clutched Mark's letter in her pocket throughout the day, but she still hadn't read it. He'd stolen her life right out from under her, and his only attempt at an apology was a letter to her new employer. She hoped it was an apology, at least.

"This works out well. I have to get home early for Ben today."

"I'd like to meet him," she said.

"You will." He grinned all the way to his eyes.

They were silent as Jesse drove onto the freeway and they left the high-rises of downtown behind them.

"Your dad bought in a good area, near the university. It's one of the better neighborhoods, so I guess we won't have to worry about your being home alone."

"My dad is good at real estate." He wasn't great at being

there, but he was good at business. "Jesse, did you do anything with packaging yet? Did you ask them about my scent?"

"You didn't read the letter yet?" Jesse looked at her. "From Mark?"

She shook her head and noticed how uncomfortable he seemed with her answer.

He pulled the car off the freeway and to the side of the road by the brown grass. He met her gaze with his steely blue-green eyes, and she realized that she trusted him. But then, she'd trusted Mark too. Maybe, as Sophie suggested, she wasn't the best judge of character. But she had no reason to *mistrust* Jesse, and he was only her boss.

"What's Mark's story?" he asked.

"Pardon?" she asked, wondering why he'd pulled the car over.

"What's Mark's background? How was he suddenly able to qualify for your job when he couldn't originally get a job in Paris—or at Gibraltar?"

"He's a brilliant chemist." She turned in her seat to face Jesse, who looked skeptical. "He really is. But he grew up poor, and he had this deep need to follow the money. At first he thought the money was in big pharma, but he gave up that dream when he saw the prices on designer fragrances. He thought he could produce them more cheaply and start his own business."

She didn't tell him why pharma had rejected Mark and killed that dream. She vowed that she'd be more careful with whom she shared things from here on out. She'd given Mark all the ammunition he'd needed to take her job and her fragrance.

She wouldn't make that mistake again no matter how trustworthy someone appeared.

"Why did you pull over?" she asked.

Jesse looked at the road. "I wanted to give you a chance to read Mark's letter. I want you to reassure me you haven't given up the fight for the life he stole."

"Why?" she asked. Jesse's personal interest in her seemed strange at best.

"Because I know what giving up a dream does to a person, and I need to know I'm not helping steal yours. It may not make sense to you, but you just have to trust me. I don't want you to stay for the six months if it's going to cost you the dream."

In his eyes she saw truth, but also something more that she couldn't identify. "I haven't given up the dream. I won't give up the dream, but I'm a woman of my word and I'll stay until the stockholders meeting."

"I appreciate that."

"What about your dream? Is that what I am? A reminder of what you gave up?"

A shadow fell across his eyes. "My dream is for Ben. That's enough for me."

"I hope so," she said, but she thought his voice seemed awfully hollow. Grief hadn't left him for a moment, and she prayed that if her presence did anything, it would teach him to dream again.

"I don't want to make this about me. You were telling me Mark wanted to start his own business. Did he?"

She squirmed in her seat, anxious for him to get on the road and take the attention off of her. She was afraid she'd let it slip that she couldn't smell, afraid he already had an inkling of her issue.

"Mark needed capital to get started. He was doing sales for that reason, and he thought I could support the rest with my job here. That's why I was a little worried he'd steal the formula for Volatility!"

"Does he have the formula?"

"Most of it. I kept one ingredient out of it. It's my favorite scent. One I've never told a soul."

"Why would you keep that from him if you were marrying him?"

She shrugged. "I must have had an instinct, which tells me that maybe I overlooked a few things about my fiancé. It's the top note. It would be the first thing he smelled, and if he ever really knew me, he'd have known it from the beginning. I never made a secret of why I loved this scent. My guess is that Mark has claimed Volatility! as his own. That's why my best friend, Sophie, sent the sample to my old boss. They won't produce it if there's even an inkling that another nose designed it."

"What is the note?"

"If I told you that, I'd have to kill you."

"You want to get back to Paris. I want to keep my job and feed my son. For now, we have to trust each other. I trust you to keep your scent to yourself."

She swallowed past the lump in her throat. She didn't think she had a choice. Not at least until she patented the packaging for Volatility! Which Mark may have already done. He had stolen her last shred of dignity; what wasn't he capable of?

"Jesse?"

"Yes."

"I—" She bit at a fingernail. How could she tell him she didn't have the skills he needed to save his job? "Is there an archery range in town?"

"A—what?" He started the car up again and merged back onto the freeway.

She felt oddly comforted by Jesse's triumph over tragedy. Life went on. His situation made hers feel relatively mundane, and she vowed to pray for his full healing and understanding that there was nothing he could have done to save his wife.

"I shoot when I'm nervous and need to think. I want to shoot until I figure my way out of this. I need to regain Arnaud's trust, and yet I feel so betrayed by my mentor. How could he give my job to Mark, of all people?"

"Don't you have to move in first?"

She realized she sounded crazy, but in her defense, he wasn't sounding like the sanest man on the planet either. The two of them had been thrust into each other's lives, and for now, they needed one another. "I guess."

"I'm not going back to the office today. Do you have a ride in tomorrow morning?"

She paused. She didn't want to be any more indebted to Jesse than she had to be. "Yes," she said. A taxi was a ride.

Jesse's cell phone rang. "Excuse me a minute." He glanced at it, then pressed a button. "Hey, Abby. I'm driving; let me put you on speaker."

"Jesse, do you think you could swing by earlier than five?

Spike is already here, and he's rented out the dance studio for us tonight. Can you believe it?"

Daphne liked the sound of her—and her voice sounded remarkably like Sophie's.

"He's so romantic!"

Daphne had to admit, she couldn't imagine a guy named Spike renting out a dance studio. Sometimes people didn't fit their names.

"Where'd he get the money for that?" Jesse sounded just slightly judgmental.

"Jesse! It's none of your business where he got the money. Can you come by earlier or not? Spike wants to get me a new pair of dance shoes before we go."

"I was already planning to work from home, so yes. I've got one errand to run and then I'll be there."

"Okay, but hurry!" Abby's voice radiated joy.

Daphne remembered when she used to sound like that. She wondered if she ever would again. "She's in love!" Daphne said.

"Don't remind me." Jesse rolled his eyes. "Why do women want the bad boys?"

Daphne laughed. "He can't be too bad if he rented out a dance studio. That's all *Dancing with the Stars*, not Kid Rock."

"He wears a lot of leather and chains. Rides a motorcycle."

Daphne smiled, imagining the likes of Spike in Jesse's house. "He sounds like a picture. I'm not sure about the bad boy fetish, though. I tend to go for the clean-cut sort who have trouble keeping jobs and other big commitments. Like their wedding day.

Then I shoot arrows at a target and pretend it's their faces." She shrugged. "If I figure out the bad boy thing, I'll let you know."

Jesse raised a brow. "But that sounds like a bad boy. He just came in sheep's clothing."

"Then I haven't figured it out yet," she said.

"This is Highway 48. You'll take this to work." He paused for a minute. "What are you going to do for a car? You said you had a ride?"

"I, uh, meant a taxi. I figured I'd do that, or find a bus route. That's what I did in Paris."

"Something tells me that our public transportation isn't quite up to the Metro."

"Jesse, if we're going to trust each other, you have to trust me to take care of myself and get to work on my own. I'm a big girl."

He nodded. "Fine. But the last time I left you to yourself, you came back to work with a giant lip."

She laughed. "I went to find an ear, nose, and throat man. I mistakenly found a Botox man."

"And you let him do that to you?"

"He said my lip was cockeyed, and I thought, you know . . . maybe Mark had noticed and—"

"Say no more. I get it. Sorry. I tend to baby people."

"It's nice to be babied," she said honestly. "But I'll be fine."

"You must be close to the country club in this house." He stared at the GPS system on his car and exhaled. "You have no idea how great that is. I can tell Dave you're safely part of Dayton society."

She smiled. "I thought Mark might show up at the house,

but I guess if he's safely in Paris at my job, I don't have to worry. Apparently he and my dad had a disagreement about whose house it is. My dad left a message on my phone not to let him in."

"That's why you didn't come here. Here I've been pushing you, and it's not safe."

She waved her hand. "It's fine. My dad left for Europe on business, so he can't be too worried. If Mark did care to fight for his share of the house, it might be epic. He loves a good battle. Though I'm sure there's a mortgage attached to the house, and that will be all mine."

As they drove into the neighborhood shaded with canopied trees, Jesse stared at her. "Do you always just settle with what you're dealt?"

"I might ask you the same question. If we didn't both take what was handed to us, would either one of us be here right now?"

Daphne couldn't look at Jesse's handsome profile any longer. His presence calmed her like the scent of freshly cut flowers. If only she could truly capture his scent and know who he really was. His warmth and the depth of his own background made her want to succeed at Gibraltar. Not simply as a stepping-stone back to Paris and the fragrance industry where she belonged, but because she wanted good things for Jesse Lightner. He seemed to deserve it.

"This is your street," Jesse said. "Does it look like you imagined it?"

"It's gorgeous! I wish I could smell that tree!"

"What?" His face contorted, and he opened the window.

"You know. I don't know what kind of tree it is, so I wouldn't know its scent."

"It's a honey locust. They're everywhere here in Ohio. You'll have to get familiar with the scent. Maybe it will inspire something like Volatility!" He laughed. "How does Honey Locust Mist sound?"

"It sounds very romantic." She giggled. "Okay, it sounds like a trashy air freshener, but I admire you for trying."

"Atta girl. Bring me some of that Paris snobbery. That might save Gibraltar yet." He pulled the car to the high curb and got out. He left the car running while he pulled a branch down and ripped off a twig. It was the second time he'd stopped the car, and she marveled at the gesture. Mark never stopped the car. No matter how she might have needed to stop, he always had an excuse to keep going.

Jesse brought the twig back to the car and handed it to her with a flourish. "My lady."

She lifted it to her nose, but nothing happened. "Mmm." She focused on the row of trees at the curb and pointed. "Look at how the houses are set up off the street. It's perfect." All of the houses seemed old and well maintained. They were two-storied and clapboard on the outside and had a cottage feel to them. "I feel as though I've just entered Mayberry." She raised her hands in the air. "I can't believe I own my own home! Well, and a mortgage too, but I own my own home, Jesse!"

He grinned. "Tell me how excited you are after you shovel the driveway the first time."

"I can afford to be independent here. Maybe that's why Mark walked out on me. I didn't need him, but I was too swoony to see it. He did me a favor." The way she felt around Jesse only highlighted what had been wrong in her relationship with Mark. She'd never felt at ease with him but always as though she had something more to aspire to.

"Swoony, huh? Gibraltar didn't need him either." Jesse smirked.

"The address is 2250. Oh, Jesse, it's that white one there!" Her mood dropped as he rolled into the cracked asphalt driveway and she got a closer look. "That's it?" She suddenly wanted to shoot her bow. Preferably straight into the house.

The roof was missing a few shingles and bowed slightly in the middle, like a slightly over-loved sofa. The garage stood separate from the house with its door askew. The regular door to the house hung on its hinges in an unnatural way, and she turned her head to get some perspective. She tried to remain upbeat. "I'm sure it has great bones."

"Yeah. It's the best neighborhood."

"Is it just me, or is the state of the foundation a bit wonky?"

"I'm sure it's just our perspective. Let's go see it."

But Daphne was just sitting, staring wide-eyed at the For Sale sign. It had *AS IS* written across it like a bad beauty pageant sash.

"It's like it reads *Miss Congeniality*," she murmured. Her hands were moving strangely in her lap, as though she was knitting with invisible needles.

"What are you doing?"

"Oh. I knit when I'm nervous. I don't really knit much anymore, but my hands still go into action when I'm nervous."

He stared at her as though he couldn't believe she could get any stranger.

"I know," she said. "I'm a knitting, bow shooting, human bloodhound. You were expecting normal?"

Jesse laughed and got out of the car. He came around and opened the car door for her and held out his hand. She felt his touch like an electrical pulse to her system. She looked to him, and he pulled his gaze away immediately.

"It's absolutely the best neighborhood," he said, sounding like a used-car salesman. "Let's go see these great bones, shall we?"

The change in his tone completely shut down the sense of intimacy they'd established in the car, and to Daphne it felt like a stinging rejection. Suddenly she just wanted to be alone. She'd been stupid to think that she was ready for even a working friendship with a man.

"I've got this," she said. "I know you have to get home for your sister." She took the suitcase from Jesse as he yanked it out of the backseat.

"Are you kidding me? I have to see the place. You can't tease me and then leave it to my imagination."

His voice was so light, she wondered if he had any idea how his kind concern for her dreams and his lighthearted banter confused her. She thought he didn't want her there, but he acted as if he did.

"You don't strike me as a man who's into interior design."

"*Au contraire.*" He grinned. "Did you like that? That's my

only French. I'm very interested because you, my newest acquisition at work, have said that you create on emotion. So I have incentive to see what the emotion is within that house."

She exhaled. "I hadn't thought about that." It made sense that he was concerned for her as a commodity.

"Daphne, it's a nice house. You should have seen our first place. Oh my, all we had were pilfered milk crates and a hand-me-down couch. You wouldn't want it all done for you, would you?"

"But you got to pick it out. Right?" She needed to look to her heritage again. "I shouldn't look a gift horse in the mouth. Wait. As a Greek, should I look a gift horse in the mouth? That's how they got into Troy, right? But if I were *in* the gift horse, then—"

Jesse gazed at her. "Do you have the keys?"

"I'm rambling again."

He nodded and took the keys from her. He tossed them into the air to catch them again. "I feel like we should have some kind of ceremony. Hey, do you have one of those bottles of Volatility! in your suitcase?"

"In my purse," she said and rifled through her bag.

"Grab it. Let's spray the doorway." He shrugged. "You know, like carrying a bride over the threshold. It seems like we should mark your first house with something. You know, scent-wise."

Her expression dropped. She hadn't needed the reminder that no one would be carrying her across a threshold anytime soon. Perhaps ever.

"I'm sorry. That was insensitive. Hannah always said I failed at Romance 101. I guess she was right, but since I'm your boss, you can't say so."

She laughed. Somehow that made her feel better. "Mark excelled at it, so take that for what it's worth." She thought if anyone overheard their strange conversation that day, they would think the two were more than just colleagues.

Jesse peeled off his suit jacket and kicked at the bottom step. Like the roof, the crumbly concrete porch bowed slightly in the middle, worn down by nearly a century of foot traffic.

"You can just leave the suitcases here," she said at the base of the steps.

"I've got them," he said, following her up the stairs. The landing wasn't big enough for the two of them. He used the keys she'd given him and opened one of the locks, but one remained stubbornly closed.

"Oops, sorry," she said. She pulled another key out of a small envelope her father had given her and inserted it into the lock, jiggling it until the doorknob gave way. She felt a hot rush of air, and for the first time since she'd lost her sense of smell, she felt thrilled to be without it. She could only assume that it smelled as bad as it appeared. Air shouldn't, in fact, "appear" at all.

Dirty gray carpet met up with scarlet walls, and judging by the markings, the former owners had loved to perform auto care in their living room.

"Go ahead," Jesse said, standing on the small stoop contained by a black iron fence. "I'll do the honors." He took the small cobalt bottle and sprayed the threshold.

"I don't think there's enough of that to go around. In fact, I don't think if I took every bottle I made for the wedding, there'd be enough to go around. I have a bit of a cleaning fetish, and I think that's going to be a problem."

"You do? A cleaning fetish *and* a bow-and-arrow habit?"

"Well, I didn't know I had a cleaning fetish until this particular moment, but yes, I obviously do, because as I look around I have the increasing desire to smell bleach."

He maneuvered around her and stepped inside. "Come on in, the water's great." He took her hand and pulled her in, setting the bottle of cologne on an old mahogany ledge originally made for a telephone.

The house was the proverbial last straw. "I don't think I can stay here." She wanted to call Arnaud that very moment and beg her old boss to have mercy on her soul and bring her back to Paris. Even at the cost of working alongside Mark. "Where are the great bones?"

"They're here!" Jesse said with false enthusiasm. "Look, you can knock this wall down." He looked up at the ceiling. "Well, not this one, it's load-bearing, but certainly that one over there."

The room was a series of choppy smaller rooms with walls in the way of any path one would naturally take through a house.

"You know how Dickens got paid by the word? I think this architect got paid by the awkward barrier." Daphne stared at the dingy gray carpet, the water-color walls, and the solid mahogany staircase that stood right in front of the entrance and wondered what on earth her father had been thinking. "That staircase belongs in a mansion. Not a house this size."

"Maybe they got a deal on it."

"Stop being so positive!" she snapped. "It's a dump, and you know it."

"It's—it's got potential," he said.

"Where? Where does it have potential?"

"Maybe the kitchen. Let's go see."

They walked around the staircase and through the living room and came to what was supposed to be the kitchen.

"There's no refrigerator."

"An easy fix."

"Do you think that oven works?" She looked at the ancient stove.

"If not, you can probably sell it for a pretty penny. People love that style."

"All these depressing ocean colors make me think Moby Dick is going to burst through that staircase at any moment and tell me he's won. Then he'll consume me for dinner."

Jesse laughed. "You women are such drama queens. Is this the kind of emotion you create on? I'd hate to know what the male noses are like. I doubt I could take them."

"If you mean to imply that I'm prone to histrionics, my best friend the psychologist could have told you that. If you didn't have an ulterior motive for keeping me here, you'd see this house just the way I do."

"I don't need your best friend to sort you out. It's more fun to find out for myself."

"The kitchen is depressing," she said. "Let's see the rest." She stepped back into the room and felt swallowed up by the solid dark-wood staircase with only a small octagon-shaped window, framed in the same wood, to provide light.

"It has some nice details," he said. "Let's go see the upstairs."

He held out his arm, and she thought how those simple niceties were worth a great deal. He should definitely get married again.

She climbed the steps into a loft-like room with original hardwood floors, scraped and degraded by a life without maintenance.

"Imagine these floors redone," Jesse said, ignoring the filthy scarlet curtains against the chlorophyll-green walls and the air-conditioning unit hoisted lopsided in the window.

"Hmm," was all she could think to say. "Let's go back and see the downstairs again." She burst down the stairs with the best of hopes in her heart, and this time she noticed the tea-stained lace curtains against the brothel-red walls in the dining room.

"Jesse, it's a disaster. This isn't like my father at all. I mean, he's cheap, but he likes the good life. It's like there's been some kind of mistake. I can't believe he expected me to just move in like this." She caught sight of the hall closet underneath the staircase and opened the door. Wrapped wedding gifts stood atop each other. There was a realtor's card on top of the pile.

"Open one," Jesse said. "You'll feel better."

She took a box from the top of the heap and tore open the white and silver wrapping paper. She opened the box and pulled out a crystal brandy snifter. "I don't drink," she announced. "But I can't even keep milk here, because I have no refrigerator!"

He shook his head as if searching for something positive to say. "That's it. Get your stuff. You can't stay here. There's no furniture, for one thing. Didn't your father think you'd need at least a bed when the two of you arrived?"

"I doubt my father wanted to think about that," she quipped.

"You're not staying here," he said. "It's not habitable. Gibraltar will put you up in a hotel until you can rent a place."

She cringed. "It really is that bad, isn't it? I thought maybe I was just acting spoiled. But my apartment in Paris was four hundred years old, and it was in a lot better shape."

"I'll call the hotel," he said. "Do you want to stay in the same place you did last night?"

She lifted a corner of the carpet up and saw real wood beneath. "These can be redone."

Jesse didn't look convinced. "Not tonight, they can't."

She'd done everything she was supposed to do her whole life. For once, she wanted to do something that wasn't expected of her. "I'm staying," she announced.

His phone trilled again. "What is it, Abby? . . . I'm coming. I'm working, and you're buying dance shoes. A little perspective." He clicked off the phone. "I can't think of a man in Dayton who would let you stay here alone tonight. Your father obviously hasn't been here. He must have counted on Mark to do some work."

She smiled. "Jesse, go home. I'll be fine."

"Do you smell gas?" he asked.

"No," she said honestly. She didn't smell anything. But she imagined old houses had more than their fair share of scents, so at this moment not smelling might be a gift. "The house has been closed up for a long time."

"I'm going to check around back and make sure it's turned off. Why don't you get back in the car?"

"Jesse, I'm not going anywhere. I'm fine. You're my boss, but I'm an adult. I assure you that when backpacking around Europe during my summer internship, I stayed in places a lot worse than this. We're winning, remember? This is the last stop on the loser train, that's all."

He looked at her as if he didn't believe her. "I have to go."

"I know. I'll be fine. I know how to check the gas. Go! Before Abby hates me like Kensie does."

"Abby isn't the sort to hate. Put my cell number into yours, so I know you can call me if you need anything." He took her cell phone from her and programmed his number into her contacts. Then he walked to the kitchen and fiddled with the stove knobs. "Everything's off."

"Just go! I can take care of myself."

"You'll check outside though? Just to be safe?"

She moved in front of the back door. "I will. Go!"

She felt paralyzed under his stern gaze. He stood by the door, and it was clear he didn't want to leave her there alone. She wondered if she didn't give off an air of incompetence. It felt strange to have someone she barely knew care more about her well-being than the man she'd been set to marry.

"You're good people, Jesse. I'll be fine." She walked through the house and opened the front door. He walked out and left her alone.

She leapt into the air. "My first home!" No roommates. No surly fifty-year-old Greek man at the dinner table in an ambush blind date. And no Mark, a man who said all the right things but had no actions to back the words up.

As Jesse backed out of the driveway, she wondered what his whole story was. How had he lost the VP job at P&G? Had he been like her? Destined for greatness, only to have life give him a reality check?

"I wouldn't make your cologne dark and sensuous like Mark's," she said, her breath fogging up the window as she pressed her forehead against the pane. "You're better than that."

Maybe that was the key. Discovering someone's true scent nature.

When she was very small, Daphne's grandfather had lived with them. He was an invalid who rarely left his room, and she wasn't allowed to visit him without express permission from her mother. "Don't go bothering Grandfather" was the common refrain, but Daphne never felt as if her grandfather didn't want her there. He clung to her every word as if it were gold.

On summer mornings she'd be sent out to play to "give the house some peace." But if she opened the door to the fresh scent of rain, playing outside wasn't possible. On those special days, Grandfather was all hers. The scent of rain meant puzzles, board games, and unbridled attention.

That's what Jesse's scent was like, she thought. Unexpected and redeeming, like a summer shower. Like a fresh start, with the freedom to be who she was meant to be. The scent of rain.

Or perhaps losing her sense of smell had addled her brain completely.

# Chapter 10

W*hat a day.* Jesse's world was falling apart, but for some reason, he couldn't wipe the smile from his face. He thought about the ray of light that seemed to emanate from Daphne, and his worries seemed far away. At work he had so many balls in the air, and they were all in danger of coming down. New products, bigger budget, more expectations, and a beautiful young nose that he needed like a hole in his head. But the very thought of her made him grin. From her crazy archery bow to her putting salt in her coffee, there was something about her that mystified and warmed his heart.

He hurdled away from her house feeling the pressure of the time constraints on him. So much work. So little time and resources. And yet he felt drawn back to the house and guilty for leaving her there. Where was her father? Who would let his daughter move into that rattrap without so much as a stick of furniture or a refrigerator? How was she supposed to eat dinner? Breakfast? Suddenly her choice in husband material didn't seem so mysterious.

"I never should have left her in that house," he said aloud. Anger rose within him and burned his throat. "God, I'm putting her in Your hands. That place is a nightmare!"

Hadn't that been Hannah's issue? Why couldn't women ask for help if they needed it? If a man stepped in without being asked, he got accused of being overbearing. He was convicted by his thoughts. It was too late to help Hannah. As for Daphne, she had her whole life spread out before her like an open road. For her, Gibraltar was just a short detour. He wanted to give her a solid foundation before he sent her on her way to success.

As he pulled up to his house, the sight of the front lawn littered with Ben's plastic toys warmed him. Ben made everything worthwhile. Jesse's inability to take household goods to the next level paled in comparison.

Abby sat in the porch swing with Ben at her feet. At the sight of Jesse's car, the little boy popped up to come running, but Abby was faster. She swept Ben off the ground while he waved.

"Daddy's home! Daddy's home!"

Jesse waved back and pulled into the driveway. He got out of the car as his son wiggled out of Abby's arms and bolted toward him. He raised Ben high into the air. "There's my boy!" He kissed his son's pudgy cheek. "What did you do today?"

"We went swimmin' and I had a waffle with lots and lots of serwup. I watched Thomas after lunch, but then Thomas got stuck in the tunnel."

"Thomas got stuck in the tunnel?"

Ben nodded, and Abby walked toward them, picking up

littered toys as she came. "That tunnel being the heater vent. Thomas is still stuck in the tunnel."

"You dropped Thomas down the heater vent?"

"Thomas went into the tunnel." Ben shrugged his rounded shoulders, as if the toy train had suddenly developed a mind of its own.

"That sounds like a fun one to try to retrieve."

"Don't bother. Spike has already been here and tried. I think Thomas has officially parked himself in a tunnel of eternity."

"Daddy." Ben grabbed both of Jesse's cheeks and turned his head. "Daddy, I want Thomas back. He's scared in the tunnel. It's too dark. You can get him out."

Abby shrugged. "Good luck with that. I've got to go get ready. Spike will be back soon."

Abby was nearly twenty-nine. She'd always been slightly pudgy, but in that cute way that made her look as if she'd never lost her baby fat. She had a beautiful face, with deep-set sapphire-blue eyes and baby-doll red lips.

A caretaker by nature, she had a history of picking terrible boyfriends, ones who needed parenting more than the responsibility of a relationship. It was as though they came out of the oven half-baked, and she was determined to get them to rise correctly. A waste of time in his opinion, but like most little sisters, she didn't give much credence to his opinion. He wanted someone to take care of her the way she took care of others.

He followed her into the kitchen.

"Spike can barely afford gas for his hog right now. The shoes are a present because he did some handyman work at the shoe store and they couldn't afford to pay him. So I'm getting new dance shoes. Isn't that sweet?"

"The barter system is alive and well, I see. Abby, you're not getting engaged tonight, are you? That isn't what this is about, me coming home early? Can't you see you deserve better than this?"

"Do you have any cash?" she asked, ignoring his questions.

He shifted Ben to one side and pulled his wallet out of his back pocket. "How much do you need?"

"Twenty?"

He pulled out a bill and handed it to her. "What time are you coming home?"

"Thanks. Spike and I did want to talk to you about something."

He didn't like the sound of that. "Can it wait? I have a pile of work in the car, and I can't imagine what Spike has to say to me that I'm ready to hear today."

"Why don't you like him anyway?"

"Do you really want the answer to that question?"

"Yes." She walked away from him and took the steps to the living room. She opened the wooden box and dumped Ben's toys inside. "Seriously, what's not to like about him?"

"Besides the excess of leather and chains? I just wish he had a job and a real car. I hate seeing you putting that bucket on your head and driving off in the open air on that motorcycle. I've already lost my wife. I can't lose you too."

Ben made the sound of an engine.

"You're the one always telling me about God's will. If it's God's will that my head ends up splattered on the pavement—"

"Abby!"

"Sorry. Ben, Auntie Abby isn't going to get hurt." She turned back to Jesse. "Now you're judging people by what they wear and they drive? If Spike doesn't drive a sedan, he's not husband material? Seriously, that's Christian? Besides, if someone were to judge you by what you wore, they'd think you'd wandered off the set of *Mr. Rogers' Neighborhood.*"

"This is a nice suit!" he protested.

"For a fifty-year-old man, it is. In your case, it looks like you're in the suit we buried Dad in."

"Don't change the subject, Abby. Spike has no life plan. Don't fight me—look at reality. How is a man like that supposed to take care of you? Your life is your own, but I'm old-school when it comes to marriage. I believe if a guy can't afford a ring, he can't afford to be married."

"Fair enough, but we're not getting married, so I don't see what you're going on about." She threw the last toy into the box and slammed the lid shut. "Look at reality? You mean, the way I asked you to do with Hannah?"

At the sound of his mother's name, Ben looked up. He knew enough to know the name changed the mood of his home.

"Which should tell you, sometimes love blinds you to certain realities, and that's not a good thing. Unless you want to end up like me, a pathetic middle manager at a sorry company working for a man who doesn't know the first thing about running in the black."

"Just because you're miserable doesn't mean I will be."

"I'm not miserable, Abby. I'm saying the reason God gave

us the Bible is so we could see how people messed up and try to do better. Actually, you don't even have to crack the Bible. I'm right here as your warning sign."

"You are maddening!" she said through her teeth. "Ben, tell your daddy to worry about Thomas in the tunnel and let Auntie go get ready."

"Yes, Daddy. Get Thomas." Ben nodded his head up and down and bent down to look through the vent's holes for his long-lost wooden friend.

Abby disappeared into the hallway but stuck her head back into the living room. "Remember, I saw how special Hannah was from the beginning, but she had all those crazy allergies. Would that have stopped you from marrying her?"

"What does that have to do with you not listening to me about Spike? Hannah had allergies, not a history of unemployment."

"I'm only saying there are no guarantees in life, Jesse. It's impossible to see all the details sometimes. Spike and I are happy. Isn't that enough for now?"

*No*, he wanted to tell her. It wasn't enough. A man who could afford to put gas in his hog still wouldn't be enough. "You just don't know how special you are, Abby." He lifted the vent off the floor. "Tell her, Ben. Tell her she deserves the bestest ever! Hey, is there a craft shop nearby where you could get knitting stuff?"

"What?" Abby peeked her head around the corner.

"You know, knitting stuff. The new hire knits when she's nervous, and today in the car she started knitting when she didn't have any needles."

"Are you making her nervous?"

"What? No. I just thought she'd be less, you know, quirky if she had some knitting needles in her hands."

"Take her Hannah's knitting basket. It's in the hall closet. No one here is going to use it."

"She also does archery."

"Who does? The nose?" Abby asked.

"Daphne. Now who is calling her the nose?"

The roar of Spike's chopper could be heard vibrating their city street. "Don't say anything. I'll be right out," Abby said.

Jesse put the vent back and followed Ben out to the front yard. Spike came into view on one of those ridiculous choppers where his arms were perched straight up, like he was being held up in a robbery. The roar of his engine tore down the street like a tornado.

Jesse walked with his son toward the motorcycle. For all of Spike's faults, he was good to Ben.

Ben clambered onto the motorcycle's banana seat in front of Spike. Jesse was sure it wasn't called a banana seat, but it looked just like the one his sister had had as a kid.

"Hey, Spike, big plans tonight, huh?"

Spike cradled Ben in one arm and pulled him back, then removed his helmet. "He's going to be riding before you know it."

"Not if I can help it. Abby says you need to talk to me?"

"*We* need to talk to you." He looked down at Ben. "Later. When Ben's in bed."

Jesse got a waft of gasoline off the bike, and the small detail struck him. *The gas!*

He had smelled gas at Daphne's. Something hadn't been right, but he'd been in such a hurry to get home, he'd ignored his first instinct. The memories shot through his mind now like a meteor shower, and it all made sense. It wasn't a simple cold as he'd suspected. It had to go deeper.

Daphne had said nothing about the overwhelming stench of spoiled milk in his car. She hadn't commented on the soured smell of garlic in the Italian restaurant. Nor the strong fennel scent that wafted off the minestrone. In fact, the only odor she'd referenced since arriving was the baby powder in his office, which he'd tried to use to sop up the week-old spilled Sippy cup that morning.

"I smelled gas!" Jesse said aloud.

"Pardon, bro? No worries. I just got gas. Spilled some on the bike."

"Huh?" Jesse stared at his sister's boyfriend. "No, not now. I'm thinking out loud. It's been that kind of day."

He wondered if the stress of moving and adjusting might have blocked out the gasoline smell from the normally meticulous nose, or if it was something more. She was hard to read as it was. And he didn't know her well enough to wonder if she was acting strangely. The fact was, he had to check. He couldn't afford another regret in life.

Hannah's sensitive soul had been too tender for the world's pain. If he'd done a better job of protecting her, maybe she never would have needed the pill for sleeping that had been substituted with the deadly antibiotic. All the signs had been there for postpartum depression, but he'd been so ecstatic over Ben's birth that in his bliss he failed to notice the warnings. What kind of new mother couldn't fall asleep at a moment's notice?

Hannah couldn't sleep. Every hiccup and sputter kept her awake, and she needed one good night's sleep. Rather than hear any subtext in her request, he'd called the doctor and gotten the deadly prescription.

He lifted Ben off the bike and looked to Spike. "We've got to run. Got an urgent errand. Tell my sister to lock up."

"Motorcycle!" Ben reached toward the bike. "I don't want to leave, Daddy."

Jesse swung Ben up in his arms and sprinted toward the car. "Sorry, buddy. Daddy has to do something." He opened the passenger door, pulled up the front seat, and plugged Ben into his car seat. "I'll make it up to you."

He sped the roads back to Daphne's house, convinced he'd look ridiculous, but unable to turn off that inner voice that shouted *danger*.

# Chapter 11

Daphne didn't know where to start. The project of the house was overwhelming, and without her most important sense, she probably didn't know the worst of it. Her cell phone rang, and by the Rascal Flatts song she knew it was Sophie. She welcomed the interruption.

"Sophie!"

"Hey, Daph! How's the new job?"

"I think it's going to be okay," she answered honestly. "I have a boss who looks like he stepped out of a BMW ad, but he drives an American hatchback and has a missing wife. But he had my back at a horrible meeting today, and I think we have a great idea for his new product."

"That's not good, though. Missing spouses are never good."

"Well, she's not alive. But it was an allergic reaction. There was no foul play."

"So he says."

"He said I could Google it, so go ahead if you don't believe it. Now his sister lives with him, and he has a son. You see what I'm getting at, right? I attract circus acts, not people, into my life. Everyone has to have a story."

"Maybe you should have been the psychologist."

"Maybe that's why you're my best friend."

Daphne could tell that Sophie wasn't saying everything she wanted to say. They'd known each other for too long, and she recognized that another shoe was about to drop. "What is it, Sophie? Just spit it out already."

"I wanted you to have more time to heal before I gave you any bad news."

"But this is my life, so that isn't possible."

"Mark is making it impossible. I have to tell you."

Daphne slipped the letter out of her bag. "I've got a letter he wrote to my boss. I've been waiting all day to read it. Are you proud of me? I didn't obsess."

"I am proud of you."

She searched for a place to sit down and went to the lone piece of furniture near the small living room window: an old sewing table that had seen better days.

"Daphne?" Sophie said. "Mark took your job at Givaudan."

Daphne nearly fainted with relief.

"Daphne?"

"I thought he might have, but I didn't want to believe it."

"You're okay with it?"

"Of course I'm not okay with it. Why do you think I'm denying the reality by not reading the letter?"

"Don't get harpy, I'm only asking."

"Mark wasn't qualified for my job," she said. "Not at Givaudan, with their training center. I don't understand it, but it's an enormous company. Arnaud's sway must not have reached whoever hired Mark."

"Actually, he's working for Arnaud."

"No." Daphne shook her head. "He's not!"

"He is."

The betrayal she felt was worse than that she'd felt on her wedding day. Something was wrong with this picture, but she couldn't think about that now.

"Arnaud knows you, Daphne. It's only a matter of time before Mark proves himself to be the fake he is. I just wanted you to hear this from me, and not someone else."

"Why would he do this, Sophie? Wasn't leaving me at the altar enough?"

"Do you want my professional opinion? Or my opinion as your friend?"

"Whichever one says that he's a psychopathic lunatic who shouldn't be on the loose and he must be painfully good at what he does or he never could have fooled me."

"Yeah. That's it."

"I don't understand. It's like he's personally trying to destroy me. What could I have done to him to make him hate me so?"

"Nothing. You didn't do anything, Daphne. This is about him."

"I did everything right, Sophie. I gave up my job for love. I let my father help us buy a home so we'd have something. Why is this my reward?"

"Because there's evil in the world, Daph. Plain and simple. And Mark seems to have more than his fair share of it."

She wanted to believe it was all about Mark and his own inferior personality traits, but how did one give up all responsibility for someone systematically taking away the things that mattered to her? If she were anyone else, Sophie would tell her to look within to see what she'd done for her half of the dynamic. And maybe she'd say it yet, when the pain of rejection wasn't so unrelenting. But it was nearly impossible to believe Mark didn't have a motive, the way he'd gone about things.

"But you missed it, Sophie. You're a professional, and you missed it. How will I ever know what to look for if I missed every possible sign that this man was going to leave me at the altar and take away the one thing that mattered to me?" That wasn't fair. If she were honest, she'd admit that she'd given the job and her dream away for the price of love. What she thought was love, anyway.

"I don't know what Mark's motives were, but I plan to find out if it's the last thing I do. I feel that if I can understand him, it will help me somewhere down the line in my professional career. I never liked him, but that's not enough to provide a diagnosis or to have seen any of this coming. I feel like if I could have seen it, I'd be worthy of being a psychologist."

"I think it would make you worthy of being a psychic, and no one expects that of you."

"I haven't told you the worst part," Sophie said.

Daphne wasn't sure she could take the worst part. "Worse than losing my sense of smell? I can't think of anything that's worse than that."

"Me either. It's who you are. I think of all those nights you never drank or ate the spicy food while we all indulged, and it doesn't seem fair."

"I'll get the name of a doctor, a real doctor," she told Sophie. "I'll go to the library after work tomorrow. I'm going to rent a car until I figure out what my next move is."

"Before you plan your next move, I have to tell you something. That's not the house your father bought."

"What?" Would the sources of betrayal never end?

"It seems the house you're in isn't the one your father planned to buy, but rather a case of bait and switch. Mark bought a different house and kept a large chunk of the intended down payment."

Daphne looked around the shack of a home. This made sense.

"Your father hired a private investigator to figure all this out. He couldn't bring himself to tell you, though. He feels like he should have done all this before the wedding."

"Mark had to be planning this forever, Sophie!" Leaving her at the altar was the tip of Mark's iceberg. An iceberg that he'd planned and molded and shaped into a sparkly facade of love.

"It will be over soon. Your father is handling it in court. I'm coming out to help you get situated. You'll get past this, Daphne. It's just a valley on your way to the top of the crest."

She wished she believed that. "I have a headache. I'm going to lie down for a while." She looked around and wondered where she planned to lie.

"Hold tight. I'm coming, and we'll get your new life started. It's going to be beautiful."

"I'm going to call Arnaud. I have to ask. Of all people, I can't believe he'd betray me with Mark. Even my father, I can see his motives with money. It's always been all about winning with him. But Arnaud? That doesn't make any sense." She slid down the wall and leaned against it. "I'll be fine, Sophie. You and Gary don't have to coddle me."

"We do," she said. "We love you, and we don't want you to wear this. It doesn't become you."

Daphne hung up. It had to be her. This wasn't happening to anyone else. She looked up at the ceiling and saw the brown soil marks where water damage indicated a plumbing problem. Upstairs, she'd seen the same thing and dismissed it rather than believe she'd need to replace the roof before winter approached. The scent of rain was decidedly less inspiring when it came through a moldy Dayton rooftop.

She needed to change out of her work clothes. Her slacks and the carpet, circa 1955, did not mesh with one another. She unzipped her suitcase and found a pair of jeans. Her head was pounding, and she needed some water. She hoped the tap water at the house was fit to drink, because that was all she had.

First she checked the time in Paris by calculating it from her watch. Then she plugged her cell phone into the wall, thankful she'd at least had the forethought to turn on the utilities before she'd arrived. She prayed to be strong enough to hear whatever Arnaud had to tell her, even if it was why he'd betrayed her, and she dialed Paris.

*"Allo, Arnaud Polge. Qui est al appereil?"*

She warmed at the sound of his familiar voice.

"Arnaud, it's Daphne," she said in English, and he switched over to her native tongue.

"Daphne, where are you?"

"What do you mean, where am I? I'm in Dayton, Ohio." She drew in a deep breath. "You hired Mark," she said.

"*Oui.* You did not tell me your boyfriend, ah, husband, had the same training as you. I completely missed it on his résumé the first time. Why didn't you tell me, so that I could give him a job too?"

"I did tell you. I told you everything about him, and you said he didn't have the experience for any of the jobs in the Paris region."

"Ah, but your husband—"

"He's not my husband, Arnaud. He's not even my boy-friend." She felt the heat in her face as she told him. "He left me at the altar, and you gave him my job!"

"No! You left the job so that you could get married."

"To *him*! I left the job to get married to him, and he's there! You've given him my job, which I quit for him."

"No! I hired him so that you would come to me. I thought you'd be arriving with him. You are not here?"

"No, I'm not there. I'm in Dayton, and I'm in trouble, Arnaud."

"You will come back here. To France. And Madeleine and I will care for you. We will restore you with good food that's easy on the palate and love. My foolish pride made a mistake letting you go, but now your boyfriend is here. You can have your job and be happy, no?"

"I can't come back, Arnaud." What good was a nose who couldn't smell? "I've made a promise to my employer here."

"I said there was no job for you here. Things change. Tell him this and you will come back to us."

Her head ached. Something didn't make any sense. Arnaud was acting innocent, but she knew that man like she knew the scent of her favorite Paris café, and he didn't miss a trick. Something was very wrong. "I need to go."

"*No! à Dieu ne plaise.* I would never betray you, my best student."

"*Je t'apprécie vraiment.* I love you, Arnaud."

"Daphne!"

She heard the fear in his voice, but she felt too tired to respond. Her head ached, and she needed to sleep. Just a small nap before . . .

"Daphne, come back to Paris!"

*Paris. She awoke in Paris. The scent of fresh rain filled her senses, and under that a foundation of freshly baked bread. She inhaled the sensations around her. The wonderfully old buildings surrounded her like a warm raincoat. She was in the Fourth District with its beautifully elaborate architecture, its quiet embrace. Night was falling, and the City of Light was just starting to sparkle and soon would reflect off the River Seine under its magical bridges.*

*Someone in a clown suit handed her a baguette and a bouquet of balloons.*

*"Merci," she said.*

*The clown nodded.*

*She walked down the rue de Bourg Tibourg, two walls of*

*antique buildings on either side cradling her in their familiar warmth. A man in a tuxedo walked three dogs toward her, and as he approached she felt an overwhelming warmth from his presence. As if he gave off a ray of light with his very being. He glowed from basking in God's love. As he approached, the city noises disappeared, and all she could sense was the scent of fresh rain. The dogs had vanished.*

*"Where have your dogs gone?" she asked.*

*As he got closer, she recognized Jesse's mesmerizing blue-green eyes and felt the warmth of his glow. "They've gone home," he said.*

*She released her grasp on the balloons, and they rose into the night sky. She held only the baguette. "Are you hungry?"*

*Jesse came toward her and put his hands around her face. He began to kiss her, and she dropped the baguette to the cobblestones below. His hands pulled her closer yet, and he hungrily showered her with kisses. He pulled away, and suddenly he was yards away, only the glow of him remaining.*

*"Perfect love casts out fear, Daphne," he said as he disappeared completely from her sight.*

*"Jesse! Come back!"*

*"Perfect love," the voice said again. She looked down at her feet, and the baguette was gone too. She ran across the cobbled streets searching for him.*

*"Jesse!" she yelled again, but nothing would bring back the image. The warmth. She was alone . . .*

# Chapter 12

Ben hummed in the backseat while Jesse sped the short distance back to Daphne's house. He was probably making a fool of himself, but he couldn't afford to take the chance. He'd rather Daphne think him a soppy idiot than second-guess himself ever again. Living with regrets was the worst curse. Far worse than showing a person you cared—even if the person did find you off your rocker.

"Daddy? Can we go to McDonald's for dinner?"

He glanced back at his son. "After we do what Daddy has to do, yes, we can. I owe you that much. Are you going to have chicken nuggets or a hamburger?"

"Nuggets," Ben said decisively. "With lots of ketchup."

Jesse pulled into Daphne's driveway and turned to Ben.

"Can you be a big boy and wait here a minute?"

Ben nodded. "French fries," he said.

"I'll be right back, son." He clambered out of the car and rushed up the crumbling concrete steps. The door was unlocked, and he pushed it open. "Daphne!" The smell of gas was stronger than ever, and he could kick himself for his stupidity. For ignoring his instincts again. "Daphne, where are you?"

He found her on the floor in the living room. He held his breath and lifted her from the age-old carpet. Cradling her in his arms, he rushed out the door and ran down the steps. He placed her on the overgrown grass and called to his son. "Ben!"

"Yes, Daddy."

"Ben, take my phone and call 911. Remember how we practiced it?"

Ben scrambled out of his car seat and waved the cell phone to show his father that he could do it.

Jesse's shoulders tightened at the responsibilities before him. He had to turn off the gas. He had to get Daphne breathing again. He had to get Ben out of here, lest the gas should have any reason to explode.

A stranger walked past him on the sidewalk. "Sir, sir!" Jesse called. "Can you come help me?" The man kept walking as if Jesse were insane. The scene ate at some distant memory of his own, and his hands curled into fists instinctively.

Ben appeared at his side with the cell phone in his hand. "Here, Daddy."

Jesse took the phone. He quickly gave the address and explained the scene. The dispatcher wanted him to remain on the line, but Ben's frightened expression forced him to tell the woman he couldn't wait.

"Daddy, what's wrong with the lady? Is she sick like Mommy?"

"No, buddy." He put a hand on Ben's shoulder. "How did you know Mommy was sick?"

"Auntie Abby told me. She said Mommy got sick and had to go to heaven. Jesus wanted her right away."

He felt for Daphne's pulse. He knew enough from lab rules that administering CPR could prove dangerous if she'd inhaled dangerous levels. He prayed for the ambulance to get there with oxygen.

"Ben, get over by the sidewalk. I don't want you near the house, all right? The lady's going to be okay."

"First we hafta pray." His son closed his eyes as though prayer was the easiest stance in the world. "Jesus, make this lady better. You already have my mommy in heaven, and that's enough. Amen."

Jesse's heart swelled with pride and his eyes filled with tears. His four-year-old son had the faith of a giant. He followed up with his own prayer and asked Ben to sit on the grass by the sidewalk. Jesse gazed on Daphne's clear complexion and smoothed the loose tendrils of dark hair. Her skin appeared sallow, with deep, purple marks under her eyes. Her falsely full lips looked fuller. She sputtered and coughed then, and took short, desperate breaths.

"She needs oxygen." Jesse lifted her into a better position, where her body wasn't bent and her throat had clear access to the summer air. "Daphne," he whispered. "It's Jesse. Breathe, Daphne. Take a deep breath for me." He bent over her and thrust a breath inside her. Her sleepy eyes blinked heavily.

"Jesse," she said groggily. "Do you smell the scent of rain?"

"I smell it, Daphne. Squeeze my hand if you can hear me."

He felt the slightest pressure and exhaled his relief. He couldn't have said why someone he barely knew meant so much to him already, but it was apparent. This wasn't any act of a Good Samaritan. He cared. More than he wanted to. More than he ever wanted to again.

An ambulance pulled up, with a fire engine close behind. Two EMTs jumped out and came toward him.

"She inhaled gas. There's a leak."

"Is the gas off?" called a firefighter.

"I didn't have time," Jesse answered.

"How long was she in there?" asked one of the EMTs.

"I don't know."

"You need to get the kid away from the house. Smell's still pretty strong."

Jesse crossed the lawn and picked up Ben, still berating himself. Why hadn't he turned the gas off before he left?

"Daddy, can we go to McDonald's now?"

"Soon, honey. Right now our car is blocked by the fire engine. Let's take a walk down the street until they finish their job."

"That lady is like Snow White, Daddy. You kissed her and she came back to life."

He reached down for Ben's hand. "That's called CPR, Ben. She didn't have enough breath of her own, so I gave her some of mine."

"Like a magic kiss."

"Yes, I suppose." He took Ben's hand and walked away from the house while the firefighters secured the place and the

EMTs helped Daphne. The scene ate at him. If he'd listened to that still, small voice, none of this would have happened. He called the gas company from his cell and reported the leak, even though the fire department had probably already taken care of it. He had to do something useful.

He looked back toward the house. Daphne was sitting up now, leaning on a kneeling fireman. Although he'd seen her breathing, in his heart he'd panicked at how close she'd come to being consumed by the house. By his own misgivings and dawdling.

"Is she going to be okay, Daddy?"

"She's going to be fine, Ben. Just like you prayed."

He looked down at his son in his red-and-white striped T-shirt and blue shorts, each decorated with an orange fish. Abby really was an excellent mother to Ben, and he felt grateful his sister had been there for him. He squeezed Ben's hand and bent to lift him. "She'll be fine," he said again.

"Can we go to McDonald's now? We could ask the firemen to move the engine."

"The firemen are still busy doing their job. How about if we just wait a little while longer?"

Ben stuck his lower lip out. "I'm hungry now."

Neighbors were gathering outside, responding to the wail of sirens. An older man walking a husky came up beside them. "What's happening?"

"Gas leak," Jesse said.

The older man shook his head. "I knew that house was bad news. Heard a young couple bought it. I told my wife I hope they had that place inspected."

"I don't really know."

"Is that the girl who lives there?" The old man jutted his chin toward Daphne and the scene of firemen.

"Yes. She works for me. Her name's Daphne." Jesse knew he was rattling on.

"Looks like she's going to be okay. Your boy like dogs?"

Ben nodded enthusiastically.

"This is Kodiak. He likes kids. You want to pet him? He only lets really special kids pet him. Boys like you."

Ben struggled to get down, and Jesse set him on the sidewalk where he was face-to-face with the giant blue-eyed dog.

Something gnawed at him about seeing Daphne on the ground like that. He remembered Mark's words in the letter: *"A man would have to be crazy to marry into that family."* He had to admit, the warning touched a nerve. Hannah had been so sensitive, and he hadn't been prepared for that. What if he wasn't prepared for his feelings for Daphne either? Then it would be true that he'd had his one and only shot at love.

"Ben, we need to go now."

"Nice-looking woman," the old man said. "Hope they can get that house up to code, but they've got a long road ahead of them. Remember that old movie *The Money Pit*?"

"No," Jesse said.

"That's what these two got themselves. A money pit. No one's lived in that place for years."

"It looks like the fire truck is moving. Nice to meet you, Mr.—"

"Riley. Ed Riley."

"Nice to meet you, Mr. Riley. Jesse Lightner. I'm sure we'll be seeing more of one another someday."

"Count on it. Your boy here can help me walk Kodiak. Dog needs a lot of walking."

"Come on, Ben. Let's get to McDonald's, then Daddy's going to have Mrs. Weimer watch you. Daddy has something to do."

"You said you'd help me with the big Legos tonight."

"I did, didn't I?" Well, first he had to go to the hospital.

He needed to tell Daphne to take the next two weeks off and get her life sorted out. Clearly, she was no use to him as a nose anyway, but he felt betrayed. First, by Dave in hiring her, and now by Daphne. She let him believe she'd been forthright with him, that she was a woman of her word—when, in fact, her word obviously meant very little. A lie by omission was still a lie. There was no other explanation for the day's events. Daphne Sweeten had lost her sense of smell, and perhaps her way.

In any case, he wasn't about to let her wake up alone in a strange place. At least he told himself that's what it was about. But inside he knew there was more to it than that. He didn't want Daphne to feel alone. He forced the word *ever* away.

# Chapter 13

Daphne awoke in the hospital. Her head pounded, and she groaned in pain. She hadn't felt any pain in her dream—she'd been in Paris, dining on luxury cheeses and pasta in truffle oil with no worries for her palate. She'd even kissed her dream man—and it was not Mark. It was—

"Daphne?"

She looked to her right and felt herself turn scarlet at the sight of her boss. "Jesse!" she said, certain he saw right through her and knew how she'd dreamed of him in a most unprofessional manner. "What are you doing here?"

He lifted a small basket and set it beside her on the hospital bed. "I brought you some things, like my iPad. So you can play Angry Birds. I thought it was the closest I could get you to the archery field for now." His jaw was tight, and though his words were friendly, his demeanor was not. He wouldn't look at her directly.

"No, I mean, what am *I* doing here?"

"It seems you had a gas leak in the house." He went to the window and fiddled with the curtain. "I found you unconscious in your living room. Do you want to tell me how that happened? You said you were going to check the gas."

"I must have forgotten."

"You can't smell, Daphne." He turned toward her, hands on his hips, suit jacket pulled back. "Go ahead, tell me I'm wrong. If not, what were you thanking me for after the meeting when Dave waved those scent strips in front of you? Don't tell me the story you told him about being nervous. You accepted my help, so I figured you knew." Jesse's voice was stern. Annoyed. "I gave you a chance to tell me after the staff meeting, when I pulled over on the freeway, but you didn't. If I hadn't listened to my gut, you would have been gone."

"I hoped maybe you'd forget, or you'd just think I was off my game—and really, that's what I hoped it was. When I saw your interaction with Dave, I worried for your job if I didn't live up to what my résumé said about me. I was afraid you'd be held liable for me."

"Did you think to worry that if you'd turned up dead, I'd have yet another inquiry into why young women seem to slip into heaven when they're with me?"

"I—" She stammered to find the words. "I never thought of such a thing. I was going to tell you!"

"Like you were going to check the gas valve."

"You have to understand, I thought I'd have my sense of smell back any minute. I wasn't trying to deceive you. I was only buying my nose some time."

He scratched at his head. "Do you know how close Gibraltar is to running out of capital? Do you know the difference your salary makes to my bottom line? When did this happen?"

"After my wedding. After what should have been my wedding. That's why I think it has to be temporary. It's just a stress reaction, and when I gain control of it, I'll be fine."

The sting of tears gnawed at her, but she clamped down tightly on her jaw to keep from breaking down. Professionals didn't cry, but the way Jesse wouldn't look at her made her feel ashamed that she'd been secretive to protect herself without regard to him.

"I wish you'd told me." Jesse's dress shoes clicked on the hospital floor as he paced the small room. "Though I suppose I knew it, on some level."

"What do you mean?" She hadn't let on that there was anything missing from her senses.

"That's why I was at your house. I was checking on you because I couldn't get past the idea that you couldn't smell that gas. It was strong. But there were other clues."

"There were?"

"My car smells like a small rodent died in it. Ben threw a sippy cup under the seat, and I found it a few weeks later."

"Oh dear."

"Then there was the salt in your coffee and the sugar in your soup."

"They use odd containers at that restaurant."

"Anne told me that you don't drink coffee. It's too strong for your palate. She'd asked me to approve a green tea for you to drink during the day."

Sheepishly, she looked up at him through her bangs. "I was still able to put together a decent sample for you at the restaurant. I thought I'd rely on my chemistry background until the scents came back."

"Instead of a base note of oak moss, it seems you used oatmeal."

She sank into her bed. "Oh." Things looked bad. She'd believed that her chemistry skills would pull her through. No wonder he thought she was a con artist. She wasn't able to do the job, and she'd lied rather than admit it.

"Jesse, this isn't like me, you have to understand. I'm usually honest to a fault, but I was afraid. You didn't think a nose would help your staff. But I know it will."

"When I find one, I'll let you know." His jaw twitched, and his set expression told her there was little reason to say more.

"I understand," she said curtly.

"You understand? Do you understand what it was like for me to find you crumpled on your floor?" Jesse looked pained as he dropped his forehead in his hand. "You didn't have to be perfect, Daphne. You could have told me your circumstances, and I would have given you time off. Why did you come here early if you knew that you couldn't smell?"

She didn't have an answer. None that would suffice. And she knew after one day that Jesse wasn't confrontational. She'd taken a perfectly reasonable man and turned him against her. "I'm sorry that things worked out this way. Look at the bright side: you'll get your funds back in your budget."

"I'm not worried about the—" His face got red, and he stopped and drew in a deep breath. "I don't care about the money,

Daphne. Not anymore. I care that you put yourself in a stupid situation rather than ask for my help. Was I that frightening?"

She wanted to tell him that at the moment he was, yes. "I'm used to taking care of things myself, and you barely know me; why would this time be any different for me?"

"Because I'm not the guy who stood you up at the altar. I would have helped you if you'd only asked. I care about my staff. I cared about you immediately. Enough where I wanted you to get out of Gibraltar as soon as possible before your dream died. You don't belong here. A few months under Dave, and you'd forget about all that and believe there were no other options for you. Trust me, I've seen it happen time and time again. I wanted to give you a way out, and you thanked me by lying to me."

"I don't understand any of that. I'm here to do a job. The fact that you're preparing for me to leave it on the first day doesn't make any sense to me."

Jesse stood to his full height. "I don't imagine it does."

She'd forgotten that he hadn't experienced the romantic dream she'd had. It seemed as if they were speaking, but not communicating a thing, and she struggled to get through to him how truly sorry she was. She could have paid with her life, didn't that say anything to him?

"I haven't read the letter from Mark," she admitted. "But just like Dave has a way of twisting the truth, so does Mark. It sounds as if whatever he may have accused me of, you believe wholeheartedly."

If Arnaud, who loved her like a father, believed Mark, what was to stop Jesse from doing the same? She had to find a place to start over and get out from under Mark's shadow. She wouldn't be a victim for one more day.

Jesse wanted to say something more. She could read it in his expression, but then the line of his brow darkened and his brusque voice returned. "I have to get home for Ben."

"Will you at least let me explain *why* I didn't tell you?"

"I know why you didn't tell me. Mark's letter explained it all. My only problem was I was taken in by those deep blue eyes of yours. My fault, not yours."

"Taken in . . . Jesse!"

He may as well have slapped her. Mark had already helped her to feel unworthy in love, and now Jesse joined Arnaud in implying she was unworthy as a nose besides.

"You've been here for two days, and my world is already crumbling around me. Do the math, Daphne."

"You can't blame me for that. You didn't even want me here, so what could I have done to upset your world?"

"I'm glad you're not hurt. You can return the iPad before you head back to San Francisco. Or Paris. Or wherever it is your story hails from. I'll have Anne send your things. Keep her posted on your address if there are any moves."

Her head was pounding, but she cared more that Jesse had lost faith in her. "But it's our turn to win! Remember?"

"It's Gibraltar's turn to win. As you know, Gibraltar has a no-tolerance policy for bulking one's résumé, and we hired a nose."

"Jesse, you're not firing me?"

"You never really started, so technically I'm just not hiring you."

She nodded. "I won't let any of you break me. I'm not who you all seem to think I am, and I will prove it to you. To all of you."

"There's nothing I can do for you at this point; it's company policy. If you can prove to Dave that you can, in fact, discern between five thousand different scents, the decision will be up to him. As far as I'm concerned, I have my budget back." He started for the door, and she saw the tight muscle in his cheek tremble. He turned and faced her again. "Sophie's on her way. HR got her number from your emergency info and called her. It's been a pleasure, and I wish you all the best in your future endeavors," he said coldly.

"I do possess that skill, Jesse. I promise you. On my honor as a Christian. It's just temporarily out of commission. Would you fire someone for having the flu?"

The muscles in Jesse's face twitched. "Mark wasn't qualified for a job with us, and yet he's now working at Givaudan? That's where you want to be anyway."

"What about the stockholders? What about Dave?"

"That's my worry."

"Don't you understand? This is how Mark makes things look when he's involved. He makes the truth look crazy, so that only his story makes sense. My mentor assumed he'd be bringing me with him. That we'd both decided to go to Paris."

"Your same mentor who originally couldn't find a job for him?"

"You're right," she stammered. "It doesn't make sense. I don't understand it myself, but that's how things get when Mark is around. I never understood it until I was away from him, but now I see how the manipulation is unnerving and I always felt crazy because he worked it that way."

She felt soiled with shame, and for a moment she questioned her own background. Without her sense of smell, it seemed nothing more than a shaky dream.

Jesse gave an exasperated sigh. The way he looked at her as though she was guilty of something terrible made her feel broken. She wanted to run, but the fact was, she had nowhere to go. Even if she went back to Paris now, Arnaud had been tarnished by Mark's version of their history, which no doubt undermined Daphne's own truth. Her father purchased her a house in Dayton, Ohio, so that her parents could get on with their lives. Something they'd both seemed to want to do since they'd sent her to boarding school at fourteen.

"Do you need anything else before I go?" Jesse asked.

What she needed was for him to believe her, but she could tell by his expression that her wish would go ungranted.

"I'm fine. Go on about your life. Take your iPad. I don't want you to accuse me of stealing that too." She held the tablet out toward him.

He reached for it. "Your phone's on the nightstand. I brought the charger and I left you Hannah's knitting basket, so you don't have to pretend-knit with your fingers. You get a better product if you use yarn."

"Thank you," she called toward his back, unsure what to make of his visit. It had felt like nothing more than a chastisement.

Jesse walked out of the hospital room, and a nurse walked in wearing black, white, and red Elmo scrubs.

"I'll need your blood pressure."

Daphne heard the rip of the Velcro cuff.

"Are you ready to eat something?"

"Yes," she said.

"You're in the pediatric wing. We're out of rooms in the adult wards tonight. You'd think it was a full moon with how crazy it's been."

Daphne allowed her arm to be manipulated while she looked at the sweet basket of knitting goods and wondered what on earth she might have done to upset Jesse. Was it only that he knew she couldn't smell? That she was a fraud? Or had Mark gotten to him the way he'd gotten to Arnaud?

"You knit?"

"Only when I'm nervous," she answered honestly. "I haven't done it for a long time."

"You knit hats? Beanies?"

"Sure," she said. "Well, I used to. I suppose I'll actually need them here in Ohio. I'm from California, and I didn't need a knit hat too often."

"If you knit the small ones, we have a group that meets here and knits caps for the new babies. They meet in the basement on Saturdays. The hospital supplies the coffee and donuts. Though the women usually bring something homemade. If you're new in town, it's a nice way to meet people."

Daphne smiled. At this rate, ladies who knit in the hospital basement might be the only set of friends she had anywhere on the planet. She waited for the nurse to get her reading and stared at the basket. So Jesse's wife had been a knitter. She had to get that dream out of her head or she'd never be able to look him in the eye . . . not that she had any reason to worry about running into him again.

Her lot in life felt sealed. As if she was destined to fall in love with men who didn't want anything to do with her. Maybe that's what the dream meant: she lived in a fantasy, and *reality* was precisely what Jesse—and Mark—had just given her. She could claw and clamber for them, or accept that no man she ever wanted would want her back. She was meant to be like her namesake: Daphne, the maiden of Greek myth who was turned into a laurel tree, determined to remain a virgin.

"Eighty over fifty." The nurse ripped off the cuff. "A little low, but we'll get you back up and running in no time. You were lucky someone found you in that house. I'll tell you, the way they sell real estate these days, you'd think it was perfectly acceptable to kill the next tenants."

"I think my former fiancé signed off on any inspections."

"As in he didn't do them?" She clucked her tongue. "You're good to be rid of that one then. One thing you don't need in this lifetime is a man you have to take care of. Trust me on that." The nurse exited on those words of wisdom.

Daphne was about to dig into the knitting basket when she heard the nurse's voice again. "You too, Anne! So nice to see you. Say hi to Roger for me."

Anne from the office appeared in the doorway with a

bouquet of peach and yellow roses. She was wearing a gray sweater set with jeans that were too short and clunky nurse-like shoes. Daphne could hardly believe it was the same professional person from the office.

"Anne!" She tried to contain her excitement so she didn't sound so desperate. "This is so nice." She took the roses while Anne rearranged the plastic water pitcher for a makeshift vase.

"Do you know what they charge for these water pitchers in a hospital? It's criminal."

"No, I . . . haven't been in the hospital before."

"Let's hope this is the last time. Jesse was worried sick about you."

"I don't think he was," Daphne said. "He was pretty angry when he left."

"That's how men get when they can't control everything around them. You're only reminding him of his weakness. They hate that."

"No, it wasn't his weakness. There was a gas leak at my house, and he told me before he left that he smelled it. I think he was angry he had to come back to the house."

Anne narrowed her eyes. "You didn't notice the smell?"

"I just assumed the house had been locked up for some time, so—"

"Never assume anything where gas is involved." Anne dug into the huge canvas bucket bag that hung over her shoulder. "I brought you some muffins. The food in here is terrible."

"I haven't eaten yet, but thank you."

"This isn't only a social call."

"No?"

"My husband, Roger, and I would like you to stay with us until you get back on your feet. He'll get a team together to look at the house and make sure everything is up to code so you can move back in."

"Anne, I should let you know that Jesse fired me."

"No, he didn't. Don't be ridiculous."

"Yes, he did. He had good reason, too."

"He can't fire you. Dave would have his hide." She sat down in the chair beside Daphne's bed. "You'll stay with us. The church men will check out your house. I won't take no for an answer."

"I couldn't do that to you, Anne. I can stay at a hotel."

"Darling, this is what people do for each other. Someday you'll be in a position to help someone else, and then you'll pass it on. Don't rob me of my chance to play the Good Samaritan. That would be unkind of you." Anne smiled.

"You don't understand," Daphne protested. "I'm pretty used to being on my own."

"Roger and I are used to having people in the house. In fact, it's too quiet when we don't. No missionaries visiting right now, so we have plenty of extra room. We offer good food on the table and lively conversation. You can even attend our Bible study on Thursday nights. It will be a perfect way for you to get to know a little about Dayton."

"Anne, really, I . . . My best friend is coming."

"She can stay with us too."

Once again, others had come to her rescue. Daphne's

darkest thought of the day was that maybe Kensie, the model-like marketing manager, had been right about her. Maybe she *was* just overeducated and of no actual use in the real business world. And Mark, Arnaud, and Jesse had seen the light.

# Chapter 14

J esse pored over the marketing reports again, searching for some element that could help his forecasting, but as usual, Kensie's ideas were all based on her assumption that everyone who bought laundry detergent or diapers, or anything else for that matter, was just like her. She used a focus group of one. Between her extensive use of the dry cleaner and her lack of children, Kensie was hardly Gibraltar's core demographic.

Dave tapped twice and entered the office. "How's the next product cycle going? Got that winning idea yet?"

"Sporty laundry detergent. For winners."

"Not bad," Dave said. "That one of Kensie's?"

"Mine. With Daphne's help. I gave her the emotion of winning."

"I like it. When's she coming back, anyway?"

Jesse looked down at his desk. "She's not."

"She's not what?"

"Daphne's not coming back."

Dave's brow furrowed. "What do you mean?"

"I mean that she padded her background. She's not capable of doing the job, and you know how HR is about that. I had to let her go." He kept scribbling to avoid the look on Dave's face.

"And you didn't think to inform me of this? What did Anne say?"

"Anne? Why would she care what I do with my department?"

"Well, Daphne's going to stay at her house. Until her church fixes everything in that dump she bought that nearly killed her, I assume."

"She is? Anne didn't tell me that."

"Maybe Daphne told her you fired her. I want you to go and get her back."

"Dave, it's my department. I'm not going to let you undermine me again. What authority will I have now if I go running and beg her to come back?"

"You'd have *your* job."

Jesse clenched his hands into fists, but at the sight of Ben's picture, reality stared back at him. It was a tough job market out there. Like it or not, he'd have to go schlepping to Daphne's side and beg for mercy. Which he didn't deserve, after the way he'd treated her, like some scheming manipulator.

"I'd like Daphne to be utilized after the product is selected. She's got no experience with product marketing, as you can see in that ridiculously shaped bottle she had her wedding favor in."

"Where did you see that?"

"You left it on your desk."

He hadn't left it on his desk. Of that, he was certain, but he didn't let on. "Did you smell that cologne?"

"Nah," Dave snorted. "I don't wear that froufrou stuff. We need something we can market to the men of America. The reason the beauty division doesn't make cologne is that men don't buy it. Did you talk to beauty at all?"

"They make shaving cream. We make laundry soap. Smell this." He reached into his desk drawer and pulled out the bottle Daphne had left him.

Dave pulled back. "I don't want to smell it. We're not a perfumery. We make practical products for middle America."

"So which of those practical products would you like Daphne to make smell better? Because I think the soccer moms of America would love for their sons and daughters to smell like winners, don't you?"

Dave tapped the desk twice. "If you believed that, why did you fire her?"

Jesse knew the real reason he'd fired her, but there was no way to admit it without labeling himself a giant jerk. He'd fired her because seeing her unconscious that day on her front lawn had nearly killed him. He couldn't take on that kind of responsibility again—couldn't handle another pair of eyes looking up at him with trust.

He could just tell Dave that she didn't have her sense of smell. That would be it. But he couldn't betray her, couldn't hand her over to Dave's wrath. That would make him no better than Mark. Or Daphne's own father.

"Get her back here and have her work closely with Kensie on this sporty thing."

Jesse couldn't take it. "Dave, Kensie doesn't know what the heck she's doing. She hasn't had one successful product launch, and her marketing reports don't prove themselves once the sales reports come back. I need to see some hard numbers to make this work."

"It's all a crapshoot," Dave said. "You think anyone knows what's going to be successful? It's a weak man who blames his team for his losses."

"Blames my team? Dave, I can't work like this. You won't let me run with my own ideas, but you give me a marketing manager with no real experience, and I'm supposed to make something of it. My hands are tied. And now you don't want to let Daphne do what she does best."

"What are you coming after me for? You're the one who fired her. Take some responsibility!" Dave was on a roll now. "Don't turn this on me because you don't know how to fix it. I've given you nothing but assistance to make this quarter big, but you keep coming up with excuses. It's always someone else's fault. The buck has to stop here, you understand?"

Jesse understood perfectly. He was done running on fear. If he blew it this quarter, he was going to blow it by trying something different. Not one of Kensie's ridiculous, twentysomething ideas. Jesse was practically shaking, but he wasn't going to back down. He would take the bull by the horns—the cedar, bergamot, neroli-scented horns. He stacked the marketing reports on his desk and tucked them under his arm. "I'm going to work in the lab."

"Thatta boy. Light a fire under that systematic way of yours." Dave smiled as though he'd won the battle.

Which he had . . . but Jesse intended to win the war. If he didn't, Gibraltar would be no more.

He practically ran to the lab, where he found Willard and John each working separately in a corner of the lab. He set the marketing reports down and donned a lab coat, some gloves, and a pair of safety goggles.

He headed to one of the hoods and turned it on. "What are you working on?"

"Same old. You got something?" Willard asked.

Jesse looked to John, who tended to be the more rogue of the two. "I need some manganese heptoxide."

John's eyebrows rose. "Are you planning to blow something up?"

Jesse lifted the marketing reports. "I am."

"I'll do it," Willard said with glee. He got two bottles off the shelf and mixed the tiniest amount of two chemicals under the hood. The raw whirling sound would cover any unexpected noise.

"Here." Jesse handed him a manila folder, which Willard touched to the solution. An explosive fireball took the entire marketing plan up in a matter of seconds, and he and Willard laughed like boys in the backyard playing with fire.

"I'm doing the next one," John said. Number two went up with equal force and laughter.

"I assume you want the pleasure of doing the final reports," Willard said.

"I do," Jesse replied. He lit the other two on fire one by one and washed his hands of Kensie's curse.

"You should have done that a year ago," Willard said.

"Everyone should have done it a year ago. We're not doing lollipop-scented dish soap, and there will be no more cotton-candy-flavored cough syrup. We're starting a new team as of today." He pulled out the bottle of Daphne's cologne and set it in front of Willard. "I want an idea that goes with this scent. We'll do a mock-up by the next staff meeting. If I'm going down, I'm not going without a fight. And I'm not going while backing fruity, flowery air freshener. I've had enough!"

"I think Popeye has just eaten his spinach," John said.

"Darn straight. It's about time someone did."

For some odd reason Jesse didn't think about Ben, or what tragedy could befall his family if he lost his job. It was time he trusted his gut. Life wasn't for sissies.

John stared at the ashes that blew under the hood. "What are you going to tell Dave?"

"I'm going to tell him we have the product to put Gibraltar back on the map."

"Daphne made this?" John asked.

Jesse uncorked the stopper. "Yes."

Willard breathed in deeply and nodded. "That's nice. Real subtle-like, and she's got her notes down. I don't smell an ounce of alcohol or any of the binders in this."

He passed the bottle to John, who lifted it to his nostrils and sniffed deeply. Then he swirled the bottle like it was a fine wine and did it again. "You want a masculine scent for a household product?" he asked.

"I want that scent for a product. Laundry detergent. Sporty for soccer moms of winners. Lighten it with some citrus maybe, so it's not so masculine."

"Did Daphne give us the rights to the product?" Willard clarified. "And are you sure it's hers?"

Jesse was certain it was hers, and for that reason alone he owed Daphne an apology. Whatever happened in Paris, whatever Mark had done to get her job, Jesse was certain she'd been the victim. If he never trusted his gut again, he was sure of that.

"This isn't the way we do things, I understand, but we're being set up to fail. If we go down in a blaze of glory, I want you all, including Daphne, to have something on your résumé that shows creativity and a marketable scent. You agree that's marketable?"

The two men nodded in unison.

Willard smiled broadly. "You feel a responsibility toward Daphne already, hmm?"

"Willard, it's not what you're thinking. I made a deal with her about staying. Then the minute I doubted her, I reneged."

"You're a charmer."

"She's in love with her ex-fiancé and still trying to make her way back to Paris. I'm just trying to help you all get where you want to go before we're all fired."

"I hope that won't happen," Willard said. "I don't want to go back to the big boys. I like my quiet lab."

At that moment the door opened and Kensie pushed her way in. She glared at the three of them, then focused on Jesse. "You! What did you say to Dave?"

"I have no idea what you're talking about."

"We're a team," Willard said. "But we haven't had one hit since we went with your marketing plans, Kensie. So we're trying our own thing. The lab has just gone rogue."

"We'll see about that." She turned and stormed back out.

Willard shook his head. "I pity the man who marries that girl. I imagine she'd call the cops if you left the toilet seat up."

"She's only doing what she thinks she has to do to survive," Jesse said. "It's a shame she learned so much from her superiors."

John cleared his throat. "So, you're not interested in that new girl, are you?"

"Daphne? Of course not."

"Good," John said. "I think I might like a girl like that. Scientists who look like her are usually more apt to be supermodels in a music video, but she's the real thing. She's got brains and beauty."

"I've met plenty of pretty scientists in my day," Willard said.

"No," John said. "You just lost your eyesight a long time ago, and probably imagine they all look like Daphne to build your own ego. Trust me, they don't."

Jesse tried to act unaffected by John's announcement. "Well, make sure you follow the employee handbook for any dating within the workplace. The last thing we need to do is give Dave the chance to fire us before we've tried our revolution."

"Aye aye, captain."

"But first, I've got to go hire her again."

The men stared at him.

"You understand she's leaving as soon as she can to go back to Paris."

"Even better. No commitments," John said, his eyebrows wiggling.

Jesse would personally hand Daphne back to Mark Goodsmith before he'd let her near John's clutches, but the truth was, he had some major groveling to do. He wouldn't blame Daphne if she wouldn't give him the hot air off her breakfast after the way he'd treated her.

# Chapter 15

Daphne was released from the hospital the following day. Anne picked her up in a giant Buick and drove her across town to the quiet suburb where she and Roger lived.

"I don't know how to thank you for this, Anne."

"Then don't," Anne said simply. "Roger went to the airport to pick up your friend. Sophie, right?"

"Yes, Sophie."

"How do you two know each other?"

"She lived near me when we were kids, but her parents moved out of the city before we got to middle school."

"And you stayed in touch? That's amazing."

"You'll see why when you meet her. She's pretty fantastic. She wrote me letters the whole time I was away at boarding school. Real letters too. It's not like we had e-mail."

"She sounds wonderful."

"She is. I don't know what I would have done without her. I didn't have a lot of friends in boarding school."

"That sounds like a lonely life, Daphne. Did your parents travel as missionaries when you were growing up?"

Daphne's face felt hot as she explained her parents in the best way she understood. "My parents were pretty important people. They weren't home very often, and they did a lot of entertaining. So they thought it best that I get a good education without having to be quiet every time they had a dinner party."

Anne turned, her mouth dangling open. She promptly snapped it shut.

"It's all right. Really. Lots of kids all over the world go to boarding school, Anne."

"Oh, I know. I just never met anyone who actually did it." Anne's eyes welled. "I'm sorry."

"It wasn't a big deal," Daphne said. There she was again, trying to make it better for everyone else.

Anne wiped her eye with the back of her thumb. "I'm sorry," she said again. "I just can't imagine sending my babies away. It was hard enough to do it when they got old enough to get married." She laughed. "That's why I had to go work for Gibraltar—so I'd have somebody to mother."

At the name of Gibraltar, Daphne felt the sting of rejection all over again. "I'm glad Sophie's coming. She'll help me figure out what I'm supposed to do next."

"I think you're supposed to sit still," Anne said. "Daphne, from the sound of it, you've spent your entire life moving from place to place. It's time to make a home, don't you think?"

"That's what I thought, but I think God said no when my fiancé bailed on me and then took my job in Paris. With Jesse firing me, I have to consider that maybe I'm not supposed to be here in Ohio either."

"A person needs roots. How can you ever feel settled if you're always in a new place?"

"I don't think I've ever felt settled. I imagine that would be foreign." She forced a laugh.

"I'm going to have a talk with Jesse."

"I wish you wouldn't. I don't want to be here if he doesn't want me. It turns out he didn't want me to begin with. Dave forced me on him." She settled back into her seat. "Sophie's the only person who ever really wanted me around. I thought Mark did, but turns out I was wrong about that too."

"Well, Roger and I want you. We're looking forward to having you, and Roger is excited as all get-out to get started on your house. He's one of the few men I know who love honey-do lists, and the truth is, I don't have anything left on mine. As it is, he practically makes the bed before I get out of it. If I'm not careful, one of these days I'm going to be molded into hospital corners."

Daphne couldn't imagine what it would be like to be married to a man who made the bed. She scrutinized Anne's profile and tried to find some key, some understanding that unlocked what made her so lovable. The woman had the same sweet nature that Sophie did, but Daphne could never be like either of them. Her hopes for a settled future dwindled with each suburban house they passed.

"It must be hard not to have answers as to why Mark didn't show up that day."

Daphne nodded.

"There were no warning signs?"

"I'm sure there were many, but I missed them. I loved him."

"That's why they say love is blind. Was he a believer?"

Daphne nodded. "He went to church with me whenever we were together."

Anne flattened her lips as if that didn't offer any proof.

"Well, maybe not. But I felt like a princess whenever he was around. He laughed at my jokes. He knew everyone, and he has this way about him that makes people feel important when they're with him. And he wanted to marry me." Her countenance fell. "I thought."

"How long were you engaged?"

"A year, but a lot of that time I was still in Paris finishing up my perfuming degree. We met in chemistry. At UC–Berkeley."

"It's probably too soon to know what you learned from that relationship, but I have learned from every relationship in my life. Even the ones that hurt me severely."

"You had someone hurt you like this?"

"Well, not exactly. I've had pastors I trusted turn out to not be as truthful as I liked. I've seen men I really admired hurt my husband to get ahead. I think that hurts more, when someone hurts Roger. Or my children."

Daphne stared out the window and tried to memorize the markers they passed, see how the town was laid out and where she might get groceries if she needed them. She felt ridiculous staying with complete strangers. She didn't need to be taken care of; she was ready to get back to work. Or work on getting back her sense of smell. Something that gave her a renewed sense of purpose.

"I'm not saying my experiences compare to being left on your wedding day. Just that when people let us down, it's not always because we did something to deserve it."

"I'll never understand what I did to Mark to warrant his treating me that way. As if I were nothing more than something on the bottom of his shoe. I loved him. And even after what he did to me, I can't bring myself to hate him."

Anne patted her hand. "Someday someone will be worthy of that love, dear. Mark wasn't."

Daphne wondered if anyone had called Mark to tell him of her near-death experience. Would he have cared if she'd died in that rattletrap he'd bought? Would he have taken any responsibility for it? She hated to admit that she still hoped the man she loved might return to her. But had that man ever existed at all, or had she simply created the perfect hero and he fit the suit?

Maybe the hero in her dream—her boss—was meant to represent a different way of looking at life. When she had time, she'd try to figure out what it all meant. Dreams never meant what literally happened in them. She knew that she didn't harbor romantic thoughts toward Jesse.

While she was in the hospital, Daphne had asked the doctor about her lost sense. They ran a few tests—she didn't want to think about the cost—but all they'd concluded was that her issue was "psychosomatic." A cold way to put it, she thought. She supposed if there was any way to reframe the gas incident at the house, besides the fact that she hadn't been blown to smithereens, it was that her timely passing out had spared her the humiliation of seeing Jesse rescuing her with full cognition.

Also, a neighbor, Mr. Riley, was apparently a nice man who'd told Jesse he'd keep watch over the house until she returned. She liked that neighbors still did that. It almost made her want to get a newspaper so someone could collect it when she went on vacation. Maybe she could find a way to make Dayton work, even if Gibraltar hadn't.

"Here we are."

Anne's house stood in a quiet neighborhood with other ranch homes just like it. Sixties, pale yellowish brick halfway up the exterior walls, and the rest white stucco. As they drove up, Anne's husband came out the door as if he'd been waiting for them with one hand on the doorknob.

"Well, this is our bloom—Daphne, is it? Welcome, welcome!"

Roger had the essence of Santa Claus. If Daphne had to give him a scent, it would be Irish Spring soap. He was a man's man— big, lumbering, and with a full head of hair that he'd obviously tried to dye into the brown family.

"Welcome to our home. Your friend Sophie's plane has been delayed, but she called from Denver to tell me she'd take a taxi when she arrives. You Californians are so worried about putting people out. We *like* to go to the airport. It makes us feel like world travelers, doesn't it, dear?"

Anne agreed.

"Thank you, Roger. I hope I'm not going to be here too long. I won't be any trouble."

"Nonsense. Hasn't Anne told you? We get lonely when it's just the two of us. Now, I had a contractor go over to your place this morning—"

"Roger, let her at least get into the house."

"Sure, sure." He went right on speaking as they walked inside. "You know, Daphne, it appears that the stove was hooked up wrong. It was just leaking little vapors all along, ever since it was installed. It wasn't original to the house, so obviously some do-it-yourselfer didn't know what he was doing. Never play with gas or electricity, Daphne. Most everything else— Oh, and plumbing. You don't want to mess with any of those things. They can cause so much damage if you don't know what you're doing."

"Roger!" Anne chastised. "Let her into the house."

"She's in." Roger took Daphne's bag.

The house had a low ceiling and was filled with antiques and collectibles on doilies. Everything seemed breakable, and yet it all had obviously made it through the last fifty years. Against one wall there was an enormous elaborate upright piano that looked like it belonged in a church.

"I'm going to put you and Sophie in the boys' old bedroom, so you can be together. That's all right, isn't it?" Anne said.

"It's perfect."

"She should be on the plane by now," Roger said.

Daphne could hardly wait. If she didn't talk to someone about how she still couldn't smell—someone who couldn't fire her—she might go mad. Daphne wasn't the kind to keep secrets; it was almost worse than losing her sense of smell. She felt like such a fraud, and yet as much as she trusted Roger and Anne, she didn't know what Jesse had said to Gibraltar about firing her. Considering that she had lied, she figured he had the right to tell whatever story he liked.

Anne pointed to a huge stack of post boxes in one corner. "Those are your wedding gifts. I've got them boxed up and ready to send back—I assumed you were sending them back. They were in the hall closet inside the house."

"Yes, but—I planned to write thank-you notes and tuck them inside. My mother would kill me if I didn't say a proper thank-you."

"No problem. I tucked in a note saying you'd had a small accident and I'd be handling things if they had any questions. I think it's best to give everyone as little information as possible to cut down on the gossip."

"Wow, you thought of everything." They walked back to the living room, and Daphne sank into the sofa, wondering what she'd do with all the time on her hands. "I'll never be able to thank you."

"Never mind," Roger said. "If we only do for people who can do for us back, we have our reward in full. Isn't this what St. Paul said? 'Care for the women and orphans'? With your parents off in Europe, you qualify as an orphan. Even if it's only temporary."

Daphne smiled, but inwardly she winced. She'd always felt like other friends' parents parented her while hers were off at opera openings and fund-raisers. Being in a warm, comfortable house only made her think of what she'd thought she'd have with Mark. She'd purposely picked a man who didn't have aspirations for high society—but apparently he'd had more than she imagined.

"Let me show you to your room," Anne said again. "It's right this way."

They walked down a dark hallway and came to the end

of the passage. The room was small and stuffed with furniture from every era. There was a dresser from 1950 or so, big and blocky, and two twin beds without headboards, and an antique rocking chair that looked like it belonged on the front porch of an old-fashioned general store.

"I hope you'll be comfortable here, but if you need more space, you can take the room next door as well." Anne sat on the bed. "Daphne, I haven't heard you release a breath since I picked you up. Relax. People here like to take care of their neighbors."

"It's just—I'm not helpless. I can go with Roger to work on the house."

"I don't think you realize just how much work that house is going to be. But speaking of work, I'm going to call Jesse and find out what the story is."

"I wish you wouldn't. He had his reasons."

"I don't care what his reasons are, he didn't give you a fair shake." Anne acted as though something disagreed with her. "You should just go and get settled anyway. Don't worry about a thing."

How did she argue with that logic?

"By the way, a letter came for you at the office from your ex-whatever-he-was." Anne pulled a blue envelope off the dresser. "Jesse didn't want to give it to you, but it is yours. Yet I agree with Jesse: I can't think of any excuse that would suffice for what that man did."

"He didn't want to give it to me?" For some reason, the news made her hopeful. She'd searched for the letter that Mark sent to Jesse, only to find it inexplicably missing.

Roger appeared in the doorway, and Anne drew him into the discussion.

"Roger, tell Daphne she doesn't need to have the whole kit and caboodle of a husband and family to settle down. She's never had a home. Now she has one."

"A right nice one too," Roger said. "You've got a nice neighborhood and a good solid structure. Just needs some loving care."

"And the ability for me to pay the mortgage. But Sophie sent my cologne sample to my old boss in Paris, so I'm hopeful something might come from that." She wasn't really, but what point was there in saying so?

Anne crossed her legs and rested her hands on her knee. "Well, Paris, that's a pretty strong draw. Dayton probably can't compete with the likes of Paris. But I'd wager that Jesse could hold his own with any decent man in any society."

"Jesse fired me, Anne. Remember?"

"He what?" Roger shouted. "But Anne told me that Dave hired you; how is it that Jesse can fire you?"

"That's just what I said!" Anne cried. "Roger will get to the bottom of this."

"No, I wish you wouldn't. Roger doesn't even work there."

"But he's Jesse's pastor," Anne said, ignoring Daphne's groan. "I'm going to start lunch. My man gets like a bear if he doesn't eat. Can't allow guests to see that happen."

"I have a hard time believing that Roger ever gets mad."

"And I have a hard time believing Jesse was ever angry with you, so I guess we'll have to trust one another."

There was that blasted word again. But without a car, a

place to live, or a job, Daphne supposed she had little choice in the matter. In any matter. She stared at the letter from Mark, and all she wanted to do was rip into it.

"I'll have Roger bring in the knitting basket, and you can knit until it's time for lunch."

"I really don't like to knit anymore. Jesse was just being nice. I'll help with lunch. There's nothing wrong with me. Please don't make me sit in here and do nothing. I'll go crazy."

"All right. You read your letter and then come find me in the kitchen." Anne grasped her wrist in a show of warmth and left the room.

Daphne lifted the blue envelope to her nose, hoping for a whiff of the cologne she'd created for Mark, but again she smelled nothing. She'd been on her iPhone all night in search of a reason for stress-induced anosmia but couldn't find any such disease. The causes of a lost sense of smell were generally more serious than stress. She didn't have any sort of cold or infection, so it couldn't be that, and the gas leak hadn't happened until afterward, so it wasn't toxically induced. The loss had been sudden. And complete. Which also didn't bode well for finding the cause.

If she'd only lost part of her sense, the future would seem brighter, but it wasn't going to be something she could hide for long. Even if she didn't work at Gibraltar, what else was she capable of doing with her background?

She slid her fingernail under the blue-lined envelope until the seal gave way, then she took a deep breath and unfolded the letter. Typed, not handwritten. She clutched it to her chest. "At least you typed a full letter and not a text."

"Are you talking to me?" Roger had reappeared with the knitting basket that seemed to follow her around like a stray dog.

"You startled me. No, I was just narrating my letter for myself."

"Talking to yourself is a sign of insanity."

"I think it's just a sign of working in a lab by oneself with lots of solvents." She grinned. "Tell Anne I'll be out in a minute."

"Take your time. She doesn't like help in her kitchen anyhow." Roger dropped the basket near the door and shut it behind him.

She sat down on the bed and read, *"Dear Daphne:"*

"Colon? He used a colon in my Dear John letter? That's just wrong. I was going to marry a tool. A comma would have been totally sufficient, and much friendlier."

Dear Daphne:

Before we were about to get married, I contacted the chemical and flavor companies in Paris because I knew how desperately you wanted to stay there. I think you know what they told me. They weren't willing to overlook my past and the short time I did in big pharma. I think we both know how that came to be common knowledge, and I want you to know that I forgive you. Arnaud, being a good man and a friend of yours, agreed to meet with me and hear me out. I admit I lied on my résumé to get the job in Dayton, but here I was able to tell the truth. It's unfortunate that by then you already had the job in Dayton in formulation. That left a place for me here in Paris, and I jumped at the chance. I saw it as fate.

I'll be attending the perfumery school in my off-time and learning the tools of the trade, but I needed to get to Paris for the job. My reputation is not what it once was, and my license makes it difficult for me to formulate in America. With you in Dayton, and me in Paris, the writing was on the wall. If only you hadn't told Arnaud about me, none of this would have happened. I obviously need more money to live in Paris than I would have in Dayton, so I took more money from the down payment your father gave us for a house. Now we can both live on that money. It's funny how life works out, isn't it? You wanted to settle down, and I wanted to explore the world. This way, we both got our way.

You'll forgive me one day, as I've forgiven you. I know you will, because you have such a godly heart, sweet Daphne.

Mark

She needed to vomit. She ran to the hallway to find the bathroom and expunge the feelings and everything else inside.

After a few moments there was a knock on the bathroom door. "Daphne, are you all right?"

"I'm fine, Anne. I'll be out in a minute." She ran the cold water and splashed it on her face, using soap to wipe away any memory of Mark from her life. The letter hadn't explained why or how Arnaud had given Mark a job now. And Mark said nothing of Arnaud's having a job there for her too . . . Something about that missing information made her very suspicious.

The knocks came again, more insistent. "Daphne, open the door."

Daphne flushed the toilet, splashed more water onto her face, and patted it dry. "I'm sorry, Anne. I can't remember the last time I threw up."

"I think we should take you back to the hospital."

"No!" Daphne said. "It's not that. I—"

The doorbell rang.

"That must be Sophie." Daphne brushed past Anne and scurried to the living room where Sophie's wide smile and familiar squeal met hers.

Roger covered his ears. "Well, my goodness. You'd think you two hadn't seen each other for a decade. What's it been, four days?"

"Six, but who's counting?" Sophie hugged both Anne and Roger as if she'd known them forever. "Thank you for taking my precious Daphne in. You're not going to want to get rid of her, she's so much fun! Wait until you watch football and she has to ask you the rules over and over again. It's as though she grew up on another planet."

"Sophie. You're supposed to say something nice about me."

Sophie laughed. "Your house will always smell lovely with her here, and she can cook the best soups for winter you'll ever taste. There, good enough?"

"I don't plan to be here in the winter, but I do promise to make some gumbo in return for room and board."

"Sophie, why don't you get Daphne to her room? She's not feeling well."

"No?" Sophie asked.

"I'll explain it all. Let's give Roger and Anne their house back for a bit while we catch up."

"Are you hungry, Sophie?" Anne asked.

"No, I ate on the plane. Cost me a fortune, but a girl's gotta eat. Thank you, though."

"After I feed Roger, I'm going back to the office. I'll run by the post office and mail out the wedding gifts."

"You did all that, Anne?" Sophie said. "That would have taken me months. I want to hire you for after my wedding."

"Except you will actually *have* a wedding, and nothing will go back except the thank-you notes," Daphne reminded her.

They walked to the back room, and she took Mark's letter from atop the dresser and handed it to Sophie. "He knew I'd understand," she said breathily, with the back of her hand to her forehead, "because I am such a godly woman."

Sophie unfolded the letter. "He used a colon in a Dear John letter?" She skimmed it quickly, then tossed it aside. "I love how he tries to make this all your fault. And then announces you're godly, so you have no choice but to forgive him."

"Well, I don't have to. I think I'm entitled to hate on him for a good week at least."

"A month. A good month, then it's time to get on with life." Sophie sat down in the rocker and leaned back. "I don't understand what he's accusing you of."

"I told Arnaud why Mark was in sales and not chemistry any longer. Because, you know, his license got taken away after he did all that stuff in college. I was trying to be forthright, so he'd know the issues up front, but that came back to bite me in the bum."

"Yeah?"

"The information made it to the Web over there, and Mark

got banned from European chemistry as well. So I don't really understand how he can be working there. Arnaud can't know the whole story. The sales job at Gibraltar was all he had, but they found out that he lied about being at Chlorox, so that backfired on him here."

"All of this is going to backfire on him. Listen, even if you did make the mistake of leaking the information—" Sophie's nose wrinkled. "How did you make that mistake again?"

"Well, you know I don't drink because it messes with my palate? Well, Arnaud's wife had served this fabulous fruit punch, and I'd never tasted anything like it, and—"

"You did not get drunk."

"Apparently I got a little tipsy and talked a bit. The punch was called sangria. They never told me it had alcohol in it. When something tastes like grape juice and no one explains to you that's to cover up the huge doses of red wine—at least I think it's red wine—well—"

"I find it hard to believe with your taste buds you couldn't recognize it had alcohol in it."

"I know. Mark said the same thing. But I swear to you, I didn't taste it. I don't know if it was a really light wine or what, but I just kept talking like there was empty air I had to fill, and I have no idea what else I said." She smiled. "I do know we had a team archery meet that afternoon, and I was banned from my bow."

Sophie kicked her shoes off. "It's still not your fault. He did what he did. You only told that he did it. The fact that he makes it all your fault only helps me diagnose him more readily with narcissistic personality disorder."

Daphne threw a pillow at her.

"He may have been a brilliant chemist, but there are laws for a reason. He always thought himself above the rules. Did Gibraltar know about the sanctions against him?"

"Not as far as I can tell, but Arnaud did, so I can't imagine how he got that job."

"That has nothing to do with you. He's got all the signs."

"Personality disorder or no, he's working for Arnaud now."

"Then that's Arnaud's problem, not yours. You have enough of your own here."

"Arnaud says there's a job for me, but you know I'll never be safe with Mark there."

"You have your sense of smell back?"

"Shh! Not yet. But my boss, Jesse, found out, and he fired me already. So I don't have a job here either. What I mean is Mark has probably already destroyed my reputation somehow to save his own."

"You're not going to Paris, Daphne. Mark is dangerous. He's probably a sociopath, and he's certainly NPD. And that's a professional opinion, so I wouldn't discount it."

"You can make all those diagnoses from one short colon-ized letter? Sometimes I don't know whether you've had too much schooling or you're just watching too many Lifetime movies."

"Lifetime movies are based on true stories. They've got a lot of movies, so that should tell you something. There are a lot of psychopaths out there, and some of them are really handsome and really charming."

"If he's dangerous, I can't let Arnaud be in danger. What if he wants Arnaud's job? Now that I know what he's capable of, I feel like no one is safe. It's my job to warn them."

"Arnaud is a smart man and can take care of himself. When are you going to understand, you have to take care of *you*. Not the entire world. You're a genuinely nice person, Daphne, but Mark needs to take some responsibility for himself. You need to let the whole thing go. He's not your problem anymore."

"Well, he's still sort of my problem if I don't have a job here."

There was a knock on the door, and Sophie opened it by reaching from the rocking chair.

"Jesse's here to see you," Roger said.

"Jesse the boss?" Sophie asked with her brows raised. "Oh, I'm anxious to see if he's as hot as you described."

"That was before I got to know him. This is the boss who saved my life and then fired me."

"Bring him on!" Sophie said, rising from the chair. "Then we'll take care of Mark."

# Chapter 16

J esse waited on his pastor's porch like a bad date on proba-
tion. He paced as he waited for Daphne to come to the
door. Anne and Roger obviously knew about the firing—that
would be the reason he wasn't invited in—but both were too
polite to say so.

In the midst of the emotional turmoil at the hospital, he had
failed to see the repercussions of firing Daphne. He'd thought
he was doing her a *favor*, actually. She didn't want to be there,
and this would only hasten her route back to Paris, where she
clearly belonged. Unfortunately, Dave hadn't seen things in the
same light, and so here he was. Groveling. On bended knee, if
necessary.

The door opened. Daphne moved like liquid in a form-fitting
pair of yoga pants and a bright pink sweatshirt. Her dark hair
lay over her shoulders. All his original reservations came back in
force. It would be better if she left and got on with her life.

"Hi," she said, and the moment seemed intimate until he

saw her redheaded shadow behind her. "Jesse, this is my best friend, Sophie."

"We talked on the phone yesterday." He held out his hand.

"Was that before you fired Daphne? Or after?" Sophie put a hand to her rounded hip, and Jesse knew his apology would prove useless.

"Daphne, can we talk?" He met Sophie's steely gaze. "Alone?"

"I'll be back in a minute, Sophie."

Daphne stepped out onto the porch, and Jesse drank in the full view of her and questioned himself all over again. What was he doing here? How long would he answer to Dave's every whim? But then Ben's hopeful face swam before his eyes. He couldn't afford to take his eye off the target, no matter how difficult it became.

"I made a mistake," he said. "I didn't have the right to fire you. And there's no reason we can't use the ideas we came up with and more until your sense of smell comes back. It's the first time I've been excited about a product since my first quarter at Gibraltar."

"Okay." She stared up at a tree while she answered him.

"You're not going to make me beg? Get on my knees maybe?"

Daphne frowned. "I wouldn't do anything that made you feel like a loser, Jesse."

Her words socked him in the gut. He'd fired her. What could make her feel like more of a loser than that? Other than being abandoned on her wedding day, of course. "I deserved that."

She blinked a few times, and he watched as her lashes fluttered up slowly to reveal the deep blue of her eyes. He shook the vision from his head and stared at Roger's perfect green lawn.

"Did you tell Dave why you fired me? You had a good reason."

He sliced his hand through the air. "Just don't. Don't make me feel any worse than I already do. I didn't tell Dave anything, because the truth is, you can do this job without your sense of smell. It's the way you create. I have to admit, I was wrong. What you do works for me."

"I was afraid that the cologne I made for Mark was my swan song. I'd never do another thing. But then we made our deal, and I felt like I could create again." As she looked toward her feet in her summer sandals, he noted that the pink toes matched her wedding manicure. It made him feel like a heel all over again.

He could see Sophie watching the two of them from behind a curtain in Anne's house. "I think your friend wants in on this conversation. Maybe she thinks you shouldn't take the job again."

"Why don't we ask her?" Daphne opened the front door and called to her friend. "Sophie, you may as well come out." She turned back to Jesse. "She's a psychologist, so she doesn't like to be left out of a good conversation."

He felt as though he was in junior high school and Daphne's decision to attend the dance with him depended upon the good graces of her friend. Did everything in the world have to be decided by committee?

Sophie's nature seemed soft and friendly toward the world, but perhaps not toward him at the moment. There was a way of the world within her; he imagined that her wrath would be thorough. He could only imagine what Mark must have felt.

"You may as well know. I'm here to offer Daphne her job back. It seems that I was hasty in my decision."

Sophie crossed her arms. "That's nice. Are you going to take it, Daph?"

"Yeah." She shrugged. "Jesse inspires me. I think we'll work well together."

Sophie stared at him skeptically. "If you say so."

"Do you want her to take the job, Sophie?"

"Does it matter to you?" she asked.

"It does," he said. He didn't want to be put out in the same rubbish bin as Mark.

"Maybe Daphne should come home. Where those of us who love her can take care of her."

"No one could take better care of her than Anne and Roger. They're incredible people."

"They are," Sophie agreed. "But when she goes home to her own house, I worry it will be too quiet for her."

"What does Daphne want?"

The subject of their conversation seemed lost in her own thoughts, as if she'd missed the whole thing. He found that strange, because not a lot escaped Daphne's attention.

"Huh?"

"Do you want to stay in Dayton until Christmas? Keep our deal?"

"I don't understand," Sophie said. "How could you fire her yesterday if you already had a 'deal'?"

"I'm not feeling good again," Daphne said. "Would you excuse me?"

She walked into the house, leaving Jesse and Sophie standing face-to-face in silent mortal combat.

"She's too sensitive for the world," Sophie said. "I worry about her."

That was exactly the reason he wanted Daphne to go. He couldn't be responsible for her. He had too much on his plate already. Not that Dave would ever understand that. He never took the responsibility for a thing unless it was accolades that involved the press or attention.

*It's for Ben*, he reminded himself.

"I'll take care of her," he blurted.

Sophie laughed. "Like her fiancé took care of her?"

"I'm nothing like him. Daphne lied to me and I overreacted, that's all."

"You made a deal with Daphne that you reneged on, and now you're telling me you'll take care of her? Mark said the same thing before he took her job in Paris. Do you want her to wait around for the other shoe to drop?" Sophie crossed her arms in front of her. "Daphne can take care of herself. She's made do with makeshift family her whole life."

"She doesn't have to do that here. I overreacted, but I don't intend to do that again. She has an ability that's valuable to Gibraltar."

He hated that he was defending himself and Sophie was defending Daphne. It should never have come to that. Why hadn't he just said he was so mad at her that night because he'd almost lost her too? The first woman who'd broken through his armor since Hannah. Why hadn't *he* told the truth?

Sophie's arms were crossed in front of her. "Daphne's very loyal. To a fault, I'd say. And I wondered what kind of man wrestled a promise to stay out of her so quickly."

"We made a deal, that's all." He looked away from Sophie's prying eyes.

"But the deal was off when she made a mistake?"

"Sophie, there are so many reasons I want Daphne to get out of here, but none of them has to do with me. *I* want her to stay, and I wanted that when I first laid eyes on her, which scared me. Six months seemed like a fair time frame for both of us."

Sophie nodded, and as if his hour was over, she disappeared into the house.

Jesse stood alone on the front porch wondering how it was that his life had been turned upside down by a nose.

On June 27 Daphne was officially starting work at Gibraltar for the second time that month. She'd prayed for her sense of smell to return in that time, but as of that morning, her black tea still went down like warm, flavorless rust-colored water.

"Not tasting is getting old."

"Quit complaining," Sophie said. "You're getting a free pass on dieting. I'm jealous. I mean, if broccoli tastes like chocolate cake, there's no temptation to eat the real thing. By the way, Anne and Roger are bringing a group here tonight to pray over you."

"Do they know why they're praying?"

"They probably think you're depressed since being dumped."

"I am depressed since being dumped. As far as I know, boils have not yet appeared all over Mark's face, and Arnaud hasn't said a thing about Volatility! You're sure you sent it to him, right?"

"I'll bet you anything Mark claimed it as his own, and he's trying to recreate it."

"He'll never figure out the top note. It's something I made myself."

"So that's a good thing. Focus on that instead of the taste thing. There's still color and texture to enjoy."

"Trust me, broccoli is not chocolate cake. Still, it would have been helpful if I'd lost it before the wedding. Do you know how hard I worked to fit into that gown?"

"It was worth it. You looked like a million dollars, and I put your pics all over my Facebook page so that Mark can eat his heart out."

"Don't kid yourself; Mark hasn't been stalking your Facebook wall. He replaced me a long time ago." A loud bang resounded from the roof. "I'm so tired of all this work. I mean, don't get me wrong. The men from church have been fabulous, but I'm ready to have my house back."

"At least we're here and not in Anne's back room. God love her, she and her husband talk a lot. I thought you might explode over there."

"I almost did, which makes me feel like the worst person on earth. They would do anything for anyone. Surely I should be able to put up with some conversation from two people

216

who are housing me, feeding me, and helping me get this house in shape."

"I'm just glad you found a church home so quickly. That has to help, having some fellowship to look forward to."

"All those potlucks, and I've still lost eight pounds."

"Don't rub it in," Sophie said. "All I want to do in this heat is eat."

"I'll get air-conditioning eventually."

"I think you'll get everything eventually. This place is going to be good for you. I can feel it." Sophie smirked. "Though you're going to be watching babies until eternity as payback."

"It's a win-win. I love the church nursery, and I love seeing all these people give up their time for me! Their spirit reminds me not everyone is like Mark. I'd rather be an eternal optimist and get burned again than forget there are people like this in the world."

Sophie hugged her. "I'm proud of you, Daph. My baby girl is all grown up. She doesn't need me anymore."

"What would I have done without you? Look at this place!" She allowed her eyes to rest on the new, pale yellow walls and thought how beautiful the hardwood floors would look when they were refinished. Luckily, she had very few pieces of furniture to move. "You're a good painter. If the psychology thing doesn't work out, you'll always have that."

Daphne hadn't painted for fear her nose would get worse, if that were possible. From an outsider's perspective, she was sure she looked lazy. Sophie and the men of the church had done all the hard labor, and Daphne almost felt like she'd explode with gratitude.

"You'd be there for me," Sophie said. "But if I were you, I think I'd rather have the help of that hottie Brad. He seems very interested in hanging around more than necessary. I'm not sure I'd have the strength to ask him to leave." She laughed. "If he doesn't rekindle your interest in Anne's church, I don't know what would."

"They're all wonderful. But Jesse hasn't shown. Did you notice?"

Sophie nodded. "But I saw the way he looked at you on Anne's front porch. Something tells me that his staying away is harder on him than on you."

"Now who's the eternal optimist?"

"You were pretty close to Arnaud and his family," Sophie said. "I thought that's how it might be with Jesse."

"I'll never understand how Mark wins time and time again. How could Arnaud believe I could come and work side by side with Mark after what he did?"

"Well, aren't the French known for their liberal thinking? If anything, he probably thinks you're a baby for staying away." Sophie rubbed a dust cloth over the windowsills.

"Mark just has that magic in him that keeps people from seeing past whatever he says."

"That makes him sound like the Antichrist."

"Well, if the pitchfork fits . . ." Daphne checked her reflection in the mirror.

Sophie's eyes widened. "Speaking of Jesse, I've heard his praises sung a lot this week."

"Don't even go there. I made him a deal, and now I just worry that I'm going to need him a lot more than he needs me.

I look forward to being inspired again. He knows I can't smell, and yet he still sees the possibilities."

"Keep steaming when you get home each night and don't neglect your prayer time. Nothing is going to clear your stress away like prayer." Sophie sat down next to her. "And when Anne's group comes to pray for you? Keep an eye on Brad. Those eyes are sure to do something for your health." She handed her the mug from the side table. "Finish your tea."

"Maybe he's going to do it when I get there in person."

"Do what?"

"Fire me again. Legally, he probably has to do it in person."

"And maybe the cows in the field are going to fly home and paint the rest of your walls blood red. Could you worry about something that has a basis in reality?"

"Such as?"

"Such as why your friend and mentor, Arnaud, won't return your calls." Sophie put the tea cup down. "I'm still worried about Mark being in Paris with your fragrance. He stands to make a lot of money on that if you don't claim it, Daphne. You know you have a hit there."

"I do, but I plan to patent it here with packaging. I'm telling you, he won't get the last ingredient. It makes all the difference."

"But if he patents it with Givaudan's packaging, you're done for. At least make a claim about it being yours, will you? If Arnaud had come to your wedding, he'd already know it was your fragrance, and I wouldn't worry—but as it is, I worry that I sent the fragrance right into Mark's hand. He played me like a fiddle."

Daphne couldn't worry any more than she already had. At some point, she had to rest in the fact that God was in control.

Between the repairs and her hospital visit, she was in debt for nearly ten grand, not counting her mortgage. Leaving Dayton was financially impossible. She felt justified, though. Like Cortez burning the ships.

"By the way, Mr. Riley brought more casseroles over," Sophie told her. "He was here bright and early this morning. I think his wife is determined to fill that fridge for you."

"More? What does Mrs. Riley think I eat?"

"Daph—one more thing. Gary got me a flight home for tomorrow morning," Sophie said.

The words Daphne least wanted to hear, though she had to admit Dayton had welcomed her with open arms. Anne and her husband, Roger, had made her feel more at home than her own parents ever had. She had more help at the house than she knew what to do with—including a lot of single men.

Still, the prick of tears stung behind her nose at the thought of being without Sophie. "Who is going to diagnose Mark every day and make me feel better?"

"I'll send you a DSM-V of your very own. You can be a private pseudo-psychologist in your own home." Sophie smiled. "Which, by the way, isn't half bad. You made some nice finds at the secondhand stores, and your church filled in the rest."

"My church," Daphne said out loud. "I guess this is where I am for now."

"Paris isn't big enough for you and Mark. Until you find out how he got that job, you just need to heal without him anywhere near you."

Daphne nodded.

"You've got that far-off look again. Stop it, Daphne. You don't miss Mark. You only miss the idea of him. Remember that."

"Thank you, Doctor."

"As soon as I'm out of here, you'll have more time to get your new life going. And don't forget to work on that packaging for Volatility! It's too good not to sell, Daph, but you've got to do your part and protect it. But first, protect yourself."

"I thought that was your job. If you want to be near Daphne Sweeten, you must pass muster with Dr. Sophie. She will run a short battery of mental health tests at Stanford, and we'll be able to go forward from there."

"I think you're going to like living alone. And everyone is so friendly. I think I've met more of your neighbors here this week than I've met in five years of living in Palo Alto."

There was a knock at the door.

"Mr. Riley's already been here this morning. Who could that be?"

Daphne opened the door to a young man in a hoodie and jeans. "Daphne Sweeten?"

"Yes."

"Have a nice day." He handed her a thick envelope and hopped off the stoop to a waiting car.

She stared at the official seal. Was it really necessary that her father had the lawsuit arrive in that fashion? Unless he was suing her too. She ripped open the envelope.

"It's Daddy's lawyer." Her parents didn't have time to check on her well-being, but they had time to start the lawsuit process and make sure Mark paid in full for their humiliation. Which in her father's language meant loss of money. *That's where you hurt a man.* She ripped open the contents.

## SUPERIOR COURT OF THE STATE OF OHIO
## COUNTY OF MONTGOMERY
## PLAINTIFFS: GEORGE SWEETEN

*And*

## DAPHNE SWEETEN

*V.*

## DEFENDANT: MARK GOODSMITH

On May 14, 2011, GEORGE SWEETEN entered into an agreement in good faith with his former future son-in-law (MARK GOODSMITH)...

Yada, yada, yada. "At least he's not suing me. But good luck getting a penny or a rock out of Mark. He'll just slither into Switzerland with a secret bank account."

She continued reading. Daddy alleged fraud and wanted his twenty thousand dollars returned, along with another five grand for emotional suffering and lawyers' fees. *Who suffered?* She supposed it didn't count that her distress included nearly being asphyxiated. Her father had selective awareness skills. But then, emotions didn't count in the game of money.

She tossed the official letter on the unfinished wood floors. "He bought the wrong house. Can you stand it? How did I ever buy that this was a God-fearing man?"

"Delusion is a powerful drug," Sophie said. "I'm adding delusional to my diagnosis of narcissistic personality disorder, along with passive-aggressive and avoidant patterns."

"Mark's got a lot of letters behind his name. Think he can fit it all on stationery?"

"I'm serious, Daphne. Get healthy. Listen to your body and stop second-guessing yourself. I think you knew the truth all along."

Everything she had, her talents, her relationships, her family life in San Francisco, had been stripped away while her debts and connections to Dayton grew. Even if she wanted to go back to Europe, her chances of doing so dwindled by the moment.

She had a home now.

She had a car payment now.

She had a Visa bill with extensive repairs and medical bills.

As she went out onto the cement porch, a light summer rain began to sprinkle on the driveway. "Sophie, look! It's raining." She breathed in deep. "It's a sign. The scent of rain." She raised her arms and let the small droplets of water hit her. "I think it smells better here than it did in Paris!"

"You can smell?"

"No, but I'm imagining it. And it's better. Everything is fresh and renewed. I'm right, aren't I?"

Sophie nodded. "You're right."

Daphne stepped back inside and tightened the belt around her new forties-style khaki skirt with its oversized buttons and slid into her oxford pumps. She felt classically stylish—like a sexy professor—and she was glad she'd taken the time to dress well that morning. She needed the confidence boost.

In her new outfit, all traces of the former Daphne Sweeten had been washed away, like a summer rain cleansing the pavement.

# Chapter 17

Daphne entered Gibraltar with a confident stride, ready to make the most of their sports detergent and live up to Jesse's expectations.

Anne was already behind her desk when Daphne arrived. "Daphne, how's the new place?"

"Oh, Anne, it's perfect. I can't wait to have you and Roger over for dinner, and I won't even have to cook. Mrs. Riley down the street is pelting me with casseroles."

"Good, you need to gain some weight."

Daphne couldn't say that without her sense of smell and taste buds, the casseroles were only a mushy, unnatural texture, and she hadn't found herself hungry. She saw Jesse walk into his office. He stole a glance at her and promptly turned away. "Jesse's here early."

"He's always here early." Anne stared up at her over the rims of her glasses. "Why don't you go see him first? I know he's been waiting for you."

Daphne walked down the lengthy hallway to his office and rapped on the open door. "Good morning."

"Good morning. I trust you're feeling better."

"I am feeling better, and it was good to have the time to move in properly. I'm sorry I didn't plan that too well. I guess I was just too anxious to get out of San Francisco."

"That's what I do for a living. I streamline processes—and yours looked like it could use some tweaking." She smiled, and he started to laugh.

"What's so funny?"

"*I streamline processes.* Gosh, I sound so full of garbage. I think I've been here too long. Shut the door."

She did, and then focused on his desk. "Your desk is so clean. That's a sign of mental illness."

"Who says that?"

"Sophie. But she says a lot of things, and sometimes I think she overanalyzes. Maybe you're just neat."

"Let's go with that."

"No," she said. "The first day you had all those marketing reports on your desk—that's why I thought you were messier."

"That's what I want to talk to you about. Have a seat."

She sat.

"The marketing reports are gone."

"Oh."

"Willard and John are creating a product out of your scent. We're presenting it at the next staff meeting, which will have the board involved."

"Does Dave know?"

"No. He thinks we're making sexy fabric softener because it's Kensie's idea. He thinks yours is on track for next quarter."

"Gee, thanks. But we're not?"

"I don't know. Maybe we are. This is *you*, this fragrance. I assume that means there's emotion involved and that might resonate with buyers. Like the sports detergent. All I can smell is the scent of winning. What emotion do you feel when you think of Volatility!?"

"Right now? I think of volatility, because I know my ex is trying to figure out the last note. But when I was creating it, I thought of love. I felt singled out and special, like I was the luckiest woman alive. I didn't understand what I'd done to be worthy of such love. I felt treasured. Now . . ." She paused. "What I feel most is not rejection, but a loss of innocence. I don't know that I can ever believe in love that wholeheartedly again, and I worry I won't be able to create on that emotion ever again. But you showed me that we can come close. It's not all emotion."

Jesse's brows were raised, and she felt the heat of the Ohio summer, though the building was well air-conditioned.

"I did it again," she said. "I'm talking too much. I'm nervous."

Jesse's eyes were locked on hers. He cleared his throat and wrote down some notes on a notepad. "What else makes you feel like that?" He met her eyes again. "Besides love."

"God. When I'm in worship and I just feel the connection between the two of us. And I know—" She stopped. "Wait— you mean winning? What makes me feel like that?"

She was pouring out her heart like she was in a therapist's office. She'd spent too much time around Sophie for the last two weeks. This man didn't know her from toilette water, and she felt his patience wearing thin.

He nodded. "I'm trying to make the most of what you do. I want to create a scent around an emotion, but I think we need an alter ego for Volatility! I have an idea, if you can think of a way to feminize that cologne for a female fragrance."

"Feminize Volatility!, you mean?"

"If you're comfortable with that. I just thought it would be easier than starting from scratch. And in case Dave doesn't like the first two ideas, I want to have backups."

"That's great. Great." Equal parts excitement and anxiety tore through Daphne. She wanted to use her signature scent, but she also wanted to get back to Paris with it. This presented a happy, Mark-free answer. She could prove her process. Prove that she'd created it and owned it, but it wouldn't do her any good without an actual product.

"Dave and Willard have been working on ideas, but so far they have nothing. They're two old bachelors, so I'm not sure the 'treasured' emotion comes into play unless it's from one of Dave's game controllers. Or maybe Willard's ham radio. So . . . my idea. The reason I need two . . ." He held his hands up for punctuation. "Dog shampoo!"

"Dog shampoo?"

"We could have a dry dog shampoo as well, for weekly spritzes. A whole line of them, really."

She didn't want to be offended, but her signature scent . . . for dogs?

"Hear me out. Dogs give you unconditional love. They

make you feel treasured. Volatility! is the perfect scent for a freshly bathed pup. We'll have to come up with the perfect name—we don't want anything that makes you think *wet dog* when you're thinking about how much they love you and you want to treasure them. It will work for both sexes, but if we wanted to expand the marketing, we could have a pink brand and a blue brand."

"You came up with this?" She blinked. "You don't even have a dog, do you?"

"I don't know how I didn't think of it before, actually. You made the scent for Mark. Mark's a dog. It's a natural fit."

Daphne felt utterly wistful. "When you were kissing me in that dream, you had a dog. Three of them, actually." Her mouth stopped moving.

"What was that?" He looked up from his desk, where he'd been scribbling a note.

"I was thinking about marketing."

"A line of dog products. I think that might work, Daphne. We've got some solid ideas for the staff meeting. Maybe Dave was right about you."

"Well . . . good. Thanks."

"Why don't you get started on the female version? Your fragrance lab is all set up; you should be able to start mixing for the sample. Work with Willard on a formula. He can keep a secret."

She couldn't wait to get to the lab. "I've done a mock-up for the detergent. Sophie helped me with it at home, and I think you're going to be happy with it. Sophie said Gary would use it, and he's pretty manly."

"Daphne, I know this wasn't the idea you had originally for the cologne."

"No, but it's more important to be a part of something. We can fix this division."

"Dave can't know anything about this until we present the ideas with your samples at the staff meeting. So that means Kensie can't know about it either. As far as they both know, we're working from the marketing plans."

"Which are?"

"Now dissolved into a giant fireball worthy of a Bruce Willis movie."

"Very nice," she said, impressed by his creativity. "That's a process that eliminated a lot of other processes."

"I told you, I'm all about procedure. The lab staff meeting is this morning, so find out what John is working on and talk about that."

"I can't lie," she said. "What if Kensie asks me?"

"You won't be lying. You'll be working on that too."

She couldn't believe she'd blurted out that comment about her dream. "Jesse, I just wanted to—"

He didn't let her finish. "Let's not do this. Let's keep this strictly professional."

"Sure. If that's what you want."

He went back to his notepad, and she took her cue to leave. As she walked silently back to the elevators, she passed Anne's desk.

"HR still needs a couple more signatures from you when you get the opportunity today. Oh, and you have some mail this morning."

"I do?"

Anne handed her a familiar blue envelope. Mark's careful script was written on it, and instinctively Daphne traced the letters with her fingers. It was easier to get rid of a harsh reality than a well-crafted fantasy.

When she opened the letter, a photograph of Mark and another woman floated out. Daphne bent to pick up the picture and looked at the woman beside him. She was almost as tall as he was, and she had beautiful red hair that fell in ringlets over her shoulders. She wore a mermaid ball gown but didn't begin to have the figure for it. Daphne took a sick satisfaction in that—which separated her from Mother Teresa by more than a wide margin. Mark's new woman looked like someone who could play field hockey handily. Not his sort at all, and that made Daphne worry for the stranger. What did she have that Mark coveted? And would she be smarter than Daphne had been?

"Are you okay?" Anne asked her. "You look as white as a ghost."

She stared at the photo. Mark had his arm around the woman's waist, but in a way that made him look like a male model who had to go to a dance with his cousin. He wore an aqua shirt, and his dark hair rose due to an overabundance of gel. But the way his dark brown eyes looked at her from the photograph made her understand why she had believed in him. Why she still wanted to believe in him.

His power over her almost bordered on supernatural.

She knew her emotions were pointless. Stalking him on

Facebook, checking his status, looking at his picture—all these would do was prolong her suffering and remind her that he must have never loved her. Unrequited love might be romantic in old movies, but in real life, it stunk like a sulphur spring.

Shockingly, the letter itself was longer than a sentence. Which told her he must want something more than an apology this time. She only had to look as far as his comma for that confirmation.

Daphne,

I've had time to think about that first letter I wrote you, and I was wrong. You weren't to blame for word getting around. When the DEA blacklists a chemist from being able to purchase supplies, it's not a liability any company wants to take on—you would have aided and abetted a criminal. I can see that now. I can also see that you understood what I was trying to do. You understood the future of pharmacology mixed with aromatherapy. I know you shared my vision.

Victoria is my soul mate. I discovered her when I took that stand-up comedy class in San Francisco. She not only believed in me, but she helped me finish my second thesis— the one you disapproved of. But I believed, and still do, that the future of medicine is in scents and mists. Arnaud has seen the light. Drugs that won't feel like drugs for the sick and the weary.

If it's not too much trouble, I'd like you to send me the formula for Volatility!, as it's become my signature scent and

I plan to make more of it at home for myself. The gift should remain with the receiver. Victoria sends her regards.

Respectfully,

Mark

Respectfully? If there was anything missing from Mark's letter, it was respect. She felt sick at his heartless words. *"The gift should remain with the receiver."* She should have kept the engagement ring.

"Daphne?"

"He's turned into Frankenstein's monster. I dated Frankenstein's monster. I almost married Frankenstein's monster."

"Daphne?" Anne got up and came around her desk.

"Mark. I think he's on some sort of substance. In fact, I hope he is, because I don't even want to think that's his version of normal." She held up the picture. "This is his new woman."

"If he's got a new woman mere days after canceling his wedding, he's not worth it." Anne took the picture from her and ripped it in half. "Get to work. He's not worth your energy. I'll be in the storage room if anyone needs me."

Daphne walked slowly toward the restroom. She needed a shower. She wanted to wash away the vision she had of Mark with a new woman. As she stepped around the corner, she saw Kensie and Dave getting into the elevator. He patted Kensie just above the behind and grasped her low on the waist, saying something into her ear. She giggled coquettishly, throwing her hair back over her shoulder.

Wasn't Dave married?

Daphne's stomach roiled, and she crumpled Mark's letter in her hand. There was so much darkness in the world, she felt she'd never create again.

Maybe there was a reasonable explanation for what she'd just seen. She needed to know that marriage meant something in the world, because right now it seemed to have no value whatsoever.

She'd just gone into the ladies' room when the door behind her swung open and Anne appeared.

Without preamble Daphne blurted, "Oh, Anne, it's you. How did you meet Roger? How did you know he was the right one?"

Anne didn't even ask where this was coming from. "He wouldn't let me think otherwise. Chased me to the high heavens until I agreed to go out with him. I hate to say persistency paid off, but in this case, it did."

Daphne smiled. "I needed to hear that. But, Anne, if I stay here at Gibraltar, do I join the ranks of the terminally single? You seem to be the only married person here."

Anne looked puzzled. "Dave is married," she said. "And Jesse used to be married. I have hopes that he'll get married again." She placed a hand on Daphne's shoulder. "As for you, we'll see about you once you get your head in that beaker. Something about those scientific concoctions. I have to wonder if you're all not brewing in a cauldron up there. But unlike John or Willard, I think you'll pull your head out once in a while."

Suddenly Daphne had clarity. Jesse, too, had loved and lost. She'd pray for him and for Ben and stop thinking so much about herself. His personal life was none of her business, but in her dream she'd felt perfect love. Love without fear. She wanted that for Jesse again. He deserved it.

Hearing Anne's story about being pursued relentlessly sounded so romantic. She'd wait for that next time, Daphne vowed. Or she'd just live with cats and sink her face farther into the beaker.

# Chapter 18

D aphne tried everything to get her sense of smell back. She owed that much to Jesse. She loaded up on lipoic acid, which according to old wives' tales and various websites seemed to help for some. All it did for Daphne was give her indigestion.

"If I'm going to have indigestion, I should get pizza out of the deal, right?" she asked her reflection.

She tossed aside the antibiotics she'd parlayed with the idea that she might have an underlying virus. She added a sick stomach to her list of symptoms.

There was a week of zinc intake and "aromatherapy" that consisted of boiling eucalyptus oil, sniffing strange concoctions like burning sage, and finally, eating horseradish and wasabi. She tried drinking nothing more than water and apple cider vinegar, prayed with funky, quiet music on low volume, and took to gardening to see if she could rouse some allergies. In all, six weeks of "cures" and still no sense of smell.

Tonight's *cure du jour* was steaming her face over a pot filled with boiling water, basil oil, and honey. While she might be sweating like a busy Italian kitchen, so far she smelled nothing. Her doorbell rang, and she lifted the towel from over her head, wiped her sweaty face, and headed to the front door.

Kensie stood on her stoop in skinny jeans, stilettos, and a whimsical scarf shirt. "Why is your face so red?" she asked as she strode into the house without an invitation.

Daphne still held the door open. "How did you know where I lived?"

"It's on the company computer system. Why? Are you hiding something?" Kensie seated herself in the living room. "I wanted to speak to you in private. You know, woman to woman. Not likely to happen at Gibraltar, is it?"

"If you expect me to keep any kind of secret for you, I'll warn you right now. I believe in doing the right thing even when it costs."

"Spare me the morality check." Kensie crossed her long legs.

Daphne closed her eyes and prayed for God to give her eyes to see Kensie in a better light. Ever since she'd seen Kensie and Dave stepping into the elevator together, she didn't trust the woman as far as she could throw her. Which wouldn't have been far.

"This is a pretty old house."

"A *pretty* old house? Or a *pretty old* house?"

"Pretty. And old," Kensie said. "Don't get paranoid on me. I can't take any more pressure than I'm already under. I've got Jesse going rogue on me and Dave breathing down my neck."

It didn't appear to Daphne as if Kensie had ever known

pressure. She was one of those women who remained cool, calm, and collected while the world tumbled around them. Somehow her scarf would always keep its proper crease and her hair would never be out of place.

"I need to know what you're working on."

"Kensie, can we discuss this at work?"

"I told you. I needed to talk to you privately."

"There are conference rooms."

"I tried to find you in the lab around six. The scientists usually work late."

"I left on time today. We could meet tomorrow in a conference room."

"Why don't you like me?" Kensie asked.

"I don't even know you, Kensie."

"But you don't like me. I'm not interested in Jesse, if that's what you're thinking."

"I'm not interested in my boss either." Some part of her wanted Kensie to come clean about Dave, but she'd known girls like Kensie. They kept their secrets close to their stone-cold hearts.

"It smells terrible in here. But I suppose you know that, being a nose and all."

"My house smells?"

Kensie rose and picked up a photo of Daphne and Sophie together at Stanford in front of the chapel. Then she flopped back on the sofa and bounced slightly at its stiffness. "New couch?"

"New and cheap," Daphne answered.

"So I'm here because I need you to cover for me—as a fellow

woman trying to break through the glass ceiling of Gibraltar." Kensie pulled her hair back in a ponytail with all the confidence in the world.

Daphne wished she possessed one ounce of the other woman's emotional strength. "Cover for you?"

"Tomorrow's the wedding show. The one you finagled your way into."

"I didn't do any such thing. Kensie, there's a reason Jesse wants me to go with you."

"Well, I'm not going to it."

Daphne admitted to herself that she hadn't been looking forward to a chummy outing for the two of them, but she felt abandoned once again. "I thought the whole point of our going was to see marketing trends." She panicked inwardly at the idea of having to comment on scent trends she couldn't smell.

"I can't go," Kensie said.

"Shouldn't you tell that to Jesse and not me?"

"I'm not telling Jesse. That's why I'm here."

"You want me to lie for you? Why didn't you just call in sick? Why tell me at all?"

"Not lie. I just don't want you to mention I wasn't there. We women have to stick together. The glass ceiling and all."

Daphne had no doubt Kensie wouldn't let a glass ceiling, or a brick one for that matter, stop her.

Daphne's cell phone rang, and she stared at her phone in confusion as the lyrics to Kanye West's "Heartless" played. She grabbed the phone off the table to see the display, and she grinned. The ring tone was clearly Sophie's doing. But she hated to admit that her heart leapt a bit at the sight of Mark's name on the caller ID. She pressed the phone off.

"Aren't you going to answer it?" Kensie asked.

"No." Daphne set the phone back down without further explanation. "Kensie, I'm not sure I'm the person to ask to cover for you. I'm not that great at stretching the truth, and if I'm asked directly, I'll spill everything like I've been tortured."

Kensie stared at her. "Are you kidding?"

"Can't you just take the day off legally?"

"Haven't you ever needed a day off? You, who took the last two weeks off after you just got here?"

"I understand, but just take the day off. I can go to Cincinnati by myself."

"You're not even past the trial period. You really can't afford to lose me as an ally."

Daphne thought that with Kensie as an ally, she might accidentally get shot in her own foxhole. "Kensie, I don't want to lose you or anyone else as an ally. But as you said, I'm still on trial. Putting me in the position of lying for you is a lot to ask, don't you think?"

Kensie changed the subject. "I guess Jesse didn't tell you about my new product."

"*Your* new product? Aren't we a team at Gibraltar?"

"I thought so, but Jesse seems to be keeping me out of the mix. I did some studies and came up the perfect new product idea. Last I heard, you'd be off Willard's project and onto this one."

"Hmm," Daphne said, so as not to give anything away. She wanted Kensie to leave so she could call Mark back, but the woman looked to be in no hurry. "Did you want something to drink?" she asked out of politeness.

"That would be great. Do you have something cold?"

"I have iced tea and some soda."

"I'll just have water."

Daphne nodded and went to the kitchen. She brought her phone with her and checked to see if Mark had texted her, but there was nothing. Disappointment swelled in her chest. She pulled the towel off her head, shook out her hair, and washed her hands before getting Kensie's ice water.

The doorbell rang again, and Daphne wondered what she'd done to suddenly be so popular. Then she remembered she was without makeup and her hair was frizzing out in all directions. So naturally she'd have visitors.

"You expecting someone?" Kensie called.

"Nope." She hadn't been expecting Kensie either, but the woman clearly needed a friend. What sort of Christian would she be if she didn't at least give her the benefit of the doubt?

"Want me to get it?"

"Sure, thanks!"

She heard Jesse's voice, and she scrambled in the kitchen for a hair band. She found a rubber band around the freebie newspaper that arrived the day before and used it to put her hair into a quick ponytail. She didn't want to look completely disheveled for her boss.

When she walked back into the living room, she saw Kensie standing close to Jesse. The two of them were speaking in low voices and stopped when they noticed her arrival.

Ohio certainly was different from Paris. People there got together after work for meals and connection, but they didn't come without warning.

"Daphne," Jesse finally said. "I didn't mean to barge in on you, but you forgot these." He held up papers with a plastic badge clipped to them. "They're your credentials for the show tomorrow. Anne left them in your box—but then we realized no one ever showed you your box."

"You didn't have to come all the way over here."

"You know I only live three blocks away. But I'm sorry—I should have called first."

Jesse stared at Kensie, and something passed between them that made Daphne uncomfortable. And people thought Europeans were complicated. She felt like Moses wandering in the desert, uncertain of the strangers she met along the way.

"Why don't you take my credentials and go with her?" Kensie said suddenly. "I'm not feeling all that great."

"Me?"

"Household products hasn't had a winner in their category for four years. You don't seem to believe anything my marketing reports tell you, so why don't you go use the bloodhound here and figure it out for yourself?"

"I—I have meetings all day tomorrow," Jesse stammered.

"It wasn't necessarily a suggestion," Kensie said. "Dave knows I'm not going to the wedding show tomorrow, so I'm sure he'd like someone there with the new girl."

Jesse's eyes flashed at the veiled threat, but he took the papers Kensie pulled from her purse. "Fine. We'll make a day of it. Daphne, you up for it?"

What choice did she have?

"Yeah, I guess."

"I'll pick you up at seven, and we'll get an early start."

She nodded. Kensie Whitman had mastered the art of manipulation, but Daphne couldn't help but examine Jesse's motives. What dirt did Kensie have on him that made him so willing to succumb to her suggestions? And why was she suddenly so willing to admit that she wouldn't be at the wedding show, when only a few minutes earlier she'd wanted Daphne to lie for her? Every move at Gibraltar felt like an emotional game of chess.

Something was rotten in the state of Ohio, and Daphne didn't need a sense of smell to identify it.

# Chapter 19

Daphne waited all night for Mark to call her back. He never did. The next morning she checked the time and accounted for the hour in Paris. She dialed Arnaud's number before she lost her nerve, though she had no idea what she'd say.

*"Allo."* The familiarity of Arnaud's voice rendered her speechless. *"Allo?"* he said again.

*"Bon jour, Arnaud."*

"Daphne?"

*"Oui.* Don't hang up, Arnaud, please!"

"Why would I hang up? You are all right, yes?"

"I'm fine," she said, though her voice cracked.

"You want to come back to Paris?"

*"Oui,"* she answered.

"You are more than welcome to stay with Madeleine and me, but there are no positions open. With the Greek financial crisis, everything here in Europe is on hold."

"Yet you hired Mark, Arnaud. Why?"

"Everyone has his reasons, Daphne. Life is complicated."

*Don't I know it . . .* "Arnaud, I need your help."

"There are no jobs."

"No, no. I have a job, Arnaud. But I need your help, and I need you to keep this quiet from Mark."

There was a pause on the other end of the line.

"Arnaud, I've lost my sense of smell," she blurted.

"Ahh. Stress, no?"

"Are there any secrets to getting it back? Is there something I can do so this will end?"

"Only prayer. Madeleine and I will be in prayer for you, and you must pray. Every morning and throughout the day. Without ceasing, no?"

"Yes."

"You cannot go backward, Daphne. God will make His path clear. We will pray."

She caught up on all the details of Arnaud's life and hung up in the same place she'd started the conversation. She was at the starting gate, but it wasn't opening, and she felt herself turning in tiny circles, going nowhere fast. Her conversation with Arnaud was more confusing than the dream where Jesse was kissing her and she was throwing away perfectly good bread.

A knock at the door announced Jesse's arrival. She glanced at herself in the mirror over her dining room table, checking her ruby red lipstick. She wore a white ruffled shirt with black piping, black slacks, and a light cotton sweater in red.

"Good morning," she said as she swung open the door.

"Good morning," Jesse replied. "Ben's in the car. I hope you don't mind, but I'm trying out a preschool while Abby's still home to get him in case something goes wrong. She's leaving town soon, so I have to make other arrangements."

"Oh, I'm sorry," Daphne said as she pulled the door closed behind her and checked the lock.

"It's going to be hard on us, but it's what's best for Abby."

She followed Jesse to his car in the driveway. Ben sat in his car seat and grinned at her.

"Well, you must be Ben. Ben, I'm Daphne."

"Hi, Miss Daffy."

"Daphne," Jesse corrected as he got into the car.

Daphne laughed. "I like Daffy better." She imagined it fit well, given her circumstances.

Ben clutched a wooden train in each hand. "Daddy, don't want to go to school."

Jesse's hands tightened around the steering wheel. "You're going to love school. I bet they have more trains than you've ever seen before."

"Do they have Clarabelle?"

"They might. How about this? If they don't have it, we'll buy it for the school so you can play with it when you're there."

"Clarabelle?" Daphne asked.

"From *Thomas the Tank Engine*. They're all named."

"Daffy, you're pretty," Ben said.

She turned around and took his plump little hand. "Thank you, Ben. You're pretty gorgeous yourself."

He grinned and covered his face.

"Can I see one of your trains?"

Ben looked at both fists, a red train in one hand, a green one in the other. After much contemplation, he handed her the green one.

Jesse raised his brows. "Wow, Percy, huh? She's worthy of Percy?"

"What's so special about Percy?" she asked Ben.

"He's my favorite. He's little like me, but he can do the job."

"I'll bet he can," she answered. She handed him back the train. "Those should keep you company all day while Daddy's at work."

"I don't want to go to school," he said again, crossing his pudgy arms across his chest.

"School is fun," she said. "They have all sorts of things to keep you busy, and before you know it, Daddy will be back."

"No," he said with a pout.

"My sister spoils him at home, so I don't imagine school will be as fun."

Daphne frowned. "With that buildup, how's he supposed to be excited about it?"

They pulled into the parking lot, and Ben started screaming. His meaning was clear: the boy did not want to go to school. But Daphne was more worried about the look on Jesse's face. She didn't think he had it in him to leave Ben.

The little boy started kicking the back of her seat. Daphne got out of the car and popped her seat forward to reach him. Ben stopped screaming and peered up at her with wide eyes.

"Ben, you are going to love school. The teachers are really nice, and they have snack time with juice and maybe some cookies. And I see you have a Thomas lunch box. Did your Auntie Abby make you a nice lunch?"

Ben, totally unnerved by her familiarity, allowed her to lift him out of the booster seat and set him on the walkway. Daphne turned back toward Jesse and motioned with her eyes for him to stay put.

As she took Ben's hand and led him toward the little yellow schoolhouse, he started to struggle. "Daddy, Daddy, Daddy!" he yelled.

"Ben," she said in a quiet voice that captured his attention. "Everyone is afraid of new things. I'm afraid of new things too, but when you try them, you discover they're not so scary, and you have more fun things to do."

He looked at her as if he wasn't buying a word of it.

They were inside the door now. "I see trains in there."

His stiff body relaxed slightly. "Thomas?"

"Well, I don't know. You're the expert. You'll have to tell me."

A plump young blond woman with an angelic face opened the half-sized gate that kept them separated from the classroom. Inside, a world of colors attracted Ben's attention.

"I'm Miss Spire. You must be Ben."

He pulled away. "I want my daddy."

Daphne wanted to pick Ben up and run back out the door, and she didn't even know the little boy. Jesse would never have had the strength to say good-bye.

"Your daddy tells me you like trains. Are they your favorites?" Miss Spire asked. She patted the sign-in sheet to indicate to Daphne that she needed to sign Ben in. She did so, and Miss

Spire shooed her away while she took Ben by the hand to see the train set in the corner. Ben didn't look back, and Daphne rushed out the door and down the steps toward Jesse's car.

"I feel like this is a getaway car."

"Was it awful?" Jesse rested his head on the steering wheel. "It was awful, right?"

"He's fine. Miss Spire took him to the trains straightaway, and he never looked back at me. He'll get used to it, Jesse."

"He's going to hate me tonight." Jesse still hadn't started the car. He stared back toward the doorway.

"What can you do? You have to work."

"I feel like I'm abandoning him."

"Start the car, Jesse."

He turned the key and peeled out of the parking lot.

"So, how about those Reds?" she said.

"No, let's talk about your future at Gibraltar," he said.

"My future?"

"I don't think you belong here."

"Pardon me? Look, I know my sense of smell isn't working, but I am doing everything possible to get it back."

"I think your nose isn't working because you're not where you belong, and your body knows it."

"As I've told you, my best friend is a psychologist, and she diagnoses everyone and their turtles. If she can't figure out why I lost my sense of smell, I highly doubt you've got the answer. No offense."

"None taken." They passed a drive-through coffee shop. "Need some java for the road?"

"I don't drink it very often. Thanks, though."

"That's actually why I came to your house last night. To talk to you about it. But when I saw Kensie there, I thought it could wait."

"She seemed as though she'd been expecting you. What were you two discussing in the doorway?"

"Sure you don't want coffee?" he asked again.

"No thanks."

They entered the freeway and she wondered, staring at Jesse's handsome profile, why he hadn't married again. Was his heart so broken that he couldn't imagine loving another? That's how she felt so far. She couldn't imagine giving her heart to another. Mark still owned it, even though he'd crushed it like a fresh tomato.

"So, no offense, but is being visited by Gibraltar employees a regular occurrence? Because I'll make sure I'm presentable at all times."

"Look, I'm sorry about that. I came over because I had an idea about the loss of your sense of smell, and I didn't want to talk to you at work in case someone overheard. When I got there and saw Kensie, I scrambled. If Kensie found out, she'd go straight to Dave and you'd be out of a job."

"Well, you just said you don't think I belong there."

"You're misunderstanding me. I think you belong in perfume. I think that's why your sense of smell isn't working. You're not where you belong."

She shook her head. "That's not it." She paused before adding, "I called Paris this morning. There's still no job for me."

He exhaled, as if annoyed with her. "When Hannah died, I

was trying to hold it together with a baby, and I was working like a madman as a vice president of manufacturing in Cincinnati. I literally lost the ability to recall words when I needed them."

"What did you do?"

"I got the message that I was in the wrong place, and if I wasn't going to go willingly, God was going to make it patently obvious. I moved up here. My sister moved in, and I took a lesser job that I could handle."

"I don't see what that has to do with me."

"Look, I missed the clues with my wife. I was so busy I didn't notice the postpartum depression. I was euphoric over having Ben. I knew that she couldn't sleep, but I thought that was par for the course."

Daphne still wasn't following. She gave him a bewildered look.

"God gave me the message to stop working and pay attention, but I didn't listen. And now Ben has no mother."

"You can't blame yourself for that."

"I can and I do. She took a sleeping pill that night to sleep, and I thought I was the best husband in the world, tucking her in and kissing her good night so she could get the rest she needed." He paused and focused straight ahead of him on the road. "She had an allergic reaction to the pill, and her throat constricted. People say it was a suicide attempt, but it wasn't. Doesn't make it less my fault. I should have checked on her. I should have been the one to give her the pill. Maybe then I would have known it was penicillin and not a sleeping pill like she was supposed to be prescribed."

"I think it's impossible for you to see that clearly. God's will is God's will, and sometimes it really stinks." She placed her hand on his wrist. "And that has to be the worst soothing statement in the history of mankind." She laughed uncomfortably.

He turned toward her and grinned. "But it was still very sweet."

"So what is it exactly that you couldn't say to me in front of Kensie?"

"She and Dave are up to something. I was hoping she'd let the cat out of the bag, but she didn't. I had this epiphany the other night when I was praying."

She raised her brows. "An epiphany?"

"If I wasn't going to notice that I couldn't be a vice president and a single father, God was going to shut me down and make me unable to do the job. Now, I'm not saying that's what's happening to you, but what if your sense of smell is shut down because you're not doing what you're supposed to do?"

"Earning enough money to feed myself, you mean?" She stared out the window. "You've been through a serious tragedy. I got dumped at the altar. It's not the same. Mostly because God did me a favor."

"Who is to say what's traumatic to an individual? We both lost someone. It was out of our control."

"If you say to a roomful of people that your wife died, everyone understands it's a tragedy—whereas being left at the altar could be the punch line of a late-night monologue. I think that's what separates our two stories."

"Regardless. My idea is that you start a perfume line for the home—but it's something you do on the side, not during the work hours when you're working with Willard. When cooler weather comes in the fall, you won't want to get out on an archery field after a long day at work. And I'm not sure you remember how to knit all that well."

She laughed. "I suppose not, but making a perfume I can't smell sounds even more depressing than a hat that unravels."

"You know the formulations, so all you have to do is find scents for the home. Things like lavender water for ironing and sheets. You find scents that would cover the fish smell in a kitchen, or freshen the sheets as if they were washed yesterday. You do this, and I think your sense of smell will return. You know, going about your business as if this never happened."

"It might have merit. What made you think of this?"

"Because when I quit my VP job, everything started working again. I moved here. My sister moved in, and life got a whole lot simpler. A perfume line for a company like Gibraltar will enable you to go back into the industry without any trouble. You'll have proven results."

"Why would you do this for me?" She narrowed her eyes. "Do you want me off of your budget that badly?"

"I couldn't help my wife, Daphne, but I can help you. I feel like that's why God wouldn't let the scent of gas die in my nostrils that night. He was giving me an opportunity to let go of what I couldn't do for Hannah."

She didn't know how to respond . . . Maybe he was reading too much into their odd working relationship. But she recognized that the conclusion made her feel warm and enveloped—just as she'd felt when he kissed her in Paris in her dream.

# Chapter 20

It took them less than an hour to get to the convention center, and Jesse enjoyed listening to Daphne's ideas for the household perfume line. It was the most animated he'd ever seen her, and he took pleasure in the fact that his "epiphany" may truly have been worthwhile. It helped him avoid dwelling on his guilt over leaving Ben at the preschool. Lots of families had no choice, and he understood that, but it felt like another betrayal of Hannah, who had planned to stay at home with him and any future children who might have come.

"He'll be fine," Daphne said, as if she could read his mind.

He exited I-75 and proceeded along Fifth Street toward the convention center. When he saw the sign posted for the Winter Bridal and Floral Expo, he suddenly had another epiphany. He knew why Kensie hadn't wanted to attend the event. It wasn't about marketing trends or floral scents at all. It was about showing Daphne just who ruled at Gibraltar and how easily she got her way. He recalled that Kensie had arranged for him to do a baby expo when he'd arrived at Gibraltar so she could inform him of her power. The woman really was heartless, but Dave thought she could do no wrong, and therefore she was a force to be reckoned with.

He pulled into the parking garage. "You going to be all right in there?"

Daphne didn't answer. She blinked rapidly as she took in the lacy, balloon-infested entrance to the convention center. "I have developed an aversion to all things tulle."

"We won't stay long." He pulled into a parking slot, and the two of them exited the car. They each took their badges and slipped them over their necks.

They were met at the door by a woman wearing a bridal gown and passing out postcards. He unwittingly took one. Daphne took it from him and slid it into a canvas bag.

"Grab as much as you can," she said. "All the stuff will remind us of things later."

He nodded and swallowed hard. "This doesn't bother you?"

She surveyed the room. "Actually, it gives me relief that I'm not here as a bride."

A woman with pink feathers somehow woven into her updo grabbed Daphne's arm and led her to a stylist's chair. "You're perfect," she said. "Come sit down for a minute and let me give you a free styling."

Daphne patted her hair. "Oh no, I'm here on business. I don't need—"

"Don't be silly. I'll make you look gorgeous."

Daphne looked wary, and judging by the woman's hairstyle, she had just cause.

The woman pulled out Daphne's severe ponytail and loosened

her hair so it fell upon her shoulders. Jesse looked away; it felt invasive to watch. He checked out the booths behind them, making a mental note of all he wanted to see in regard to colors and florals for the upcoming winter wedding season. When he turned around, Daphne's hair was piled high atop her head with baby's breath pressed into the hairstyle.

She jumped down from the chair and said thank you, but she came toward him with ire. "Let's go."

"You look good. Do you like it?"

"I look like Marge Simpson."

"Not true. Hers is blue."

"Come on," Daphne said, dragging him across the aisle.

A man in a black suit approached them. With his slicked-back hair, he looked more like an undertaker than a photographer, but he stood in front of a plethora of photographs.

"Are you the happy couple?"

"No," Daphne said.

"Free photos today under the arch," he said, waving toward a white, wooden arch riddled with fake flowers. "Come on, sir. Don't you want to help her remember how she wants her hair on her special day?"

"Marge?" Jesse said, holding his palm up to help her up the red carpeted step.

"Not alone, Homer," she said, pulling him behind her. "Can you get us together?"

"Naturally," the photographer said.

She turned to face Jesse and smiled up at him coyly. "You're enjoying this, aren't you?"

"Maybe."

"Stand behind her and put your arms around her. Don't you want everyone to know how you love her?" the photographer asked.

"Oh, everyone," Jesse said. He felt an elbow in his stomach, but she pulled his arms around her waist. He hadn't touched a woman since he'd lost Hannah, certainly not an employee, but their bond felt natural, the way they interacted, easy. Like they'd known each other forever.

"Perfect," the photographer said. "You two are naturals." He backed up. "All right, look at each another."

They did, and promptly broke into laughter.

Daphne walked out of the arch. "All righty. We've got to get moving or all the cake samples will be gone."

"Take my card. When's your wedding?"

"I'm not sure," Daphne said. "He didn't show up the last time." She winked and strode down the aisle.

Jesse just shrugged.

"Got an e-mail?" the photographer said. "I'll send you the pictures."

Jesse pulled out his business card. "Thanks, that would be great." He rushed to catch up with Daphne, who stood in front of a floral display.

"Honeysuckle. It's the color of 2012," she said. "Smell."

He leaned over and drew in the sweet scent.

"See this color on the flower? Not the yellow, the other color."

He nodded.

"It's the color of the year. Beautiful, right?"

"What is that, red? Pink?"

"It's honeysuckle. A bright pink with a bit of mauve."

"What color did you have?" he asked. "At your wedding?"

"Sapphire and gold."

"Any regrets?" he asked, before he thought better of the question.

"None. Everything was perfect." She shrugged. "Except the groom didn't show up. But other than that, Mrs. Lincoln, how did you enjoy the show?"

He laughed and followed her out of the floral section.

"What color did you have?" she asked, glancing back at him.

"I—I can't remember. I wore black. She wore white."

"Helpful." She halted abruptly in front of him.

He turned and saw a display of wedding gowns to their right.

"That was my gown," she said, pointing.

"You must have been beautiful in it."

She exhaled. "Let's go find some cake." She started collecting pamphlets and shoving them roughly into her canvas bag. He took it from her shoulder.

"I'll get this."

"Did you notice the gowns are more traditional this year?"

"No."

"That means we'll want to go traditional with fragrance too. It will affect people's moods."

"Traditional scents?"

"It probably means the time isn't right for home scents that offer something new, but you never know. Kensie might run us some marketing polls."

At the sound of Kensie's name, his gut twisted. Something about that woman drove him crazy. A conversation with her was like running through a minefield, riddled with unseen dangers.

"Let's keep Kensie out of this idea for now." He quickly changed the subject. "Do you think you'd wear the same gown again?"

"Oh, I won't get married again." She reached down for a piece of cake with pink icing and scooped up a forkful. "Want to try it?" She shoved it into his mouth, and before he could answer, he was chewing.

"Mmm." He nodded. "Daphne, you can't let a tool like that guy ruin marriage for you. Marriage is a beautiful thing."

"So when's *your* next wedding?" she prodded.

"I won't get married again. I had my chance."

"Is that really fair to Ben?" she asked.

She may as well have taken the cake knife off the table and stabbed him.

"Life hasn't been fair to Ben, but I'm devoted to him. No sense bringing in a woman to take the time he deserves away from him."

"So here we are: two avowed singles at a wedding extravaganza."

"That cake's good," he said. "Do you get tired of people telling you that you'll meet someone?"

"No one's really saying that yet. They might think Mark got lucky."

"Anyone who would think that doesn't see straight."

"My mom thinks that. She thinks if I could have kept my mouth quiet more when Mark was wrong about formulations, he might have stayed."

"Do you believe that?"

"Well, I wasn't going to let him blow himself up if he was wrong. Would you?"

He laughed. "No, probably not."

"Mark was a terrible chemist. A brilliant mind and ever capable, but he was lazy and took shortcuts without thought to consequences. He wasn't careful about ratios, not until he understood that ratios and chemistry could make him wealthy." She grinned at the thought of Mark when he didn't think measuring mattered. "One time he burned his eyebrows off in the lab."

"Really?" He couldn't help his smile.

"Took at least a month to grow back. Do you know how weird a person looks without eyebrows? It's very disconcerting to strangers."

They walked into the floral hall, and the scent of fresh blooms hit his senses. He watched Daphne carefully to see if any of the smells affected her. She bent into a bouquet of red roses and looked up. "Nope," she said.

"You can't smell anything? If a room smelled like a flower shop, would that be a warm smell?"

"Fresh. Moist, but not necessarily homey. More romantic or tropical, I would guess."

"Do you like the ideas for the home perfumes?"

"There are lots of things on the market like that now."

"Not in the household goods aisles. The benefit here is we take those grocery store buyers and grab their attention with an unmet need."

She picked up a small bouquet. "It's hand-wrapped, do you see?"

"What does that mean?"

"It's simpler. People are scaling back."

"Not on rings. Did you see the size of those things?"

"Colors. I noticed the colors. A lot of chocolate diamonds, and green ones, sapphires. That's not traditional, but it's definitely unique. And every bride wants to be unique." Her blue eyes stared into the distance.

Mark was an idiot if he thought she'd be waiting around for him to return, Jesse thought. She'd last about a week at his church's singles' group.

"You'll be back in Paris before you know it. Or maybe New York."

"You're that confident about this idea?"

"I'm that confident in your nose. That it will work when you're where you belong."

She paused. "Jesse, what if I am where I belong?"

He wouldn't allow himself to believe it. She was destined for greater things, and he planned to make her dreams come true. As some sort of redemption for how he'd failed Hannah. "You're not where you belong."

"How can you know that?"

"Don't you think you'd be able to do what you do best if you were where you belonged?"

261

"Not if God didn't want me to do it for some reason I didn't yet understand."

"He allowed you to be trained as a perfumer."

"He allowed Paul to be trained as the foremost scholar among Jews. Only to have him preach to the Gentiles." She shrugged. "Just saying."

He grinned. "So now you're going biblical on me."

"If I have to. I just think your conclusion may be premature. Yes, I'll admit, I miss perfume. I miss it badly, but I haven't had the chance to get my feet wet here. Maybe this is where I belong."

"I was a star at a young age, and that was all thwarted by circumstances that I couldn't control. I can control these, Daphne. I can get you back to Paris. Or at least as far as New York."

"For someone who thinks I'm supposedly so good at what I do, you seem awfully anxious to get rid of me."

"Do you want my help or not?"

"What does that mean? You'll give me a reference if I create a selling line of household sprays?"

He didn't want to promise anything. Already, the idea of Daphne leaving bothered him, but he couldn't offer her anything she needed.

His cell phone vibrated, and he worried that Ben was still crying, but it was only Anne.

"Hey, Anne."

"I need you and Daphne to come back to the office immediately."

"We're just getting started. Isn't Dave there?"

"Jesse, I need you to come back now. I don't want to tell you over the phone."

"It's not Ben, is it?" he said frantically.

"Ben? No, it's not Ben. Nothing to do with your family. It's an office emergency. I need you here."

"Okay, we'll head back now. See you in an hour." He took the bouquet from Daphne's hand and placed it back on the skirted table. "We've got to go. I pray it's not an accident in the lab. Anne's not usually frantic like that."

Daphne closed her eyes and prayed. "Lord in heaven, we ask for peace as we make our way back to an unknown situation. Help our fears to be worse than anything that's happened. Amen."

"Amen." He took her hand and they raced out the doors back through the bridal displays to the parking garage.

The bridal show had been the first time he'd let his guard down and really had fun in ages. He wouldn't have believed it if someone told him he'd enjoy a wedding event, but Daphne brightened the world around her.

Because of that, she needed more. She needed to go. Their new product launch would allow her to fly away like a balloon.

# Chapter 21

Daphne had fun with Jesse. Being with him felt easy, as it did with Sophie, and Daphne felt confident that while her mother thought marriage the only acceptable option for a young Greek woman, there were other possibilities. Friends made uneventful events fun. She'd had a good time at a wedding show, and if that didn't prove that her heart was on the mend, surely the fact that she hadn't checked her phone for possible texts from Mark in the past two hours would strengthen her case.

She'd make more friends. She'd invest in Dayton until the time came to leave for Paris. A huge weight lifted as she realized if marriage wasn't in her future, she hadn't failed at life, even if her mother did think otherwise. Eventually she'd get her sense of smell back, and life would be fuller and richer without the roller coaster of love.

She looked out at the passing landscape. "I can't get over how barren things feel here. There are so many buildings just left for dead along the road."

"It's cheaper to build from scratch, I guess."

It wasn't like back home, where real estate was so expensive and people were crammed up against one another. Ohio had space to spare, but even the Ohio River was subdued by its murky green tones. She missed the mountains and the ocean.

The anxiety of what might be facing them back at the office came back, marring the bright morning they'd shared.

"Anne didn't give you any idea what this is about?"

"Not a clue," he answered. "But they must not be able to reach Dave if they called me. I'm next on the ladder when we're in trouble."

The miles went by quickly, and they arrived at Gibraltar's offices in record time. "I'm glad my sister's getting Ben. Who knows what awaits me upstairs?"

"Jesse, if you ever need help with Ben, I want you to know it's no trouble for me to help. An on-site scientifically trained babysitter might be just what the doctor orders someday."

"Too true."

Upstairs, a solemn skeleton crew milled about in the main office. Anne came toward them and pulled Jesse into Dave's office. Daphne looked around for Kensie to find out what had happened, but she was nowhere in sight—which made sense, since she was supposed to be with Daphne at the wedding show.

She looked for someone else to ask, but everyone seemed to avoid her gaze and move away as she got closer to them. She decided to head to the lab.

In the stark bright white of the lab, Daphne felt at home. She donned a white coat with her name embroidered on it and headed to her station. Willard was nowhere in sight, but John, looking pale and unkempt, tinkered at his station. His eyes focused intently on his mixture.

"I assume you heard," he said.

"I didn't hear anything. What happened?" She stepped closer to his station, and he put down the mixture.

"Dave is dead," he said without inflection. "Killed in a car wreck."

Daphne gasped. "Dave our boss?"

John squeezed a drop of liquid into his beaker. "No, Dave Letterman. Yes, Dave our boss. He and Kensie had some kind of marketing meeting and got T-boned by a truck. Dave never had a chance."

"John, that's terrible. No wonder everyone's so solemn."

John shrugged one shoulder. "It's a shame. I think he was really ready to turn this company around, and now this."

Scientists left much to be desired in the empathy department.

"I—I'd better go check on Jesse. He must be devastated."

"Doubt that. He probably has himself a promotion."

Her mouth gaped open. "Jesse's not like that! He would never want to profit from someone else's tragedy."

"Relax, Daphne. I didn't mean anything by it."

"Then you shouldn't have said it."

"Whatever."

"I have to find him," she said. Once in the hallway, she ran straight into Jesse and wrapped him in an embrace. "Jesse! Are you okay?"

He pulled away and stared blankly toward her. "I'm in shock. It feels impossible. Daphne, I need you to do me a favor."

"Anything," she said.

They got in the elevator, and he pressed the button to close the doors. "I've got to call about the company insurance policy and get the payout started. I know that sounds heartless, but his wife will need it. And I need to make changes on the signing partners, that kind of thing."

"So what can I do?" she asked.

He handed her his keys. "I want you to take my car and go to the hospital."

"To the hospital?" She looked up at him, confused.

He spoke quickly, in low tones. "Kensie was in the accident as well, and nobody knows why. Anne made up a marketing meeting, but there was nothing on either one of their schedules. Did she happen to say yesterday where she planned to go today instead of the bridal show?"

"No." Daphne didn't mention the show of affection she'd seen pass between Kensie and Dave. For all she knew, it was nothing more than a friendly gesture that could be construed the wrong way. After all, what might people think if they'd seen her banter with Jesse at the bridal expo? "Is she badly hurt?"

"I don't know." He rubbed the back of his neck. "Dave's wife is on her way to the morgue to identify the body."

Daphne felt sick to her stomach. "Jesse, I'm so sorry this happened. I feel so helpless."

"Me too." He took her hand and held it until the elevator door opened. "I don't know how to say this, and there could be nothing to it . . . but if you happen to run into Kathy, that's Dave's wife, at the hospital, she'll be in shock. Let the authorities release details to her as they deem fit."

She nodded. "I understand." Daphne wished she could go back to bed and start the day over. The dark side was alive and thriving in Dayton.

Jesse faced her and took both of her hands. "I'm not covering for him if he's done something wrong. You understand that? I'm only trying to protect his wife until she's ready. She'll get bad enough news as it is."

"It might be perfectly innocent," she said. "Don't jump to conclusions." But though she hated to admit it, she had already jumped. She squeezed his hands to offer encouragement. "I'll call you as soon as I know anything."

He nodded and peered at her with saddened eyes. "We're going to make this home spray line a success. We owe it to Dave."

Daphne didn't think he owed anything to Dave, but she admired the loyalty within him that made him want to pay tribute.

# Chapter 22

Daphne hated the sour smell of hospitals. All those foul odors rubbing together: alcohol, ammonia, urine, and stale cafeteria food combined to make a murky soup of stench. For once she was glad she couldn't smell. She was happy for the errand, though not of course for the circumstances, because it kept her from thinking about Mark's call.

An older woman in a candy striper uniform sat behind the information desk, fully focused on wrapping a gift.

"Excuse me," Daphne said. She cleared her throat loudly.

The older woman finally looked up. "Sorry, dear, didn't see you there. Can I help you?"

"You're a good gift wrapper," she said.

"Oh yes, I have to be. I spend a lot of time doing it. Did you need information?"

"I'm looking for Kensie Whitman's room."

"Well now, just a minute." The woman jiggled the computer mouse, stared at the screen, then held up four puffy fingers, curved from age and yet perfectly manicured. "She's still in intensive care. Are you a family member?"

"Um, no. I'm a coworker. Her family isn't from around here, and the accident happened during work hours."

"Well, check in at the nurses' station before you go in to make sure it's all right. It's on the fourth floor."

The woman went back to her wrapping, and Daphne slowed her steps. She had no idea what she'd say to Kensie when she got into the room—if she was even conscious. Did she know that Dave was dead? Daphne was hardly the person to tell her.

She didn't want to know why the two of them had been together in the middle of the workday, and she wouldn't ask. She wasn't going to pry into anyone's business that wasn't hers. And she wanted to get in and out quickly, in case Dave's wife showed up. Daphne didn't know what she looked like, other than a distraught widow—but Daphne was the last person on earth who would cover for a man's betrayal. She was still reeling from her own.

The nurses' station was bustling with activity, but as Daphne approached, no one looked at her or offered her the slightest bit of help. The rectangular station was surrounded by rooms behind glass, and she walked around and tried to get someone's attention.

"Excuse me," she said, but the nurse walked to the other side of their containment area.

"Excuse me," she said again to another nurse, who looked at her but offered no answer. If she hadn't known better, she might have thought herself invisible.

The third time she asked, to no avail, she gave an audible sigh and headed toward the bank of intensive care rooms and read the names listed. Finding Kensie's name, she glanced behind her. When no one tried to stop her, she entered the room.

Kensie looked like a soap opera star lying asleep with her head raised and her makeup still perfect. *Why didn't you just come to work today?* Daphne wanted to ask.

Kensie was wrapped tightly and looked to be strapped to the bed from the waist down. The upper part of her looked undisturbed. Her silky dark hair was draped in front of her shoulders as if a stylist had placed it there.

Daphne put her hand on Kensie's and prayed for total healing, and for God's hand to touch the young woman and give her what she was missing. When she opened her eyes, Kensie's deep blue eyes were staring back at her.

"Kensie, you're awake! Do you need anything? Can I call someone for you?"

Kensie groaned, shifted, and groaned again.

"Can I get you something?" she asked again.

"Where's Dave?"

Daphne swallowed and looked away. She didn't know what to say. Why couldn't she just formulate fabric softener? Why did everything have to be so complicated?

"He's not here," she said honestly.

"A truck hit us," Kensie said, almost as a question.

"Yes."

"It's all over now," Kensie said, staring down at her hips, which were lodged in some kind of inflatable balloon pants.

"It's over. Now you can concentrate on healing."

"I can feel your judgment. You Christian folks always think you're a cut above the rest of us."

Daphne shook her head. "No. Jesse sent me to make sure you have everything you need. Is there family I can call?" But she couldn't let Kensie's comment pass. "You're wrong, Kensie. I don't judge you. Though you haven't been exactly nice to me since I arrived."

"So you're here, why? Because of guilt? Or because you want to show me the light?" Kensie's voice was weak, but the underlying anger was still apparent. Pain often spoke for people, and Daphne tried to drum up her compassion and see the part of Kensie who hurt, not the part who lashed out so easily. After all, she barely knew Dave, but Kensie was in for a deeper blow when she understood he was gone.

"If this happened to me, I'd be alone in here. I didn't want you to wake up alone." She remembered how Jesse had told her the same thing.

Ohio felt very different from home, where time was scheduled so tightly. It dawned on her that maybe that's what had made Europe so wonderful for her. It wasn't that everything was slower; it was that people weren't so rushed. They made time for one another. Who would have thought Ohio and Paris had something in common?

"But this wouldn't happen to you, would it?" Kensie stared down at her legs, and tears pooled in her eyes. "Because you live a charmed life. Your college was all paid for and you just go to work for the sheer enjoyment of it."

"Kensie, what exactly is charmed about my life? I'm the one who was left standing at the altar in my Monique Lhuillier dress, remember? I took a job that I didn't actually want, and I live in a giant money pit that almost killed me the day I moved in. Does that sound charmed to you?"

"You're not going to ask why I was with Dave this morning?"

"I figure if you want to tell me, you will."

"Because you assume the worst of me. People don't assume the worst of you, but they always assume the worst of me."

"Maybe there's a reason for that." Daphne shrugged. "I mean, I did watch you throw Jesse under the bus in that meeting, and—"

Kensie put up her palm, and a tear spilled down her cheek. "No more. I know what I did. Dave can be very persuasive, and I saw a way out of my debt. I was desperate."

"What are you talking about?"

"Dave and his wife needed a surrogate."

"A surrogate what?"

"Someone to carry their baby," Kensie said, annoyed. "I know, people like you don't do that, but I grew up in the wrong part of town, and I am not going back. No matter what."

"Oh. Oh!" Daphne felt struck by the information. She choked on her words, unable to form any that made sense past her initial shock.

"We had a doctor's appointment this morning. That's where we were going and why I couldn't go to the wedding show with you. I'm not what you thought I was—a girl who worked her way up. I was a girl desperate to secure my future any way I could. Dave didn't want to say anything to Kathy until he knew

I had a clean bill of health from the doctor. She's gotten her hopes up before only to have them dashed."

It was true: Kensie wasn't what Daphne had thought. And with those words, Daphne felt remorse. It amazed her what drove people. How their backgrounds came back to haunt them and put desires inside of them even they couldn't comprehend. People did things for a reason. Reasons that didn't make any sense to others unless they understood where the actions came from.

"Are you pregnant?"

Kensie shook her head. "No. No. I was just being tested to see if it was possible. Now look at me. It might never be possible. I may have screwed up my entire future for the chance to feel safe."

"Well, thank God. Kensie, you've been given a second chance at life. God understands if you want to be secure and even wealthy—there's nothing wrong with those desires. But how does your heart feel in all this?"

Kensie's eyes filled. "It doesn't feel good. I felt ashamed even being in the car with Dave alone. I was nice to him, but he took liberties he shouldn't have." Her eyes flashed. "Nothing too bad, but past my comfort zone."

Daphne put her hand on a nonbandaged part of Kensie's arm. "You know, I didn't listen to my gut once, and I ended up in front of hundreds of my closest friends and family in a wedding dress with no groom." She smiled. "Dang, I looked great, though. I mean, really, that's the best kind of humiliation, when you're dressed in your finest, with your hair and makeup done." She shrugged. "Some people get hauled off to jail in handcuffs and shown on TV in their mug shot. My experience beat that."

Kensie started to laugh. "Oh. It hurts," she said. "Was your gown really Monique Lhuillier?"

"You better believe it. And Christian Louboutin shoes with rhinestones encrusted on them. My parents spared no expense to get rid of me."

"I'm sure it wasn't that."

"Oh, trust me, it was. I was fashion perfection," Daphne said. "But something still didn't feel right. Mark was a little too affectionate at the rehearsal dinner."

"Why are you telling me all this?"

"Because I want you to remember that we never see people's worst side. We see the image they portray out in the world."

"But what will I do now? I don't know if my insurance will cover all this, and I just can't afford to take on more loans. That was my one shot to get *out* of debt."

"That was not your one shot, I assure you. I thought Mark was my one shot. I was wrong. I learned a good lesson. Maybe being an old maid, like my dad called me, is better than being married to a tool."

In Kensie's desperation, Daphne saw her own anew. Mark didn't love her. No amount of waiting around or pathetic posturing would make him love her.

"The body is an amazing healing machine. God made it that way. You'll be fine, Kensie. It's your heart I'm worried about."

Kensie scoffed. "Don't preach at me."

"I'm not in any position to preach." Daphne looked down at her lap, suddenly grateful for all she had in life. "Maybe it sounds like preaching, but that's just the way I talk. I'm not preaching at you. I'm seeing how much I have in common with you."

Kensie forced a laugh, and her hard exterior seemed to return. "I'm tired. Can you go now? You've done your Christian duty. You can tell everyone at the office that I'm all right, that I got what I deserved for being with a married man rather than at work."

"I'd never do that, Kensie. People may give us what we deserve, but God never does. He loves us no matter what. He loves *you* no matter what."

Kensie scowled. "We're not alike. Do you know how hard I had to work to even get my simple marketing certificate from the local community college? I've been on my own since I was fifteen. I finally found a place where I thrived. Then you come in, and in one day I become obsolete. Everyone listens to you like you're some kind of psychic. Do you really think you've done nothing to me? In one day you made me irrelevant."

Daphne shook her head. "Only if you are your job, and you're not. Kensie, you have everything going for you: beauty, brains, a good job. I'd give anything to have your natural grace. Your awareness. Do you think you would have ever fallen for a smooth talker like Mark?"

"Only when he came bearing cash from his wife."

"So your weakness is money. Mine is smooth words, even if they aren't real. We all have our temptations." She looked straight into Kensie's eyes. "I'm no better than you, and I believe that fully. In fact, I might trade my temptations for yours if I could have your body—which I'd never give up for someone else's baby." She laughed. "My own, maybe. Or maybe I'd just cast myself in marble and put it in the foyer so I could grow old with my memories."

She felt Kensie squeeze her hand.

"If I could have a perfect, perky nose like yours and still smell like you can, I'd take that as a gift that might earn me money," Kensie said.

A nurse with a pudgy face and a short blond bob rushed in. "Who are you?" she asked.

"Daphne. A coworker."

"How did you get in here? Her heartbeat is through the roof." The nurse grasped Kensie's wrist. "You need to leave immediately."

Daphne stood. "It's not the end," she said to Kensie. "We're going to lift each other up. You're going to stay with me when you get out of here."

"Please get out of here before I call security," the nurse demanded.

"Daphne," Kensie's weak voice called to her.

She stood in the doorway and waited while the nurse glared.

"Dave didn't make it, did he?"

She paused before answering. It was obvious Kensie knew the answer. "I'm sorry, Kensie. He didn't."

Kensie lifted her hands to her face, and her tears fell freely. The nurse motioned for Daphne to go. As she left, she glanced back at Kensie. Life was hard, but God was good. When the rain fell on the pavement, the fresh scent of renewal blossomed, and her faith went deeper than her circumstances. Anne and Jesse had showed her, and now she intended to show Kensie.

# Chapter 23

J esse's job responsibility was about to quadruple. He was
barely doing his division manager job to full capacity, and
now he'd be expected to step in for Dave until the board decided
what to do. The very reason he'd left P&G now threatened him
again. He wanted nothing more than to be a good father to Ben,
to be the kind of dad he'd wanted. And now circumstances were
creating that same scenario where he was nothing more than a
paycheck. Only Abby wouldn't be there much longer to be a
surrogate parent for his son.

Anne stepped into his office and fell into a chair. "Are you
all right?" she asked.

"I'm not going to be able to do it, Anne. Especially without
Abby." He looked down at his hands clasped on his desk. "But
she needs to live her own life."

"And you and Ben need to live yours. God won't give you
more than you can handle."

"I hate when people say that, Anne. Where does it say that
in Scripture?"

Two men in dark business suits suddenly filled Jesse's doorway. They were both older gentlemen, and Jesse had seen one too many Mafia movies to not be unnerved by their sudden appearance. The older man's face was lined and craggy, so much so that it made his face look filled with tiny pillows patchworked together. He had an enormous, bulbous nose. The younger man had a full head of white hair and dark black eyebrows that complemented his suit.

Anne regained her composure. "May I help you gentlemen?"

"We're looking for Daphne Sweeten," the older man said. "She's a nose. Are we in the right place?"

Jesse stood. "She's at the hospital."

The man dropped the briefcase he carried.

"No, no, she's fine," Jesse reassured him. "She's at the hospital visiting a coworker."

The man's eyes closed, and he crossed himself. "Where can I find this hospital?"

"I'm Jesse Lightner, her boss. May I assist you?"

"I'm Daphne's father," he said. "And this is Arnaud Polge from Givaudan."

"You're Daphne's father?" Jesse came around the desk and extended his hand. "It's nice to meet you, sir. I wish things weren't so out of sorts." He extended a hand to the other man. "And, Mr. Polge, I know of you by reputation, of course. Welcome to Gibraltar. It's an honor to have you here."

Mr. Polge nodded his response. Jesse didn't know if the man understood a word of English, but he tried to maintain composure and rely on his business acumen.

"You'll have to forgive us. Two of our employees were

involved in a terrible accident, and we're awaiting word on their condition now." He couldn't bring himself to announce a death to two unknown men in suits. "Daphne's at the hospital checking up on them."

"But she wasn't in the car?"

"No, sir. She was with me at a wedding show this morning."

"A wedding show? She just had her heart broken at a wedding a few weeks ago," her father chastised. "Did you know that?"

"Yes, but—"

"What kind of sadistic boss makes a woman go to a wedding show weeks after her groom walks out on her?"

"I would never do such a thing," Arnaud said in English.

"She assured me she was fine with it," Jesse said.

"I'm sure she did. She almost convinced us she was happy in this sweatshop, but that's Daphne. She'll tell you what you want to hear to make it easier on you. She never cares about herself first."

"Even in the short time I've known her, I'd have to concur with that statement."

Anne spoke up next. "I'm Anne. Daphne and her friend Sophie stayed with me for a couple weeks while our church fixed up her house. I hate to say it, Mr. Sweeten, but that place was not in livable condition."

"That's not what I gave her," Mr. Sweeten said. "Her fiancé was supposed to buy a lovely house on Peach Orchard. State-of-the-art kitchen and a master suite out of a design magazine."

"Not in her house," Jesse said. "I've been there. It's quite old. And Anne is right; it was uninhabitable."

"I didn't buy her that house," Mr. Sweeten repeated. "I am

a Greek man. Do you think I'd let my daughter live somewhere that was not fit for her? You insult my heritage."

Anne's soothing voice took over. "Jesse meant no harm, I assure you. Can I get you both some coffee?"

But Mr. Sweeten was still staring at Jesse. "You, the man who would take my daughter to a bridal show after what she's been through? You would insult me as a father?"

Jesse didn't have time for the drama. "Would you like to wait for her? Or should I tell her you'll meet her at her house? I imagine she'll be home early today."

"I do not know where she is living. As I said, that's not the house I intended for her."

"We'd like to go see her now if you can tell us where she is," Mr. Polge said. "She's not answering her cell phone."

"I'll take you to her," Anne said. "The hospital is just a short drive from here."

"That won't be necessary," Mr. Polge said. "We have something personal to discuss with her."

Jesse didn't like the way Arnaud acted. As though Daphne belonged to him. As though he need only say the word, and she'd go crawling back to him at Givaudan.

Daphne belonged to *him* now. At least for the next few months. If the esteemed Monsieur Polge had made the mistake of letting her go, why should he, Jesse, pay the consequences? He felt his fists tighten at the idea of anyone stealing Daphne away from him so soon, but what claim did he have on her, really? Whatever emotions were stirring in him, they were the stuff of dreams.

"You should probably just wait here then," Anne said. "She should be back soon. She's not a relative, so the hospital won't be able to tell her much anyway. We just thought Gibraltar should have a representative there for the families."

"I need to see my daughter!" Mr. Sweeten's voice filled with anguish as he spoke to Arnaud. "You told me this was for the best, but my daughter thinks I don't care. I fail to see how this is best. Her boss thinks I bought her a rattrap! And I—"

"Gentlemen, why don't you come sit down?" Anne said in her soothing pastor's wife voice. "There's a sofa in the foyer. Make yourselves at home, and before you know it, Daphne will be here."

Anne led the two men away, then came back and shut the door behind her. "They're not here to take Daphne back to Paris or San Francisco, are they?"

"I don't know why they're here," Jesse said. "But I've got to get up to the lab and talk to the scientists." He dropped his head. "I burned the marketing reports, and now what? Kensie's not here to help with packaging."

He'd make it work. He owed it to Gibraltar. To Dave. But once again, Ben would pay the price with an absentee father. He couldn't win.

"But what about Daphne? We can't lose her now."

Jesse shrugged. "We can't stop her from going if that's what she wants to do. Slave labor is a thing of the past, thank goodness."

"Jesse Lightner, if you don't put up some sort of fight for that young woman, I will never forgive you. Did you not see what happened today? Life is short. If anyone knows that, it's you. I'll bet you knew the first time you laid eyes on Daphne that she was meant for you."

"Anne, that's crazy talk. You're just upset. I've told you that if I were marriage material, I'd have a wife by now. As for Daphne—you should have seen her face when she woke up in the hospital and thought I was Mark. She positively glowed. She burst into the biggest smile I've ever seen, and then, when she discovered it was me at her side, it vanished. Of course, I was there to fire her and she probably knew it."

"This is your second chance, Jesse. You can listen to your heart, no matter how foolish it seems, or you can let Daphne go back to her old life with those two old men in Paris or San Francisco, or wherever she lands. She needs a home, Jesse. She wants to be settled, or she'll run her whole life concentrating on the details and missing the point."

# Chapter 24

"D addy! Arnaud! What are you doing here?" Daphne embraced one, then the other.

"We came to take you home," her father said.

"Well, I guess I am home. Daddy, the house you bought me—"

"I did not buy you that house. I picked out a beautiful house with a state-of-the-art kitchen and a Jacuzzi tub. Do you think your mother would allow me to buy our only daughter a fixer-upper?"

"I thought maybe because the wedding had been so expensive—"

"Daphne, I know I haven't always been there for you when you needed me, but, sweetheart, there is nothing I wouldn't do for you."

"We couldn't warn you about Mark," Arnaud said. "We didn't know who he was involved with, and Interpol would not let me tell you anything. At first they suspected you too."

"Suspected me? Of what?"

"Mark never gave up the idea of the mind-altering drugs through the aromatherapy spray. He was essentially an international drug dealer, and his stuff must have worked. He had quite an international clientele."

"But, Arnaud, I don't understand. Why didn't you tell me?"

"I couldn't," he said. "I was under strict orders. When I realized I could give Mark a job and they could get the evidence they needed, that's the route we decided to go. But it was dangerous for you, Daphne. Mark used your father's money to help fund his operation."

"I was in danger?"

"It's safe now. The dealers who were selling him chemicals have been captured. All is clear for you to come back to Givaudan."

For some reason, Daphne looked back to Jesse's office. "I promised I would stay here for a while."

"Daphne, this place is beneath you," Arnaud said. "If Madeleine could see you here, she would cry, after all the work you did to get your credentials."

"You love Paris," her father said.

"I love Dayton."

They both looked at her, perplexed. "I can't let you stay in that house. I've heard it's uninhabitable."

"Not anymore, Dad. The men from Anne's church have made repairs, and Sophie came out and painted, and it's going to be lovely. And it's mine. I don't want anything more."

She gazed down the hall toward Jesse's door, not ready to admit why she really wanted to stay.

"You don't know anyone out here. I refuse to let you stay."

"I promised, Dad. You raised me to be a woman of my word." Her shoulders fell. "And, Arnaud, I still can't smell anything. I'm not capable of coming to work for you."

"You are. I've smelled the formula for your cologne. It's impeccable. And I cannot mimic it. You did as I taught you and left an important ingredient out."

She smiled.

"You will have to change the formula a little to lower the price point, but it is perfection. To see the student outshine her master is such a feeling of pride for me." He closed his eyes and put his hand to his chest.

"You want Volatility!? We're going to use it here. In a dog shampoo."

"Of course we won't call it that. You might want to take the marketing courses again when you're back at the Institut. I'm willing to pay for the formula, but I'd rather have you back in Paris to create more hit fragrances. Your nose will come back when all is right in the world. You've been under such terrible stress." Arnaud kissed her on both cheeks. "We were protecting you, my princess. Madeleine would never forgive me if I allowed something to happen to you."

She looked again toward Jesse's closed office door, and panic rose in her at the sight, though she couldn't have explained why. It was as though a part of him was already unavailable to her. "I'll be right back," she said.

She knocked softly on the door and then pushed it open. Jesse was bent over in his chair, his head in his hands. She rushed to his side and crouched beside him. "I'm sorry about Dave," she said.

He nodded.

"Jesse—"

"Arnaud wants you back in Paris." He nodded. "You can have your scent back then. No dog shampoo and spritzer. I'm sure Givaudan will make better use of it."

"I'll have to cheapen it with a few chemicals to get it on the market, but, Jesse, I promised it to you. If you want Volatility!, it's yours. It's the least I can do." What she wanted to tell him was that if he wanted her, she was his. All he had to do was nibble at her offer.

"When will you leave?"

"Not until Kensie is on her feet. I suppose that will be around Christmas—and I promised to stay till then anyway. I'm going to have her stay with me in the house."

"What? Why the sudden love for Kensie?"

"Because I want to pay it forward. You all came around me and loved me when I couldn't smell. Anne housed me when I had nowhere to go. Mr. Riley brought me enough food for the next year. You all helped me get back on my feet even though I wasn't capable of doing what you hired me to do. I've had to reevaluate what makes me important. I always thought it was because I could smell better than anyone else, but it isn't that."

His face came close to hers, and she felt warm and tingly just being beside him. He emanated a feeling of safety, and it was lovely, better than the scent of rain. If she could bottle that, it would put Volatility! to shame.

She felt his breath tickle her ear.

"What was it then?"

"It's that when I couldn't smell at all, God's people were there to pick me up off the pavement. If God's people can love me so much, God must love me just *because*. He's created a family for me wherever I've gone."

"But when will you find a family from God that will make you settle down and stop moving?"

"What if I said I didn't want to go to Paris?"

"I'd say you were sacrificing yourself again, so focused on the details that you're missing the big picture."

"While I help with Kensie recuperating, I might help with Ben too, if you need to get the product cycle quickened." She looked down to the carpet. "Now that . . . you know . . . Dave is gone."

"You're an amazing woman, Daphne. What will I do when you're gone?" He stood over her and gave her a chaste, grandfatherly kiss.

"You've made it this long, I'm sure you'll survive," she joked. But in her heart, she wanted to tell the truth. She wanted to tell Jesse that she'd never met another man like him. "I'd better get out to my father."

"Are you sure about the scent? You won't be offended by the dog shampoo?"

"The scent is yours. I'll have to change it chemically to make it work for Givaudan anyway." She stood, and the way he looked at her, she willed him to say what he was really feeling. She felt his gaze to her soul, and with only one word of encouragement, she'd tell Arnaud to go without her. "I'll help you get the next quarter out like I promised."

He waved her off. "Don't be silly. We'll make it without you."

"Is that true?" she asked. "Your schedule is so full as it is."

They stared at one another for a long time, but neither one said more. She left his office and explained to her father that the next few days would be busy. "There will be a funeral, I'm sorry to say, and lots to do to make the product cycle."

Her father smiled. "That's my girl. A chip off the old workaholic block."

"When will you be back?" Arnaud asked.

"December," she said while staring at Jesse's door. "December is good."

Jesse came out of his office and pumped Arnaud's hand. "Congratulations," he said. "The best man won." Then he strode out of the foyer and down the hallway.

The scent of winning trickled into her memory, and her eyes followed Jesse until he disappeared into the elevator.

Jesse berated himself all the way to the lab. He was being ridiculous. Yes, he had this amazing chemistry with Daphne, but he knew enough science to know that was all just pheromones and attraction. Just because he'd finally been attracted to another woman didn't mean he needed to go off the deep end.

Yet the thought of Daphne leaving Gibraltar tugged at his heart. She'd sprinkled her *joie de vivre* like glitter. As he headed toward the lab, his cell phone rang and he answered it on the first ring. "Abby?"

"Hey, Jesse, I heard there was an accident in town. You all right?"

"I'm fine." He'd been so busy he hadn't even thought to call and check on his own son. "Abby, we're going to have to find a good daycare for Ben. I'm going to be VP for a while again."

"VP? Jesse, no!"

"I have no choice. Dave is . . . Dave is gone. There's no one else who knows the business."

"Just quit, Jesse."

"I can't quit. I have to feed my son."

"I'm not going to Cincinnati and leaving Ben with some stranger while you work your life away. What would Hannah have said?"

"I can't talk about this right now," he said. "I have to go tell my scientists the clock is ticking. They have to come up with the products fast, and there's only me to review them."

"Do you think there's no other way God can make a path for you than to work your entire life away? You're not helpless, Jesse. Yes, it's hard. Yes, you're not going to get to buy Ben all the fabulous wooden trains he wants. But that's not what he really wants anyway! Do you know he named his favorite train after you? He talks to it like it's you, because you're never here. That's the legacy you're leaving."

"Abby—"

"Don't Abby me. I've got a good mind to petition to adopt

Ben. He needs someone to be there for him, and you feel the call of dish soap is higher."

Abby hung up on him. He had to get out of the office. John and Willard would find out soon enough. He thought about the two men in their lonely lab, all alone without so much as a conversation, and he saw his future. The rain fell and it fell, but if he didn't take cover, could he really blame someone else for his standing there soaked?

Daphne led her father and Arnaud, who were in a rental car behind her, back to her charming little house. Pride of ownership welled up within her, and she couldn't imagine leaving it. When she got to the stoop, she could hear her landline ringing, and she jiggled the keys to open the door.

"Getting the phone, Dad. Check out the place." She huffed over to the phone and figured it was probably only a sales call. But it would be *her* sales call. "Hello?"

"Daph, it's Sophie."

"Why are you calling on this line?"

"I was hoping you were home from work. I have a message I think I'm supposed to give you."

"A message?"

"I read today about a woman who couldn't stop sneezing. No matter what she did, she sneezed and she sneezed. Through breakfast, lunch, dinner, and even sleeping. The longest respite she got was like a couple of minutes."

"Can we talk about this later, Sophie? It's been a long day. My dad and Arnaud are here. And Mark's in jail."

"He's where? What are you talking about?"

"And I've got my old job back."

"In Paris?"

"Yeah."

"You don't sound too happy about that."

"I'm not, but I can't explain why."

"I think that's why I had to call you. I knew that message was from God! This woman who sneezed all the time. She'd been holding in an ugly family secret. She was protecting her parents, protecting her brother, but it was wreaking havoc on her. So I was thinking, is there a truth that you need to say that no one wants to hear?"

"I don't think so."

"Think about it."

Daphne didn't have to think about it. She knew what the truth was. And the truth hurt. The truth was that the man who left her at the altar stole her job and her life in Paris. Was it so hard to imagine she'd have a physical reaction to that kind of rejection and betrayal? She now possessed what was taken from her, though . . . so why hadn't her sense of smell returned?

# Epilogue

Fall stirred within the Ohio leaves. Daphne called out to Kensie as she peered out the window. "I think it might rain today!"

Kensie emerged from the first-floor bedroom near the kitchen looking like a million. She still limped slightly, and her figure was a little rounder from a lack of exercise, but she was still the most beautiful woman Daphne had ever seen in person. And she'd grown far more beautiful inside since giving up the need to manipulate people to have control.

"You look like a supermodel, only so much happier."

"I feel like a super slouch, but I am happier. God spared my life, though I'll never understand why, and I want to make it worth His while." Kensie smoothed her hair into a ponytail and clipped it while she limped toward the living room. "What are you smiling about?"

"This reminds me of my first day back, and that warm and cozy feeling. Now you'll be like the rest of us. No more of this part-time business."

"You really are like a walking gumdrop of happiness, aren't you? Maybe if I were going to Paris in December, I'd be happy too."

"It's so exciting to be in the lab. I love watching Willard smell what I put together and tell me if I'm on target or not. It's almost more fun than working by myself. Willard is always so encouraging."

"Yes, you two have a mutual fan club. It's sickening to watch. Get that board from my room, will you?"

Daphne went to the bedroom and yanked a poster board off the bed. "What is this?"

"Open it," Kensie said with a grin.

Daphne opened the flaps to reveal the artwork. "Oh, Kensie!" There were two colored drawings of dog products. Each bottle was shaped elegantly into an Eiffel Tower with blue and black writing on one and pink and black writing on the other. "*Parisian Dog for Him* and *Parisian Dog for Her*. It's beautiful! I never imagined."

"It's going to jump off the shelves. And so will Givaudan's take on the cologne, according to your Arnaud. Isn't that wonderful?"

Daphne could hardly believe how wonderful. "My whole life I only wanted to see my perfume in a store. Not simply something I worked on, but the whole enchilada. Now I'm going to have a line of dog shampoos in a scent I created, and a cologne too. Of course I won't own either one, but I'll know they're mine. It's the pride of ownership. I did it. I mean, we did it!" Daphne hugged Kensie tightly.

"Speaking of pride of ownership," Kensie mumbled as she

pulled away, careful to balance herself upright, "I think the roof might be leaking in that back room."

Daphne laughed. "Not even that can harm my mood today. This is everything I've worked toward."

"There's more." Kensie went to the computer and turned on the music program.

"We're going to be late for your first full day of work in weeks." But she had to admit, she'd rather stay and bask in the glow of her success. She didn't want to miss a second of it, in case she woke up from her dream. "I can't wait to show the guys what you did with that packaging. If I had dreamed of it, it couldn't be better."

Kensie had started up some French music, and though Daphne liked the sentiment, they needed to get to work. Today was the first staff meeting where all the new products would have samples and artwork. Kensie represented a rebirth of Gibraltar. A baptism by fire, and Daphne couldn't wait to get started.

A car door slammed, and she peered out the curtain again. She'd grown into one of those nosy neighbors who had to know everyone's business, and she loved how she belonged somewhere.

"Jesse's car is in the driveway."

"Really?" Kensie said a little too innocently. "I wonder what he could be doing here."

Daphne turned around to face Kensie. "Are you stalling? What's going on?"

Kensie came beside her and leaned to look out the window. "It seems Jesse is on your driveway with three dogs."

"Jesse doesn't have dogs."

"Uh, he does. He has three. See?"

Daphne looked out the window again. "One of them is Mr. Riley's." But she didn't recognize the others, who had pink and blue balloons tied to their collars.

Jesse was caught up in their leashes and struggling to lead them to her door.

"I better get out there before he becomes a casualty." She opened her front door and padded down the cement steps. "Jesse, what are you doing? Whose dogs are those?"

With his free hand, he held up a clear, unlabeled jug. "It's Gibraltar's new product! We had to have at least one boy dog to wash and one girl. And this one"—he raised his brows at Mr. Riley's big white dog—"this one is just a mooch looking for a free bath. He figures his mom has fed you enough with her casseroles, and you owe her."

"It's the strangest thing. I had a dream you were walking toward me with three dogs." That was as far as she intended to go with that information.

"Is that the one where you mauled me and I had to sue you for harassment?" Jesse winked.

"You wish," Kensie called from the stoop.

"Where's Ben? He'd love this." Daphne had to admit, seeing Jesse dressed down in his roughed-up jeans and a black jacket wasn't a bad way to start the day.

"He's at daycare this morning, and he's doing fine. In fact, he didn't want to come with me. He wanted to go to school. I know when I'm not wanted."

"I'm proud of you."

"Don't be too proud. I'm taking him out soon."

"Whatever for? From what you tell me, he loves his teachers and has made lots of friends."

Jesse jerked as the dogs pulled him away from her.

"I don't know where you think you're going to give those dogs a bath, but they're not coming in this house. I just cleaned from top to bottom."

Kensie appeared beside them on the driveway, and the dogs lunged toward her. She backed away. "I'll be in the house so I don't get knocked over. Tell me when you're ready for me."

Daphne turned her attention back to Jesse, who held up one hand while he wrapped the leashes around the other. "Just a minute. I'll be right back."

He walked to his car, opened the door, and piled the dogs back inside. Then he came back to Daphne. "I didn't think that through. I wanted to show you that Gibraltar made your first genuine product. Does it feel good?"

"It feels incredible," she said. "But what did you mean about taking Ben out of school? Just for the morning, you mean?"

"No," he said as he kicked at the driveway.

She took a deep breath. "You're not leaving Ohio?" Subconsciously, she kneaded her hands together. She'd believed Jesse's stability was something she could count on. She'd taken solace in it.

"Ben and I need a change. Abby is moving to follow her own path, and there are just too many unpleasant memories here for me."

"Because of Hannah?"

"Because I let Ben down to please my boss. To make some

arbitrary numbers that were forecast by bean counters. I said that my son came first, but I threw myself into work and let Abby raise him. I'll never get those years back, and soon he'll be off to kindergarten."

"Jesse, you're too hard on yourself. You're a great father."

"I'm going to be. I'll never let another job own me like that again."

Tears welled in her eyes. "That's great, Jesse. I'm excited for you both." She ached, thinking of the illusion of love she'd created with Mark. Jesse loved Hannah in a way that survived death, and when his heart wrestled free of that love, some woman was going to get an amazing man.

Jesse lifted her chin. "You're not going to ask me where I'm going?"

She shook her head and clasped her eyes tightly. "No offense, Jesse. I don't want to deal with another loss just yet, and you and Ben . . . everyone in Dayton, have come to mean so much to me. I'm not ready to face life without all the people I love here."

He put his fist to his heart. "You're right here. With me always now because of the time we've shared."

"Mm-hmm." She didn't want to speak. She didn't even want to admit to herself that she wanted so much more from him. Just a few months ago she'd been engaged to someone else.

"Daphne."

He took her hands in his, and she tingled at his touch. With his forefinger bent, he lifted her chin and forced her eyes to the swirls of his incredible blue-green gaze. She felt the force of his intensity to her toes and clasped her eyes shut so she could remember the image forever.

"What is it?" he asked.

"I'm embarrassed."

"You're embarrassed?"

"I can't tell the difference between friendship and romance when I want more." She felt her face flame with color. "I thought I had it figured out after everyone I knew and loved saw me standing alone in a white wedding gown. But I haven't learned a thing. My feelings have a life of their own."

"That's what I love about you. You will never be good at poker, but your friends will always feel your love for them."

She forced a laugh and stepped away from him. "You'd better get those dogs back where they belong."

He brushed her cheek with his palm. "I'm not making myself clear."

"You are. You and Ben are off to start your new life, and I was very important to you while I was here." She ventured a look at his handsome face again. "You were very important to me too. I'd better get Kensie to the office."

He grasped her wrist and brought it to his lips, where he laid gentle kisses on the inside of her arm. While he kissed her, his gaze crawled upward to meet hers. "Ben and I are moving to France."

"France?"

"*Oui*. What better way for Ben to learn about the world than to submerge him in a culture and teach him while I'm at his side? It will help him understand why Abby isn't home every day too."

"But—what about your job?"

"I have a new job. Product manager at Givaudan. It seems they had an opening in Paris. As I've always said, a good product manager can go anywhere. Too bad I never listened to my own advice."

"What are you talking about? Don't mess with me, Jesse."

"If I were to stay here, Daphne, you'd never know what I feel for you and what it means to have someone support your dream. You'd never feel pursued, and Anne told me that's a must."

She didn't dare smile for fear she'd break the spell. She'd wake up, and this romantic dream would all burst. "Is this because we create so well together? You want a partner?"

He held her face between his hands and kissed her firmly on the lips. "I'm not making my intentions clear then?"

She weakened at his touch and melted into his shoulder as he drew her closer in his arms. "This isn't a dream?"

"The first moment I laid eyes on you, the thought that went through my head was, *I'm going to marry that girl.* I denied it completely, naturally, but inside . . . in my gut, I knew it was true. I could see you at my side, and that's all I could see."

"So this is about more than the business then? This is about you and me?"

"You and me and Ben. If you'll have us. I can't just bop you on the head and drag you by the hair. They don't do that anymore."

"You're sure? Don't tease me, Jesse Lightner."

"I won't, Daphne Lightner."

She let the name sparkle in her ear. *Daphne Lightner.* "Say it again."

"Madame Daphne Lightner." The dogs barked from the car, and they laughed at their romantic moment on the crumbling driveway. "I love you, Daphne."

She wrapped her arms tightly around his waist as though she'd never let go. "Jesse, I love you. I didn't want to admit it because I didn't want to be hurt again, but you make my heart sing. I love you. I love Kensie. I love Anne. I love everything about Dayton, but I get to bring the best part with me to Paris!" She drew in a deep breath, giddy with exhilaration, and the cool fall air went down smoothly. "Jesse?"

"Yeah?"

"I can smell! Honeysuckle!"

He looked around him. "Yeah. That's right. You just saw it."

She unlatched herself from his arm and plucked a green leaf from a nearby bush. "I can smell the chlorophyll." She went to his side and sniffed. "I've been longing to do this since I met you." She drew in a deep breath. "You're wearing Volatility! Oh, Jesse, I'm going to make you a better scent, a richer one! One that comes from a genuine love, one that is God-ordained and all-consuming!"

"So what is your favorite scent, Daphne? The one that's the top note for Volatility!?"

She grinned. "It's the scent of rain. Like God's mercies are new every day, the scent of rain washes away what's old and begins fresh. My grandfather used to tell me that when we'd spend rainy days together."

That was what the scent of rain meant to her, she realized. It represented her grandfather's unconditional love. Like God's, it was always faithful, ever present. As God had sent a rainbow to remind His people of His covenant, the dark clouds sent her the scent of rain to remind her that love was all that mattered, and it was all around her.

Jesse reached into his pocket, and she noticed that the black jacket belonged to a tuxedo.

"You're wearing a tuxedo jacket!" All that was missing from her dream were the clown and the baguette. The balloons were on the dogs. She looked back at the lonely little house she'd grown to love. "I was able to settle and build a family by myself."

Jesse nodded. "Maybe that was the problem. Maybe you weren't meant to settle but to find a man who loved you enough to keep moving."

"I'd go anywhere with you, Jesse, but I'll be settled wherever we end up."

He slid down to the hard concrete on one knee and held up a tiny band encrusted with diamonds. "Daphne, will you do me the honor of becoming my wife?"

"Jesse, yes!"

Small droplets of water fell on her, and she inhaled the fresh scent of rain. Jesse looked up at the sky. "I think your grandfather approves."

He stood, and they fell into an embrace under the leaking sky.

Life's clouds had a way of showing their silver linings. She drew in a deep breath and inhaled the scent of pure love.

# Reading Group Guide

1. Daphne gives up her dream job for love, only to find out it wasn't really love at all. Have you ever given up something for someone else? What did you learn from your sacrifice?

2. Daphne wanted all things perfect, but ultimately learned that the image of perfection is only that: an image. Have you ever lived part of your life like that? Where you kept your desires hidden rather than look selfish? How did it turn out?

3. Daphne's best friend doesn't like her fiancé Mark from the very start of their relationship. Has your friend ever disliked someone you dated? Did you regret not listening, or did your friend come around?

4. Our sense of smell truly is our strongest memory inducer. What scent makes you think of a memory? Is it a good memory?

5. Kensie comes off as a villain—until you see where she came from. Have you ever disliked someone, only to discover in understanding their plight, you saw their true colors?

6. The fact that Jesse lost his wife and the mother of his young child is so unfair. Have you ever wrestled with God about the unfairness of life? What did you ultimately learn from the experience?

7. Daphne's prized scent, which she thinks is the pinnacle of her creations, ultimately becomes a dog shampoo. She's excited about that, as it was created for her "dog" of an ex, but have you ever thought something was the best you could do, only to find out God had more in store for you?

8. Daphne comes to love Ohio and the people in it, and Paris and her dream job become less attractive. What's your favorite place and why?

# Acknowledgments

It's no small task to create a book, and yet the author gets most of the credit. I'd like to thank the real heroes. My editors Ami McConnell and L.B. Norton, who always go beyond the call of duty to piece things together into a working novel. I'm also grateful to Krista Stroever for her editing expertise in helping me to get unstuck at the beginning of this process. To Becky Monds for helping in the final stages and doing more of the background work. And finally, to marketing's Eric Mullet and Ashley Schneider, thank you for believing in this project and working so hard on the novel's launch.

Thank you to my friendship team, who listens to me whine when I get to the middle of each and every novel: Colleen Coble, Diann Hunt, Denise Hunter, and Nancy Toback. You girls are the best and I love you!

kristin billerbeck

an ashley stockingdale novel

what a
girl wants

All she wants is a cute Christian guy who doesn't live with
his mother . . . and maybe a Prada handbag.

kristin billerbeck

an ashley stockingdale novel

she's out
of control

Her fab new job is all-consuming, her sweet puppy can't stop piddling,
and her boyfriend has developed an aversion to jewelry stores.
Ashley's got it all together, but it's coming apart quickly!

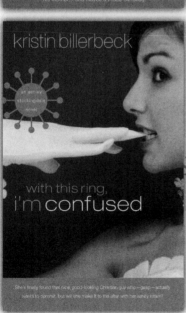

kristin billerbeck

an ashley stockingdale novel

with this ring,
i'm confused

She's finally found that nice, good-looking Christian guy who—gasp—actually
wants to commit, but will she make it to the altar with her sanity intact?

All she wants is a cute Christian guy who doesn't live with his mother . . . and maybe a Prada handbag.

The Ashley Stockingdale Series

Available
in Print and
eBook

The pursuit of life, love, and the perfect pedicure

She's **armed**—with hot irons, sharp shears, and a flair for color. She's **dangerous**—truly bad news for bad hair. And she's going to do whatever it takes to make a place for herself in the exclusive Beverly Hills salon.

splitends

sometimes the end is really the beginning

A NOVEL

kristin billerbeck

our friends devise a plan to turn Smitten, Vermont, into the country's premier romantic getaway—while each searches for her own true love along the way.

Colleen Coble,
Kristin Billerbeck,
Diann Hunt
& Denise Hunter

*Smitten*

*Love is on the way*

AVAILABLE IN PRINT AND E-BOOK

THOMAS NELSON
*Since 1798*

# About the Author

*Author photo by Michael Hawk Photography*

Christy Award finalist and two-time winner of the ACFW Book of the Year award, Kristin Billerbeck has appeared on *The Today Show* and has been featured in the *New York Times*. Her books include *A Billion Reasons Why* and *What a Girl Wants*. She lives with her family in Northern California.